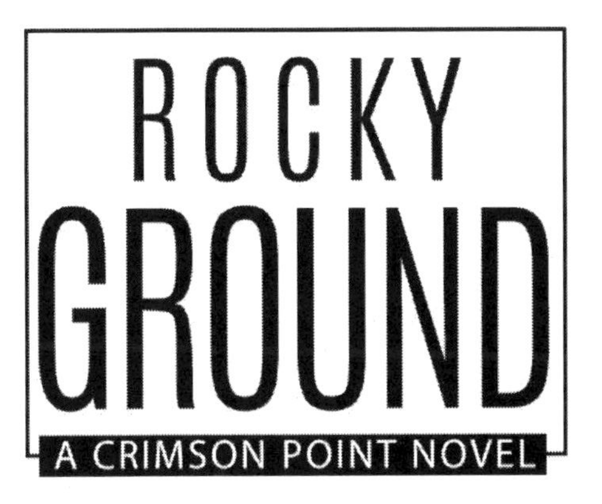

KAYLEA CROSS

ROCKY GROUND

* * * * *

Cover Art and Print Formatting:
Sweet 'N Spicy Designs
Developmental edits: Deborah Nemeth
Line Edits: Joan Nichols
Digital Formatting: LK Campbell

* * * * *

ISBN: 978-1797785479

Dedication

For Hazel, without whom Aidan wouldn't sound like a proper Scot. I so appreciate your help in bringing my Scottish Royal Marine hero to life ☺. Looking forward to Edinburgh and the Tattoo this summer! xx

Author's Note

So here we are in the final Crimson Point book. Aidan's my first Scottish hero ever, and I'm so thrilled to present you with a Royal Marine.

"*Per Mare, Per Terram*". By Sea, By Land, Captain Aidan MacIntyre's got you covered.

Happy reading!

Kaylea Cross

Chapter One

A womanizing deadbeat, a not-so-high-functioning alcoholic, and a pedophile.

The sad truths of her three longest-lasting relationships. Not exactly a track record to be proud of, or a recommendation for mother of the year.

Tiana Fitzgerald pulled the hood of her coat up as she got out of her car and dashed through the rain to the Crimson Point police station to face more fallout from her most recent disaster of a romantic relationship. Her week had already gone from bad to worse on Monday after receiving another blow, this one by mail.

One crisis at a time.

Sheriff Noah Buchanan rose from the chair behind his desk with a broad smile on his face when she knocked on his open door. He'd been so good to her and her daughter through everything that had happened. Over the past year he and his girlfriend Poppy had become her friends. "You look half-drowned," he said with a chuckle. "Come on in."

"It's monsooning out there." April showers brought May flowers and all that, except here on the Oregon Coast when it rained nonstop for weeks on end and saturated everything.

"Is Ella at afterschool care?"

"No, I dropped her off at Beckett and Sierra's before coming here." She took off her soaked jacket and draped it over the back of the chair in front of his desk before sitting and folding her hands in her lap, maintaining at least the outward appearance of calm and collected. "So, you said you had an update for me about Brian."

She still hated saying his name. Hated even more that she'd fallen for his fake charm in the first place and not seen the monster underneath. It disgusted her to think that she'd slept with him. Filled her with rage that, unbeknownst to her, he'd exposed himself to her then eight-year-old daughter, and would have molested her or worse if Ella hadn't told someone.

Ella hadn't told her. No, she'd told their neighbors, Beckett and Sierra instead. Noah's best friend and sister.

It broke Tiana's heart that her daughter hadn't trusted her, but once Ella's reasoning had become clear, she understood her daughter's decision better. Ella had been trying to protect her. That was so wrong on so many levels. It was Tiana's job to protect her, not the other way around.

"I do." Noah reached one muscular arm back into a file cabinet and took out a folder that he placed on his desk. "The latest report came back from the computer forensics people."

Her insides curdled. They'd seized Brian's electronics after he'd been arrested last spring, but they'd found a personal laptop of his only a month ago. She hadn't been shown any of the information about the ongoing investigation until now. "Let me guess—they found all kinds of child porn and a whole bunch of other disgusting stuff on his hard drive."

Noah confirmed her suspicions with a nod. "Right."

Gross. "And I'm also betting Ella's not the first girl

he's done this to."

"Right again. We identified three other possible victims. All girls, aged eleven and under, and there may be others we don't know about yet. His pattern seems to be targeting single moms with young daughters."

The news sickened her. It was horrifying to think that predators like him were walking around in plain sight, but undetected, and that she'd fallen for his act. His clean-cut, good looks and impressive professional image as a successful and highly sought-after investment banker working for a large firm based in Portland. "Well that's...disturbing."

Noah's deep blue gaze was steady. "Yes, it is." The night of the confrontation with Brian, Noah had been especially wonderful. Beckett too, whom she'd never be able to thank enough for intervening on Ella's behalf.

Tiana had arrived home that evening, clueless as to what had been going on, and walked into a chaotic scene straight out of her nightmares. Brian in cuffs in the back of Noah's cruiser, his nose and mouth bleeding from Beckett's powerful fist. When she'd found out what Brian had done, she'd wanted to rip him apart. "I can't say any of this surprises me, though. Not now."

"I showed you this because I wanted you to know you're not the only one. You're not the only person he's fooled. He's done this before and gotten away with it, at least three more times that we know of. But because Ella spoke up and he's been charged, two of the other girls are willing to testify as well."

"A tiny bit of a silver lining in this whole mess."

"Yes." He opened up the file, leafed through some papers and began to read. "The forensic psychologist's report says the usual things common to most child predators. He was likely sexually abused as a child himself and blames external factors to explain and justify his actions in an attempt to diminish his guilt. He'll also go to great lengths to hide his behavior."

"Boy, did he ever," she said bitterly. She'd been completely oblivious to what was happening behind her back.

Noah closed the file. "They're experts at it. That's why it's so hard to catch them. And they control their victims, making it hard for the people they've hurt to speak out. But not Ella." He sat back in his chair, a slight smile lifting one side of his mouth. "You've got a brave little girl there."

"I know it." She pulled in a breath and shook her head. "How do you do this job, Noah? Seeing this kind of thing day after day?"

"Thankfully around here that kind of thing is rare, but yeah, I've seen my fair share of shit. It's always harder when kids are involved. And I do it because I can make a difference and protect kids like Ella by taking the monsters off the street and putting them away for as long as possible."

If it were up to Tiana, Brian and all the other child predators in the world would rot in prison for the rest of their lives and never see the light of day again.

Noah's parting words resonated with her as she drove home to her rental house on the other side of town. If Brian refused the plea bargain that was about to be offered him—and it was sickening enough that he was being offered any kind of a deal at all—then Ella might have to take the witness stand and testify in court in front of him.

The only reason Tiana had agreed to the terms of the plea bargain was to spare her daughter that additional trauma. Ella had been through more than enough, and Tiana was determined to protect her daughter from any more harm.

That plan included steering clear of any more romantic relationships, and men in general until Ella was all grown up. Maybe longer.

Maybe forever.

Her cell rang as she drove down Front Street along the water, past all the charming wood-framed shops and businesses and the wide expanse of sandy beach and rolling ocean beyond it. Aunt Lizzie, her mother's younger sister. The closest thing Tiana had ever had to a real mother, and the only family she had any contact with. "I'm just on my way home, so perfect timing," she told her aunt.

"It's a gift," Lizzie replied in a cheery voice. "So, how did it go at the sheriff's office?"

"Depressing as hell, as expected." She relayed everything Noah had told her.

"When will you hear about the plea bargain?"

"Not sure. Last I heard the State Attorney's office was still finalizing it."

Lizzie grunted. "I hope the pedo takes it. It's more than he deserves, especially if he's molested other girls, but I'd hate for Ella to have to go through the stress of a trial to put him away."

"Me too."

"And what else? I can tell there's something else. Spill."

Aunt Lizzie knew her too well. "It's Evan."

A shocked pause followed her announcement. "As in, Ella's deadbeat sperm donor?"

The guy who'd ditched them both before Ella's first birthday and disappeared to chase women and his dream of being a famous musician. Yep. "That's the one."

"What did he do now?"

"Our mediation is over. If I don't grant him visitation—they call it parenting time here—then the court will enforce it."

"*What*?"

Tiana winced and turned the volume down on the car's Bluetooth system. "Yep. Got the letter couriered to my office Monday morning."

"That's insane. He didn't want anything to do with

Ella for her entire life up to now, hasn't paid you a dime in support, left you both to fend for yourselves, and now he suddenly wants access to her?"

The weight that had been sitting on Tiana's chest for the past several months as the start of the trial loomed suddenly grew heavier. "Yes, and since he's agreed to pay the child support he owes, the court will side with him if I keep fighting it." She hadn't gone after him for child support when he'd left because she'd just wanted him out of their lives permanently and had been willing to go without the money to get that.

"What are you going to do? Does Ella know?"

"The initial visit would be here with a court liaison to supervise. It's better for everyone if Evan and I can work out something amicably between us in terms of a visitation schedule, but since he's in California it's even harder. As for Ella, I've brought up the subject to see how she reacted."

"And?"

"She actually seemed excited about the prospect of meeting him." That had surprised Tiana. "According to my lawyer, I can't fight this unless I can prove he's a criminal or poses a threat to her. Which, given my track record with men, he probably is, and I won't be able to prove anything until it's too late."

"So you're not going to fight it?"

Part of her desperately wanted to. She wanted to keep Evan as far out of their life as possible, because as far as she was concerned, he'd forfeited any rights to Ella the day he walked out on them. "I can try, but it won't look good in front of the court and it'll burn through money I'd rather put into a mortgage and a college fund for Ella."

"God, I hate that man. Why the hell does he want to see her now, anyway?"

"I don't know, but I don't trust his motives even with the money he's willing to pay to see her." He'd abandoned her and Ella when they'd needed him most. There was no reason to let him back into their lives now. Raising Ella alone had been the hardest thing Tiana had ever done, but she'd never once regretted her decision. "I may have to come to terms with him having supervised visits. But if he tries to file for any sort of custody, I'll fight him for as long as it takes."

"Good girl."

"My lawyer's looking into what can be done about that, but right now it's all up in the air."

"Honey, the universe owes you a huge break."

"God, don't I know it. Now let's change the subject before the last of my determination to stay positive disappears and I'm forced to eat both quarts of ice cream currently sitting in my freezer when I get home."

"Is one of them mint chocolate chip?"

She smiled at her aunt's hopeful tone. "You're coming to visit this weekend, so of course."

"You always were my favorite niece."

Tiana laughed under her breath. "By process of elimination, that's not saying much, is it?" She was Lizzie's only niece.

"You'd still be my favorite even if I had twenty nieces. Which, considering the crazypants, whackadoodle family we both come from, I'm thankful I do *not*."

She grinned at the apt description. "Imagine how boring we'd have been without their influence, though."

"True. I'm still determined to write my memoir one day and sell a million copies, wind up on Oprah and all that. I'll save a few chapters for you to put in your story."

"You're too kind." She sighed. "I miss you so much."

"Hang in there, sweetie. I'll see you in a few days."

"You can't get here soon enough."

"Love you, Tia-bear."

A lump formed in her throat. Lizzie had been there for her when no one else was. She had taken Tiana in when she had nowhere to go, and given her the only unconditional love she'd known through her life. "Love you too."

She ended the call, but even the prospect of Lizzie's impending visit couldn't ease the awful pressure in her chest. Ever since that night last summer when she'd learned the truth about Brian it felt like her world was caving in.

Now she was flat-out scared. The thought of Evan trying to take Ella away even part time was enough to send her into a panic.

Rain continued to splatter across her windshield as she drove beyond the town and finally turned onto Salt Spray Lane. Tall cedars and Douglas Firs bordered either side of it, and at the top of the rise her first destination came into view. Beckett and Sierra's gorgeous heritage Victorian stood proud in the center of its ocean view lot. Warm light spilled from its windows into the gloom.

Knowing her daughter was safe and warm and cared for there put a smile on Tiana's face.

But as she pulled into the driveway, she spotted Ella sitting on the side porch not with Beckett, but with that man who worked for him—Aidan MacIntyre.

Her jaw tensed and her spine went rigid.

Hell, no.

She'd taken all she could take today, and he was the last damn straw.

Chapter Two

Here comes trouble.

Aidan would never dare say it aloud, especially not in front of Ella, but he thought it loud and clear as Tiana Fitzgerald slammed her car door shut and came marching through the rain toward them. He was used to seeing her in flowy, bohemian-style dresses and tops, but today she had on jeans and a sweater beneath her dark blue rain jacket.

"Hi, Mama," Ella called out, seated beside him.

"Hi, sweetheart." Her face was shadowed by her hood, only a few locks of fiery red hair escaping. Despite her sweet answer to her daughter, Aidan could feel the laser-like burn of her stare on his face as she approached. The woman was an arresting, albeit somewhat hostile firecracker.

"Hello, Tiana," he said, hiding a smile.

"Hi." She stopped, standing there stiffly as she faced off with him. "You're back."

"Been back a week or so." He'd been gone over three, back home to Edinburgh to visit his family for the first time in a year, and to finalize his upcoming work contract. Not that she probably cared.

He wished she would have. He wished she'd missed

seeing him around, or that she was even a tenth as attracted to him as he was to her. She was the first woman in a damn long time who had captured his interest so intently.

She nodded and looked past him to the house. "Where's Beckett?"

"Inside on a conference call."

Dismissing him, she turned her attention back to Ella. "You ready to go, sweetheart?"

"I want to walk Walter with Mac first. We were waiting for you to get here to ask."

"I told her she had to check with you to see if it was okay," he said. Ella had taken to calling him by the nickname his friends here in Crimson Point used.

Tiana's expression shuttered for a moment, then she aimed a smile at her daughter. "It's pouring rain out. We should get home. And I'm sure Aidan has better things to do than—"

"I'd love a good walk in the rain," he put in. He liked being outside, and the scenery here on the Oregon Coast was some of the finest he'd seen.

She flicked him an annoyed look and spoke to Ella again. "Well, I'm sure poor old Walter would rather stay curled up inside where it's warm and dry."

"No, it's okay," Ella said, popping up and heading for the porch door. "Miss Sierra got him a special raincoat to keep him dry. She says he needs more walks now because he's putting on weight. Mr. Beckett's been giving him too many treats." She paused at the door to grin at them. "He got in trouble for it." She disappeared inside, presumably to get Walter.

Aidan could barely hold back a smile at Tiana's impatient sigh. "She's a strong-willed little thing," he remarked.

"Don't I know it," she muttered.

"I think she comes by it honestly."

That earned him a glare, and this time he couldn't keep a straight face. He'd never had a woman react to him the way Tiana did. For whatever reason she'd made up her mind to dislike him on sight the first time they'd met last fall, and things hadn't improved much since. She seemed to be slowly, grudgingly coming to tolerate him whenever they happened to cross paths, but she didn't trust him, especially not with Ella.

That part bothered him. He had no idea what he'd ever done to get on her bad side or make her suspicious of him, but there it was. And it was a hard shot to the ego to not know whether she found him attractive or not, when he was captivated by her.

"Why don't you come out of the rain at least while you wait?" he said. "I won't bite."

She considered him for a moment, then approached the steps. On the porch she gave him a wide berth, standing farther away than necessary as she pushed her hood back to expose the glorious fall of her red waves, seeming determined to ignore him while they waited.

He wasn't going to allow that.

There was something about her that tugged at him. Since the night they'd met he'd wanted to get to know her better. He could have asked Beckett about her but he hadn't wanted to give himself away, especially to his boss. "Refresh my memory, because I seem to have forgotten." He waited a beat. "Have I done something to offend you?"

She turned her pretty, mismatched gaze on him. One eye was green, the other a golden hazel. As unique and arresting as she was. And if he wasn't mistaken, that was a blush forming in her creamy cheeks. "I'm just looking out for my daughter," she murmured, as though that explained everything.

It didn't. "I can understand that. But you don't need to protect her from the likes of me."

"Look." She glanced at the door to make sure Ella couldn't hear, then aimed that startling gaze on him once more. "It's been a long day, so excuse my lack of patience. May I be blunt?"

He inclined his head. "Please do."

"What's a single guy like you doing hanging around with a nine-year-old girl?"

The way she phrased it stunned him into silence for a moment. She thought he was some sort of deviant or something? Christ, that was an insult he'd never thought to have directed at him.

You told her to be blunt. He'd make sure not to do that again. At least not where he was concerned. "Bloody hell, you really don't think much of me, do you?"

She looked away with a defensive little shrug. "I don't know you."

No, she didn't. And just as it wasn't fair that women dealt with men judging them all the time, it wasn't fair for her to make judgments about him either. "Then come with us now and get to know me a bit. Who knows, I just might be able to improve your opinion of me a wee bit." Probably not a lot, but it was worth a shot. At the very least he deserved a chance to defend his character.

She didn't get the chance to answer because Ella reappeared at the door with Walter, leash in hand. The basset-spaniel mix's long ears drooped well below the edge of the bright yellow raincoat hood, the tips almost dragging on the wooden planks. His red-rimmed eyes stared up at Aidan with his default woeful expression.

"Awright, Walter?" Aidan asked him. "You ready for walkies?"

Walter wagged the end of his tail half-heartedly, his expression resigned. As if he knew he didn't have a choice in the matter and was trying to make the best of it.

"Just a short one," Tiana said firmly to her daughter. "You need to get your homework done—"

"I already did it," Ella argued.

"—and I need to go home and figure out something for supper." She turned toward Aidan, her expression as resigned as Walter's, and raised her fiery-red eyebrows. "Shall we?"

She sounded positively thrilled. "Aye." Aidan grabbed the brolly from where he'd left it leaning against the porch railing. He opened it as he walked down the steps, holding it over both Tiana and Ella to shield them from the rain.

Tiana darted a suspicious look at him, then murmured, "Thank you."

A bit grudging, but he'd take it. "My pleasure." He put his free hand in his pocket to keep it warm. The wind was cold and damp with the rain. "Now. Where are we off to, Ella?"

She scrunched up her nose, thinking for a moment. "The lighthouse."

"Brilliant. You and Walter go on ahead. I'll keep your mother dry under the brolly."

"Okay." Ella broke into a trot, dragging Walter behind her up the lane.

Tiana walked stiffly at his side, her hands in her pockets, eyes on her daughter.

"You said you've had a long day," he began, searching for a safe topic of conversation. Plus he was nosy and he liked to get to know people by asking personal questions.

"Yes."

"Do you want to talk about it?"

"Nope."

All right, then. Her boundaries were up and reinforced. Personal stuff was off the table for the remainder of the walk. "What shall we talk about, then? The weather?"

He was heartened to catch the slight quirk of her lips. "How about we not talk at all?"

He liked the sarcastic edge to her response. Sarcasm was a sign of high intelligence and a healthy mind. He was sarcastic as hell, so it boded well for them to get along once he broke through the ice shield surrounding her.

"Well now, that would be a shame. How will I improve your opinion of me if we don't have some sort of conversation?" He'd made up his mind to get under her prickly exterior somehow, and prove he wasn't the enemy. Tiana intrigued him. He respected her protectiveness of Ella, and the job she'd done in raising her daughter so far. And he wanted to show her he wasn't a bad bloke.

He knew only a little of her story. That she was a single mother raising Ella by herself, with no help from the father, whoever or wherever he was. That she worked fulltime as an occupational therapist, primarily with the elderly. Both things told him plenty about her character, and about the warmth and kindness she hid from him that he'd set his mind on reaching.

"Were you born and raised around here?" he asked her after a full minute of silence, unwilling to give up his quest to engage in some kind of conversation.

She cast him a sidelong glance and he was sure she was going to shut him down hard, but she surprised him by answering. "No, Idaho. But I haven't been back there in a long time. Where are you from in Scotland?" she asked, smoothly turning things back on him.

There were so many things about her he wanted to know. For instance, why she was standoffish with him, and so fiercely protective of her daughter. The latter seemed heightened to him, far more than the average mother. Had she always been that way? Or had something caused it? "Edinburgh. Have you ever been?"

"No."

"It's a bonnie country. And I'm not just saying that because I'm from there. There's no place like it in the world."

"I've heard that. But as you can imagine, I haven't been able to travel much. Been busy," she said, nodding ahead at Ella, whose little purple rain boots splashed in the puddles as she led Walter ahead of them. The pair of them made quite the picture, walking together in their raingear.

"Aye. My sister raised her two girls on her own until her husband came along just a few years ago. I saw how hard it was on her and the sacrifices she made. Being a single parent is one of the hardest jobs on earth."

"Yes," she agreed. "But it's worth it."

"Aye, 'tis. Especially when you end up with a girl as sweet as Ella."

Tiana was quiet a moment. "How old are your nieces now?"

He was heartened that she'd picked up the thread of conversation. "Fifteen and seventeen, both going on twenty-five. I've told my sister over and over that she should just lock them both away until they're thirty to keep them the hell away from all the boys sniffing about, but apparently there are laws against such things nowadays."

She gave him a wry look. "You mean you don't trust your own gender?"

He grinned. "Smart arse. We'll see who's laughing when Ella hits her teen years."

"Ah, yes. Can't wait to see what she puts me through."

"All part of the parenting adventure. You never know what's coming around the next corner."

He wasn't sure what he'd said wrong, but her expression dimmed. "No, we really don't."

The woman was as bonnie and prickly as a Scottish thistle, but he was willing to bet it hid an inner softness that would make the effort of reaching it more than worthwhile.

"Have you got any other family back home?" she asked.

"My parents."

"You must miss them. And your friends."

"I miss my family. As for my best mates..." He looked out at the sea, fighting the tide of memories that talking about them always brought. "I lost all three of them in Afghanistan a few years ago."

She gasped, looking horrified. "Oh my gosh, I'm so sorry. I didn't mean to pry."

"You're all right. Fair's fair. You may have noticed that prying is a bit of a habit with me."

A small smile curved her lips. "I have, actually."

"My biggest flaw, my mum always said. But my heart's in the right place."

"I really am sorry about your friends."

"Thank you." He would never forget them, or hearing the news that their convoy had been ambushed by insurgents. By the time Aidan's unit had been organized for a rescue attempt, it was too late.

That was his biggest regret—not reacting fast enough, not getting there soon enough. It had affected him for a long time. It had also taught him not to hesitate when he wanted to go after something.

And what he wanted now was Tiana.

They lapsed into silence again, and he was more curious about her than ever. He wanted to earn Tiana's trust and see if there was anything between them, something that could be built upon when he came back from the contract job he'd signed up for overseas.

"Ella's a sweetheart," he said to Tiana. "You've done a great job with her."

"Thank you."

They lapsed into silence again as they took the path toward the lighthouse. Just as well they didn't talk because as they neared the water the wind cut sharper across the point, threatening to turn the brolly inside out and making it necessary to shout.

Together they walked to the cliff's edge and paused

there to look out at the sea. Today it was an angry green-gray maelstrom pounding the shore and rising up to slam against the base of the cliff below. Beautiful, wild and mysterious. Much like the woman next to him.

A minute or two later, Tiana shifted her back to the wind and huddled deeper into her jacket. "We should head back," she said over the wind, ushering Ella and the dog back the way they'd come.

Aidan stayed slightly behind and to Tiana's left, using his larger body to try and shield her from the full force of the wind. "Cold?"

She nodded, her hair and most of her face swallowed by the edges of her hood that she'd pulled tight. "Freezing."

"I'll miss a lot of things about this place, but not the way the winter wind cuts through me," he said as they reached the start of the path once more.

Tiana looked up into his face, the angle allowing him to see the freckles scattered across her nose and cheeks. Adorable. Little fairy kisses, his mum had always called them. Aidan wouldn't mind kissing them himself. "Are you leaving?"

He chose not to be insulted by her enthusiasm. "Aye, end of the month. I've got a job lined up with an old mate of mine from the UK until my work visa extension is all settled." The extension he'd applied for had been denied, but Aidan's lawyer had appealed. They had a strong case and Aidan expected to hear good news any day.

"What kind of job?"

"Security contracting." He fully intended to come back here to Crimson Point afterward.

"For how long?"

"Six months or so." He'd enjoyed the break that working for Beckett's renovation company had afforded him, and he'd be sorry to leave. But he'd be sorrier yet if he didn't break through Tiana's defenses before he left. "I'll likely be back by mid-fall."

She smiled at him sweetly. "You were right about us talking more. I suddenly like you better for some reason."

Unoffended, he chuckled and pulled out his phone when it buzzed with a text message. "Sierra's wanting to know if you lasses would like to join us for dinner at their place. Jase and Molly are bringing the baby over."

Tiana opened her mouth, no doubt to refuse, but Ella grabbed the sleeve of her mother's coat, her expression hopeful. "Can we, Mama? I'm all done with my homework, and you hate having to cook every night—"

Tiana made a strangled sound and shot Aidan a look out of the corner of her eye, her cheeks turning a darker shade of pink from more than the wind. "I don't hate it," she argued, then paused. "No, you're right, I do hate it. All right, we'll stay for a bit."

"Yay!" Ella cried and broke into a jog with Walter tagging along doggedly at her heel.

"Does she want us to bring anything?" Tiana asked him.

"The answer'll be no, but I'll check for you anyway." He typed in the message, waited a few moments until Sierra's reply came back. "No, just bring yourselves."

"Okay."

Beckett and Sierra were both in the kitchen when they arrived at the house. "You guys look half frozen," Sierra said with a laugh. "Come sit by the fire and warm up."

"Don't mind if I do." Aidan loved hanging out here. The house was solidly built, and though it wasn't old by UK standards, it was for this part of the world and had a warm, homey feel that made it a comfortable place to gather.

Seated on the sofa in front of the fire he chatted with Ella while Tiana looked on, the firelight glowing on her red hair. Just the sight of her made his heart beat faster. It was an unfamiliar predicament. He was smitten, and he still couldn't tell if she found him anything but bothersome.

Jase and Molly showed up minutes later with two-month-old baby Savannah all wrapped up cozy in her car seat, and they all sat at the table together to eat. Tiana took Savannah when she started fussing, walking the curly-haired baby around and cooing to her. That natural, effortless warmth she displayed made Aidan smile. He wanted to feel it firsthand.

When dinner was over he and Tiana helped clear up in a silence that while maybe not completely comfortable, it wasn't strained, either. That was progress. Afterward he walked Walter down to the end of the lane, following Tiana as she drove Ella home.

"Thanks for the escort," Tiana said as she climbed out of her car and quickly ushered Ella up the wooden steps to the front porch. "Good night," she added over her shoulder, almost as an afterthought.

"Good night," he answered, admiring the shape of her as she moved inside.

At the door Ella turned back to him, her sweet little face shining with excitement. "Bye, Mac!"

"Bye, lass."

As the door swung shut behind them and the deadbolt slid home, Aidan smiled. Cold and wet though it might be out here, if he wasn't mistaken, some definite thawing had taken place today.

Chapter Three

"It's not looking good."

Brian sat completely still in the office chair, fighting to keep his expression impassive. "Meaning what?"

His lawyer leaned forward slightly, his forearms and linked hands resting on his desktop. "If this goes to trial, with the amount of evidence they have against you, as well as Ella's testimony... We're looking at a conviction."

Don't react. Don't let him see. Anger, humiliation and fear twisted together in a hot ball in the pit of his stomach. This was supposedly the best criminal defense attorney in the state, costing upwards of five-hundred bucks an hour, and now the man was suddenly telling him he didn't stand a chance? "Since when have you decided this?"

"Since I got a call this morning that two more girls have come forward with abuse allegations against you. They're both willing to testify."

This time he couldn't hide his reaction. He set his jaw, his face flushing hot. "Who?"

His lawyer opened a file and slid it over for Brian to see. The names jumped right out at him.

"It's bullshit." *All* of this was bullshit. He'd been put

on house arrest and had to wear a fucking ankle monitor 24/7. It was degrading. He'd lost everything: the high-paying job he'd worked so long and hard for, had sacrificed so much for. His reputation. His friends and coworkers. Even his own family had cut him out of their lives because of the charges laid against him. How much worse would it get if he were actually convicted?

Brian shook his head, struggling to keep the anger in check. He hadn't had anything important taken from him since his innocence was stolen was a kid—he'd made sure of that. He'd never been looked at with disgust before. Even his damn lawyer, who he was paying an obscene amount of money to try and clear his name, looked at him with disgust. As if he was some kind of deviant pervert who'd just crawled out from beneath a rock somewhere.

"So that's it? There's nothing you can do?" Brian demanded.

"The State Attorney's office has offered us a plea bargain."

His heart rate slowed a little, a glimmer of hope showing through the black cloud constantly hovering over his head. "What are they offering?"

"Reduced charges. Maybe even a reduced sentence if you plead guilty to all the charges."

"*All* the charges?" Screw that.

"Yes. Depending on what the judge rules, you'd be looking at a reduction of possibly a third or more of your sentence."

More blood rushed to his face, burning his skin, the volcanic anger boiling inside him impossible to repress. "I won't do it. I didn't hurt her. I never fucking *touched* her."

His lawyer's face remained impassive. "What about the other two girls? Did you touch them?"

The rage receded slightly as shame twisted his insides.

"No," he lied. But they'd been way too young to remember it. There was no way they could remember any of it, let alone prove it. Was there?

Cold sweat gathered beneath his arms and his pulse increased. How much did they remember? Or were they planning to just make shit up now because they couldn't remember the details and had heard about Tiana bringing charges against him?

His lawyer studied him for a long, silent moment. Judged him, and found him guilty. Brian could see it in those steely eyes. "Are you willing to risk adding a third more time to your sentence? If you admit to everything and take this deal, it's likely the prosecuting attorney will go easier on you. But if you refuse and force this to go to trial, force Ella and the others to testify against you..." He shook his head. "No judge is going to look kindly on that if you're convicted."

"And you think that's a foregone conclusion based on the evidence," he spat.

"Yes," the man said without missing a beat.

Brian didn't want to hear that. The "evidence" against him was stupid. Stuff they'd found on his personal computer and phone, and Ella's version of events. A freaking nine-year-old's word against his.

This whole thing was total BS. He hadn't harmed a hair on Ella's blonde head. He'd gone through way worse than she had, and no one had jumped to his defense. His abuser had never been arrested or brought to justice. Compared to what Brian had endured, Ella had nothing to complain about.

"As your attorney, I advise that you take this deal. It's the best you're going to get."

You disgusting piece of shit. The man didn't say it, but Brian knew he was thinking it. His expression and the cool look in his eyes said it loud and clear.

The lawyer opened the folder in front of him and

turned it around so Brian could see its contents. "Let's go through everything in the offered agreement first. Then you can take some time to think about it if you want." But his tone made it clear he thought Brian would be a fucking idiot not to take it.

"Fine," he muttered, crossing his arms as the man began to go through it. He wanted out of here. Away from everyone who knew what he was accused of and thought he was evil.

Listening to all the charges against him read aloud were more solid blows to his ego. He hated hearing the words, loathed the labels people now gave him.

Pervert. Pedophile.

Monster.

He was still fuming when he walked out of the office twenty minutes later. He couldn't believe he was probably going to jail, and that his life had been destroyed over a few insignificant incidents.

The Portland law office was busy. Clients filled the waiting area. To him it seemed like they all stared at him with judgmental expressions as he walked past, head high. Fuck them all. He couldn't help the way he was. The urges. And he wasn't violent.

But oh, he could see the appeal of violence against those who had wronged him.

What he wouldn't give to punish Tiana and her daughter for doing this to him—being the ones to bring the world down around him. That would fuel his fantasies for a long time to come.

The elevator let him out in the luxurious, marble-floored lobby. He stopped in the coffee shop to grab something for the road. Standing in line, he overheard the end of a conversation between two other men ahead of him.

"Thanks for flying in to meet me," the older man said

to the younger one, dressed in a business suit. Brian recognized him—a family lawyer from another firm in the building.

"I just want to see my daughter," the younger one replied. He was in jeans and a dress shirt, somewhere in his early thirties. "Ella's nine now."

Brian's ears perked up.

"I haven't seen her or Tiana in years," the younger man continued, "but Tiana hasn't changed. She's agreed to letting me have the initial visit, but she's not happy about it. I want to make sure we avoid any kind of legal battle going forward, if possible."

No way. This was Evan? Ella's father? The guy who had broken Tiana's heart when he walked out on them? He ducked his head, riveted to every word, hoping neither of them would notice or recognize him.

The older man patted Evan's back in a show of support and reached for the coffees sitting on the bar. "Don't worry, that's what I'm here for. I'll make sure you get regular access to your daughter from here on out."

They walked away, still chatting. Brian barely resisted the urge to follow them. As he waited for his order, an idea popped into his mind. Not a bad one, either. It wasn't the kind of revenge he truly wanted, but it was a start and a hell of a lot better than nothing.

He wouldn't let Tiana get away with this without retaliating.

A rush of vindication pulsed through him as he walked outside into the cold, spring rain. If he was going down, he was taking Tiana Fitzgerald with him.

****

"Do you see her?" Holding Ella's hand, Tiana anxiously scanned the passengers in the arrivals terminal at the airport.

"No, but don't worry. There's no way we'll miss her," Ella said.

A wry grin curved her lips. "True." Lizzie was impossible to miss.

"And we might even hear her before we see her."

Ha. "Also true." She bounced on the balls of her feet, about to burst with anticipation. "Gah, I'm just so excited! Can't wait to see her, it's been way too—"

A joyous cry rang out from somewhere beyond Tiana's line of sight.

Tiana went up on her toes, craning her neck to see, and an answering cry burst from her when she spotted the familiar mass of coppery curls bouncing toward them. She dragged Ella with her as she rushed forward to meet her aunt, who was running toward them in a blur of eye-popping neon pink, a jubilant smile lighting up her plump face. "Lizzie!"

Her aunt let out another excited cry and dropped the handle of her rolling suitcase, leaving it sitting in the flow of human traffic so she could pounce, engulfing both of them in a floral-scented hug that put a lump in Tiana's throat. "Oh, I'm *so* glad to see you girls," Lizzie gushed, squeezing tighter as she rained kisses on their faces. Tiana laughed. Then Lizzie stopped and cupped Ella's cheeks in her hands. "You've grown a foot since I saw you last, I swear."

Ella grinned up at her. "Soon I'll be as tall as you."

Lizzie's green eyes sparkled. "Taller, I'll bet." She sighed and hugged them again, still smiling, her suitcase forming a boulder in the stream of passengers flowing around them. "So. When do I get to see this beautiful new town of yours?"

The two-hour drive back to Crimson Point went by in a flash thanks to Lizzie's animated chatter. Tiana loved her twelve-years-older aunt for a thousand different reasons, but one of the best was how much of a free spirit she was.

Somehow she'd managed to find the strength to escape their toxic, controlling family a decade before Tiana had, and she'd even healed her emotional wounds enough to allow her a fulfilling life that gave her joy. She was Tiana's hero and role model in every way. Without her, Tiana would never have found the courage to leave her parents and her life in Idaho far behind.

Without her, Tiana would have become a victim rather than a survivor.

"This is it," Tiana said as she turned onto Front Street and the painted wooden Crimson Point sign came into view on the side of the road. "The beating heart of our picturesque little seaside town."

"Ohhh, isn't it gorgeous," Lizzie gasped, already taking pictures with her phone. "The pictures you sent didn't do it justice."

"Do you like to fly kites, Aunt Lizzie?" Ella asked from the backseat.

"I'm not sure if I've ever flown one."

In the rearview mirror Ella's eyes widened. "What? Well then we *have* to teach you while you're here."

"I'd love that."

"You hungry?" Tiana asked.

"Ooh, let's take her to Whale's Tale," Ella said. "Please?"

"I could eat an entire whale's tail right now," Lizzie joked.

Tiana parked out front of the quaint café/bookshop with a hand-painted wooden sign hanging from the roof out front boasting a humpback's fluke. "My friend Poppy owns it. Best lunch and pastries in town."

"It's nice to hear you talk about having friends," Lizzie said.

"Isn't it?"

"And cupcakes. Poppy also makes the best cupcakes,"

Ella added, grabbing Lizzie's hand and all but towing her inside.

"Oh, good. I love cupcakes," Lizzie said with a laugh.

Behind the counter in a frilly half-apron, a plum-colored turtleneck and her golden blond hair pulled up in a twist, Poppy broke into a huge smile when she saw them. "Hey, great to see you guys. And who's this?"

"Aunt Lizzie," Ella told her. "She's my mom's aunt, but my aunt too. She's staying with us for a visit."

"Poppy," she said, offering her hand to Lizzie, who shook it.

"Nice to meet you."

"You too." Poppy smiled at all of them. "So. What can I get you ladies today? Maybe afternoon tea for three?"

Lizzie looked down at Ella, shared a grin, and nodded. "That sounds lovely."

They sat at a table in the corner, and Poppy returned with a secret smile on her face. "Guess what just came in?" she asked Tiana, hand behind her back.

"I don't know, what?"

"Ta da." She produced the paperback she'd been hiding. "Katie Reus just released a new Redemption Harbor book."

"Oh! Gimme." She snatched it, flipped it over to read the back cover copy.

Lizzie read over her shoulder. "It sounds good."

"It is good. Poppy got me hooked on her stuff a while back. And she knows I'm old school and prefer paperbacks to ebooks." She grinned up at her friend. "Put it on my tab."

"You got it."

"What about me?" Lizzie asked Poppy.

Poppy stopped in surprise. "What do you like to read? Romance? Mystery? Thrillers?"

"I like them all."

Poppy pursed her lips, thinking. "I'll be right back."

She disappeared into the bookshop at the back and came back with another paperback. "Here's Toni Anderson's latest. I think you'll love her, she writes a mix of all three."

Lizzie took the book with a delighted grin. "Sold. Add it to her tab too," she said of Tiana. Poppy laughed and left to get their food ready.

Lizzie was in the middle of telling them about her latest travel adventure—riding a camel through the desert in Egypt—when the door opened and Tiana caught a whiff of a familiar scent that instantly put her on edge. Evergreen and spice and pure male confidence.

"Well now, who's this? A newcomer."

Tiana stiffened at the sound of that deep, Scottish burr behind her.

"Mac!" Smiling, Ella jumped out of her chair to rush around the table and wrap her arms around Aidan's waist. Tiana barely refrained from throwing out a hand to stop her.

Aidan stood there in a snug pair of jeans that hugged his long, muscular legs, and a blue plaid, flannel shirt rolled up to the elbows, exposing his roped forearms. A broad smile warmed his rugged face, a few days of dark auburn growth on his cheeks and jaw.

"How's my wee lassie today?" he said to Ella, giving her a fond smile that made Tiana's hackles bristle.

"I'm good."

"And who's this bonnie lady with you?" he asked, looking at Lizzie.

Her aunt was already pushing to her feet, the legs of her chair scraping against the floor in her haste. "I'm their aunt Lizzie. Their charmed aunt," she added with a coy grin.

Aidan's rumbling chuckle would have set Tiana's teeth on edge if it weren't for the strange little slivers of heat it caused low in her belly. He was outrageously hot, in a strong, masculine way, and while she might not want to notice it, she did.

She tossed Lizzie a dirty look—not that her aunt would notice or care—and shook her head. Lizzie was a terrible, notorious flirt. Most of the time Tiana found it adorable and amusing, but apparently not with Aidan. And it was absolutely *not* out of some sort of jealousy, she assured herself.

The man just…rubbed her the wrong way. All that confidence and strength combined with those looks? A flirt and a player if she'd ever seen one.

"What are you lasses up to today?" he asked, this time directing the question at Tiana.

The way his warm brown eyes delved into hers was unsettling to say the least. Whenever he directed his full attention on her, her brain stuttered.

"Just stopped in for a bite to eat on the way home," she answered, looking away. It was easier when she didn't look at him. When she wasn't forced to acknowledge his presence or the effortless, masculine appeal that heightened her awareness and put her on instant guard whenever she saw him. Men—at least the men she'd been attracted to in the past—were guaranteed to be bad news. She'd rather not take the chance again.

"We're having tea," Ella announced, sounding so pleased and grown up that Tiana couldn't help but smile at her.

"Ah. And will you be having scones with it as well?"

"I don't know—Mom, do we get scones?"

Before Tiana could respond, Aunt Lizzie reached over to pull the fourth chair out from the table. "Why don't you sit and join us, Aidan? I'll wager based on that accent you're no stranger to afternoon tea, and if you stay I'll be able to enjoy listening to you talk longer."

"Aye, I've been known to have tea and scones from time to time." His gaze moved to Tiana. "But I don't want to intrude."

"Don't be silly, we'd love you to stay," Lizzie said with an eager smile before Tiana could say otherwise.

Tiana subtly kicked her aunt's shin under the table, brining that bright green gaze to hers in annoyance. "We don't want to interrupt his workday. He's project manager for Beckett's renovation company, so I'm sure he has better things to do than sit here with us and waste time talking over a pot of tea."

"Not at all," he said, coming around to take the seat Lizzie had offered. His eyes twinkled with amusement as he smiled at Tiana. "As it so happens, I'm just on my way back from a project we're wrapping up, so I've got some time on my hands. I was going to take my lunch to go, but some lovely conversation with all of you and a cup of tea with one of Poppy's scones would be brilliant right now."

Ugh, of course it would, she thought sourly. Bah. Why did he have to be so damn hot and keep trying to be nice to her? What was he after?

Poppy came over to add his order to theirs, then brought out the three-tiered stands full of crustless finger sandwiches on the bottom plate, scones with clotted cream and jam on the middle one, and little tarts and cupcakes on the top. Tiana made an effort to be civil while they ate but not overly friendly, giving polite answers whenever he spoke to her, and he went out of his way to keep dragging her back into the conversation.

Once, Lizzie even kicked her in the shin, giving her the *what is wrong with you* look. The upward quirk of Aidan's lips told her he'd noticed the look and was enjoying Tiana's aggravation.

"Well, I've taken up enough of your time," he said at last. "I'd best be getting back into work. Old houses don't fix themselves, and we've got enough projects lined up to keep us busy for the next year and then some. Thanks for the invitation."

He dropped a twenty on the table, far more than what his portion and a tip had cost. Then he ruffled Ella's hair affectionately, automatically making Tiana stiffen and earning an adoring smile from her daughter. "Lovely to have met you, Lizzie. I hope to see you around town again before you leave."

"Likewise," her aunt replied with an admiring smile, chin propped in her hands as she watched Aidan saunter out of the café. As soon as the door shut behind him and he was out of view, she pulled her hands into her lap and spun toward Tiana with an incredulous stare. "Could you be any ruder?" she said in a loud whisper.

Tiana scowled back and sipped her tea. "I wasn't rude. I was totally polite."

"You *were* rude, Mom," Ella said, surprising her, and the hurt, almost disappointed expression on her little face pierced Tiana. "I think you hurt Mac's feelings."

Tiana barely withheld a snort at that. It would take a lot more than that to hurt a guy like "Mac's" feelings. A built, good-looking and charismatic guy like him would have no trouble finding a woman to hook up with when the urge struck him. She had no time for that kind of mentality, and certainly didn't respect it. Nor did she trust his motives.

"Honey, I didn't hurt his feelings," she insisted. "Now let's eat our cupcakes and get going so we can show Aunt Lizzie our place and the trail to the lighthouse before it starts to get dark."

To her credit, Lizzie waited until Ella was tucked into bed that night before pouncing on her. "Okay. What was that about today in the café?"

"What do you mean by 'that'?"

Lizzie gave her an impatient look. "You were outright rude to that gorgeous, friendly hunk of a Scotsman, despite him making every effort to get you to be nice to him."

"If he wanted me to be nice to him, then all he has to do is leave us alone."

"Why? He seems great. And Ella clearly adores him."

Ugh. "I don't want to encourage him, and I don't want him to get any closer than he already is."

Her aunt's coppery eyebrows rose. "Why ever not? Lord, Tia, if a man like that ever showed any interest in me, you'd find me doing the opposite of freezing him out."

"I didn't—" Okay, she kind of had. "It's…complicated." She busied herself in emptying the dishwasher, not wanting to get into it.

Lizzie was beside her in a flash, putting away the silverware as she continued. "Honey, I'm gonna tell you something because I love you."

Oh, God. Here we go.

"Don't sigh like that." Her aunt gave her a level look. "No one knows better than me how you grew up and what happened to you before you moved out on your own. I know what kind of guts that took. I also know what's happened since, and why you've sometimes got that chip on your shoulder, especially where men are concerned."

Tiana internally winced. A chip on her shoulder? Is that how she came across—cold and bitter, a man hater? "So you're basically saying I'm being a bitch."

"If that's how you usually treat Aidan and any other man who gets too close now, then yes."

She stopped and faced her aunt with an accusing frown. "*Ouch*."

Lizzie shrugged. "Hey, if I won't tell you like it is, who will?"

True. She sighed and leaned back against the edge of the counter, crossing her ankles. "You saw him."

"I sure as hell did," Lizzie said with an enthusiastic nod. "I had a full-on hot flash when he first walked through that door."

She would *not* smile at that, dammit. "Well, I've been there and done that. Guys like him. And that was before I dated the alcoholic and the pedophile." She shook her head, shaken and angry at herself all over again. "Did he seem like a predator at all to you?"

Lizzie looked perplexed. "Who, Brian?"

"No, Aidan. Because I can't tell anymore—my internal radar is either nonexistent or completely whacked when it comes to men." She'd been going to therapy about it, and though she had clarity now about why she might have chosen toxic men in the past, she wasn't convinced she could identify them going forward and wasn't going to risk it.

"Oh, stop."

She lowered her voice, making sure Ella wouldn't overhear. "No, I'm serious. I'm a disaster magnet. And twice now Ella's suffered because of it. I won't let it happen again."

Lizzie shook her head. "Well there's nothing wrong with *my* radar. Or Ella's, for that matter."

That was true. Ella hadn't liked Brian right from the start. But she'd connected with Aidan instantly.

"And so, I can tell you with one-hundred-percent certainty that the man I met today is no predator. I'd stake my life on it," Lizzie continued.

"I would've staked my life on Brian not being one, either." Worse, she'd staked Ella's on it, and been wrong.

Her aunt gave her a sympathetic look and took Tiana by the shoulders, her eyes earnest. "Baby, you're scared. Can't you see it?"

Tiana broke eye contact, unable to hold her aunt's gaze. It was true. She didn't trust herself anymore, or her instincts when it came to men. "Can you blame me?"

"No, not for being scared."

Man, she hated that she was behaving this way because she was scared. That was no example for Ella.

"But after all we've gone through, since when do you and I let fear dictate our lives?" Lizzie squeezed Tiana's shoulders, bringing her gaze back up.

"That's true," she admitted slowly.

"It sure as hell is. Now." She let go and gave Tiana an encouraging smile. "What's really going on with you? Deep down inside. Tell me."

Lizzie wasn't going to let her wriggle her way out of this. Her aunt had called her on her behavior and now Tiana had to answer for it.

She heaved a sigh and relented. "Okay, fine. I guess the truth of it is, I'm technically angry at myself, not Aidan. And I've been…" Pretty much a cold bitch where he was concerned. "A little cold to him because he's befriended Ella. Because I'm scared—" Ick. "—that he might be bad news and I just can't see it yet."

Her aunt nodded. "And?"

Man, Lizzie could still make her feel five years old. "And treating him as guilty without proof is wrong, and now you've made me feel bad," she added in a grumble.

"Honey, you were already feeling bad. You just needed to admit the root cause to yourself."

It was true. And it didn't feel good. She didn't want to be that way or have people think it of her. "Yeah," she muttered.

"No matter what you've gone through, it's not fair to treat him like the enemy when he's been nothing but kind to you and Ella. And besides, you're friends with the people he's closest to here. He even fought alongside two of them overseas, he said."

Also true. "With Beckett and Jase." Both former Green Berets. Beckett had been captain, and Jase one of his sergeants. She trusted them completely.

"Well, there you go. And wasn't Beckett the one who confronted Brian and punched him in the face that night?" her aunt continued.

"Broke his nose and split his lips open," Tiana said with a savage smile. "I wish I'd been there to see it." That whole night was a complete nightmare, except for that part. If Noah hadn't held her back, she would have added to the damage on Brian's disgusting face.

"Me too. But if Beckett hired Aidan, then doesn't it speak to the kind of person Aidan is?"

"Yeah," she admitted grudgingly. Jase and Beckett wouldn't associate with a bad person. And they would *never* have allowed Aidan to get close to Ella if they thought for a moment he might pose any kind of threat to her. They would have warned Tiana a long time ago and intervened on her behalf. That's just the kind of men they were.

Lizzie raised her eyebrows again.

She heaved a sigh, squirming inside. "Okay. *Okay*, fine, you're right. He's not the enemy. So what am I supposed do about it? Because I'm not interested in dating him, or anyone else." Not for a damn long time, anyway. If ever.

"That's such a waste, but it's your decision. In the meantime, just apologize—in person."

She grimaced, her wounded pride writhing in a sea of discomfort. "Oh, God." Anything but that.

Lizzie nodded and laughed softly. "Yep. And after you do that, maybe try explaining a bit about why you've been the way you have with him. Or even your background, if you think he's receptive to hearing it. You might just be surprised at his response."

She doubted it. And no way in hell was she telling anybody about her background. Least of all a man like Aidan. "All right," she agreed, picking up a tea towel to dry off one of the glasses still wet from the dishwasher. "I'll apologize next time I see him if the opportunity presents itself."

Her aunt glowered at her. "*If*? That's lame, Tia. No,

that's straight-up chickenshit."

Tiana made a face, feeling all kinds of defensive now that her insides had been laid open for scrutiny by the person she looked up to. "That's the best I can promise right now." She wasn't going to search him out and give him the wrong idea.

"All right, I'll take it. Now come on, give me a hug and let's go open a bottle of wine and put a movie on."

Tiana embraced her, exhaling. "I still love you even though you just lectured me like I'm a little kid. And I don't want you to go on Friday. A week with you isn't long enough."

"I lecture you because I care, and because I'm older and wiser. And no problem, I'll just cancel my bucket list cruise through the Panama Canal, South America and Antarctica and lose the fifteen grand I spent," she deadpanned.

"Good." Tiana wasn't sure what she hated more: the idea of Lizzie leaving them again, or apologizing to Aidan MacIntyre's handsome face.

Chapter Four

Four days later, Aidan left his third meeting of the afternoon twenty minutes late and jumped in his SUV to race to the next—this meeting at one of the heritage homes they were currently renovating on the other side of town. He detested being late, but the homeowner he'd just finished up with had needed extra time to go over everything and it couldn't be helped.

One of their construction crews was already on site when he arrived. They'd removed the rotten old front porch and had started framing out the addition that was going on the kitchen. If they maintained this pace and didn't run into any major problems or surprises, they might just finish up on schedule.

He grabbed his clipboard from the passenger seat and checked his phone on the way to the front door, mentally juggling his schedule. The job was fast paced and kept him busy, but he thrived when it came to logistics and organization. It was a big reason why Beckett had wanted him to come on board and take over as project manager after he'd let Carter go last year.

Their top electrician was up on a ladder installing new wiring in the ceiling they'd opened up. "Hey, Mac."

"Everything going okay?" Aidan asked him.

"Every job has its quirks and challenges," the man said with a smirk as he threaded the new wires through a hole he'd drilled in the ceiling joist. "But so far, this one's not giving us that much trouble."

"That's what I like to hear. How are the lads getting on upstairs?"

"Dunno. Been too busy to check on them."

"I'll go up there now." Hammering from above said they were keeping busy.

Three of the guys were having a grand time demo'ing the vanity and counter in the master bedroom. They'd already knocked out two walls and installed load-bearing beams to shore up the ceiling for what would become the new master suite. "Lads. How goes the battle?"

"We're finally winning," the youngest one said with a grin, his face and hair covered in a layer of beige-colored dust. "It ain't pretty, but we're winning."

Holy hell. They'd hacked the poor vanity to bits with their sledgehammers, leaving one hell of a mess behind.

"There was no other way," the senior guy told Aidan. "It's like they built this thing to be bombproof."

He studied the carnage, noting the giant holes in the walls that would all have to be replaced rather than just filled and sanded. "How much longer until you're done and cleaned up in here?" Because now he'd need to have new sheetrock installed, then have it mudded and taped before the cabinet guys and painters could do their jobs.

"Should be able to finish by tonight, maybe."

He raised an eyebrow. "Maybe?"

"Okay, by tonight."

Aidan withheld a sigh and nodded. "Fine, but none of you leaves until it's done and cleaned up. I need to have new sheetrock installed first thing in the morning."

It would still screw up the timeline for the trades he had scheduled for the bathroom, and it would definitely add to the budget. And as project manager, he got the enjoyable task of informing the homeowner that their bathroom wouldn't be finished by deadline, and oh, by the way, it's going to cost more than what was stipulated in the budget.

All part of the glamor of being project manager, but he didn't mind. He could handle stress. A necessary trait to do what he'd done in the military. And he was a people person, so it worked for him.

Although the job wasn't something he'd ever considered taking before Beckett had called him up that day, it suited him. It paid well. He didn't get shot at and his life wasn't in danger. His hours were pretty much eight-to-six with some overtime thrown in here and there when things needed to get done, but he mostly got the weekends off and Beckett was a fair boss.

Aye, he could see himself staying on long-term. He'd like to. Unfortunately that wasn't up to him, because it all depended on whether the extension on his work visa came through.

He went to another job site on the east side of town next. After dealing with some problems that inevitably cropped up with renovating an old house with an equally old foundation, plumbing and wiring, he finally drove home.

The rental he lived in was actually Noah's. When the sheriff had moved into Poppy's house next door, he'd offered his place to Aidan. Aidan had been looking for a place of his own, and since the location, timing and price of the rent had been right, he'd taken it.

He parked in the carport and was just getting out of his vehicle when his cell rang again. This time it was his lawyer. "Have you got good news for me?" he asked, starting for the door.

"Well, not exactly."

Aidan didn't like the sound of that. "They ruled against

us?"

"Worse. They rejected the appeal outright."

Oh, *shite*. Now what? He unlocked the door, disarmed the security system and stepped into his mudroom, toeing off his boots and going straight to the kitchen. "So that's it? There's nothing else to be done?"

"I'm looking into a few things. I wanted to set up a meeting with you. Are you free to come in for a meeting this Friday? I've got a colleague of mine involved in your case. I want to go over your options, and make sure we've got a plan going forward."

No, he had a thousand things to juggle on Friday. But he had to make time for this. "What time?"

A heavy feeling of disappointment hit him as he ended the call a few minutes later. He loved Crimson Point. Liked his job, his coworkers.

And he also liked Tiana Fitzgerald.

Unless his lawyer pulled off a miracle, his time here was almost up. He wouldn't be able to work in the U.S. again without attaining permanent residency first, and who knew how long that would take, or even if it would happen?

He stood at the kitchen sink gazing out at the tidy backyard. How had this happened? His lawyer had been so sure the denial would be overturned.

He looked down at his phone, still in his hand. Though he didn't want this to be the end, that's the way it was looking right now. And much as he didn't want to, Aidan had to inform Beckett that he had to hire a new project manager.

****

Beckett wrapped up his own meeting with a sense of deep satisfaction. By securing the new contract on another heritage house for next spring, the company now had guaranteed work for the next year-plus. And with word of mouth continually spreading about their work, he was even getting calls from up and down the coast. The way things were going, he'd have to bring on more admin staff and might even need to open up another office in another city on the coast to handle the growing volume.

Those were the kinds of problems he liked having.

It was almost six. Sierra would be finished at her clinic soon. One of his many faults was that he tended to err on the side of being a workaholic. Lately he'd been making a more concerted effort to knock off work at a consistent time each day so he could have dinner with his wife, trusting Jase and Mac and the rest of the management team to keep everything clicking along smoothly.

He wasn't really a romantic guy, but he tried to show Sierra every day how much he loved her and so far she hadn't complained. He'd almost lost her, and he never wanted to take her for granted.

When he spotted the neon open sign glowing in the flower shop window as he came up the street, inspiration struck. He'd get a bouquet and surprise her with it and—

He jerked the wheel to the right and slammed on the brakes when the small rock in the middle of the road suddenly moved. What the hell was it?

He got out, pausing when he heard the faint little cry coming from it. A kitten?

Frowning, he walked over to it, realizing even from thirty feet away that something was very wrong. The little gray ball was the size of his palm. Way too tiny to be on its own out here, let alone away from its mother. Its eyes were barely open.

He crouched down to pick it up, half-afraid he would hurt it, it was so small. "What are you doing out here all alone?" he asked it. It didn't appear to be injured, as far as he could tell. He tucked it inside his jacket to keep it warm and looked around, then walked to the edge of the ditch to check, just in case.

"Hell." More tiny, young kittens. All crawling around almost blindly on a small ledge above the open ditch.

He climbed down and rescued them all, tucking them inside his jacket with their littermates. "Where's your mom, guys?" A mother cat wouldn't leave her babies for long, right? Maybe she'd gone out to hunt. Or maybe—

His gaze caught on something lying at the edge of the shoulder near the flower shop.

No. The mother definitely wasn't out hunting.

He turned away and climbed out of the ditch, pulling out his phone to call Sierra while the kittens mewled and wriggled against his shirt. "Hey, I've got kind of an emergency situation here," he said when she answered. "A whole litter of orphaned kittens I just found at the side of the road."

"Ohhh. How old are they?"

Her soft heart was evident in her voice. She'd been rescuing all kinds of animals ever since he'd known her. "Young. Real young, maybe a couple weeks old, I dunno."

"Any sign of the mother?"

"She's dead. Hit by a car."

"Oh, the poor things. Where are they now?"

"Crawling all over my shirt."

She let out a soft laugh. "Is it any wonder why I love you?"

He was just damn glad she did. His life had been cold and empty without her.

"Can you bring them in right away? They'll need to be kept warm and fed."

His wife had this all dialed in. "Sure. Be there in about ten minutes." He went into the flower shop to get a box for the kittens. After settling them into it on top of his jacket for warmth, he took a towel from the back of his truck and went and wrapped up the mother cat to take her to the clinic with her babies. He placed the box of kittens on the passenger seat where he could keep an eye on them as he drove.

His phone rang as he was getting behind the wheel. Mac. "Hey, brother. What's up?"

"You sound busy. Should I call back?"

He grunted. "Just performing a standard rescue op with a litter of orphaned kittens. I gotta get them over to Sierra asap."

"Oh, well, I won't keep you then. I'll talk to you tomorrow."

It wasn't like Mac to hedge. "Something wrong?"

"No. I'll talk to you later. Good luck with the kittens."

Beckett set his phone down and started the engine, wondering what was going on. Mac wasn't a secretive guy, he was too much of a snoop for that. There was only one reason Beckett could think of for him to put off their conversation, and he hoped the hell he was wrong, but his gut said otherwise. The damn work visa extension must have fallen through. "Hell."

Mac was not only an invaluable part of the company, he was a damned good friend. Beckett would hate like hell to lose him.

One kitten made a reckless escape attempt over the side of the box. Probably the same intrepid one that had wandered into the road earlier. "Whoa there, little man," he said, grabbing it before it could fall over the edge and use up another one of its nine lives. "Hang tight. I'm taking you guys to a real nice lady who'll fix you all up."

Sierra had a soft spot for lost and wounded things. She rescued them, nurtured them and turned their lives around.

Him included.

Chapter Five

Tiana was with her last patient of the day, dreading the upcoming meeting she couldn't avoid. It couldn't be helped, however, and getting home to be with Ella and Lizzie after was its own reward for what she was about to endure.

She helped Mrs. Alvarez back into her recliner, providing support and watching for any signs that the elderly woman was about to lose her balance, mindful of the hip replacement she'd just undergone. "Easy does it."

"Yes, yes," she murmured, gingerly easing her weight back into the chair with a grimace. When she was seated she let out a relieved breath and grinned up at Tiana. "Whew. I hope my bladder holds out until bedtime. I'm not looking forward to getting up again anytime soon."

Tiana smiled back. "I'll bet. But you know how important it is for you to keep moving, for your muscles and your cardiovascular system. I know it hurts, but the longer you sit, the harder it will be to get moving again."

Mrs. Alvarez groaned. "Yes, yes, I know."

Tiana wasn't fooled by the ready agreement. "So you promise to get up when the timer goes off in the kitchen?"

The woman narrowed dark, accusing brown eyes at her. "You left it in the kitchen? Sadist."

"It's only because I care," she answered, taking a page out of Lizzie's book. Her aunt was leaving way too soon. Tiana didn't want her to go. It was so nice to have the company.

"Hmph." Now Mrs. Alvarez looked worried. "How long do I have?"

"Forty-three minutes and counting."

Her eyes widened. "Forty-three…"

"You'll thank me later, I promise. And your daughter is coming by in about fifteen minutes, so she'll help you when you need to get up again."

Tiana called Lizzie on her way out of the one-story bungalow two towns east of Crimson Point. "Hey, how are things there?"

"Wonderful, of course. Ella's just finishing up her homework, then we're going to walk up to get Walter and take him for a stroll. Who knows, maybe we'll even get lucky and bump into Aidan while we're out."

"Wouldn't that be something?" Tiana said dryly. Her aunt had asked her about him every day since they'd seen him at Whale's Tale. Tiana hadn't seen him again and wasn't going to search him out.

"Yes." She could hear the smile in Lizzie's voice. "If we do, maybe I'll invite him over for dinner. That way you can have that talk afterward."

"Yeah, thanks but no thanks. I've got enough on my mind today." The apology would happen when it happened. She had more important things to worry about at the moment.

Her aunt was silent a moment. "You sure you're up to this?"

"Oh yeah." There was no damn way she would let Evan meet with Ella without first having a face-to-face talk with him privately, court-appointed liaison supervisor or not.

"I kind of wish I could watch what happens live. I can

picture you flaying him alive with only your eyes. It would be awesome."

Tiana frowned. "Can Ella hear you?"

"Of course not."

"Good. Because I'm going to try and keep this civil, for her sake. But if he gives me any sign at all that I don't like, I'll fight him in court until I'm bankrupt and living on the streets if that's what it takes."

"That's my girl. And if you go bankrupt, you can both move in with me. I'll give up traveling and support you guys until all my savings run out."

Tiana smiled. Except for Lizzie, she'd never had anyone to support her. It meant a lot. "I love you, you know."

"Of course I know. And I love you back. You're my—"

"Favorite niece. I know."

"Well, it's true. All right, you get on the road then. I know how you like to be early for everything. You can set up camp and be waiting there for him when he walks in. Like a spider waiting for the fly to land in its web." She sounded gleeful. "I'm sending you all my love and strength. Everything's going to be fine, you'll see."

"Thanks. I'll call you after."

"You'd better."

"Tell Ella I love her."

"She knows, but I will anyway. Bye."

"Bye." A nervous bubbling started up in her stomach as she drove to the meeting location two towns to the south. She'd wanted this to be on neutral ground, where no one she knew was likely to see her or overhear what was said.

She was waiting in the restaurant at a corner table by the window when Evan walked in twenty minutes later. Even though she'd thought she was prepared for this, even though she knew what he looked like now from doing research online, the sight of him in person was still a shock.

He'd dyed his mousy brown hair dark and cut it short. He'd filled out through the chest and stomach but he carried the extra weight well and he cut a professional figure in dress slacks, shirt and a tailored jacket. The image of a professional, successful musician on the rise. Barely having any resemblance to the hard rock sex symbol she'd fallen for a decade ago.

He scanned the restaurant, his blue gaze locking on her when he spotted her over by the window. She'd chosen her seat specifically so that he would have to be looking into the light the entire time. Maybe it was a little petty, but whatever. He deserved to be uncomfortable.

Evan put on a pleasant smile that ten years ago would have made her all fluttery. Now it had no effect on her whatsoever. "Tiana, hi," he said when he reached the table. "It's been a long time."

She didn't stand or return the smile. "Evan."

His expression sobered and he sat, trying and failing to angle his chair to avoid the glare of the sun in his eyes. He settled for shifting around the table, twisting so that he was almost in profile to her. "Thanks for meeting me. It's… You look great."

"Thanks." She didn't give a shit what he thought of her looks, but she'd worn one of her nicest dresses and heels and touched up her hair and makeup before coming inside. Because she had an image to project. She was all grown up now, independent and not to be fucked with.

A server came over to take their drink orders. Tiana ordered coffee. She would have loved a double martini, but that would have to wait until she got home. Lizzie would fix her up. "So," she said once they were alone again. "Why now?" she asked, not willing to engage in bullshit small talk when her daughter's welfare was at stake.

"Why now what?" he asked, looking puzzled.

"It's been almost ten years. Why do you suddenly want

to be part of Ella's life now?"

Her directness seemed to take him aback for a moment. He cleared his throat and looked down at the table as he fiddled with his napkin. "I'm married now. My wife and I have twin six-month-old boys."

"I read that, yes."

That seemed to throw him off too. "Well, it made me think more about Ella. She's been on my mind a lot recently and I want to get to know her. I want her to get to know me and my family."

His words twisted like knives in her gut. "Let's not get ahead of ourselves." No way in hell was she allowing him any form of custody. Supervised visits were hard enough. And there was something else bothering her. "Your wife started this, didn't she? After you had the boys, she started encouraging you to find and meet Ella."

His stunned expression told her she was dead on. "She may have been the one to start the ball rolling in this direction," he allowed.

"That's what I figured."

A spark of anger lit his eyes. "But I'm here now because I want to get to know my daughter." He sighed and lowered his gaze. "Tiana, I know what you must think of me after—"

"Trust me, you don't," she shot back. There was no way he could understand what she thought or how she felt about him—the man she'd given everything to, only to be suddenly abandoned with their child without a backward glance.

He grimaced at the bite in her tone. "Look," he said, glancing around to make sure no one was watching and then lowering his voice before he continued. With his career as a lead guitarist finally taking off, he had his image to protect. She hoped the hell that wasn't another reason for this sudden interest in Ella. "I was a selfish asshole back then. I know it, and I'm not proud of it. Ella came along by surprise and I just couldn't be what either of you needed me to be then."

It's not like she'd had a choice either. Ella had been just as much a surprise to her as to him, yet from the moment she'd learned she was pregnant, there was no way she could ever have walked away from her own child. "So you took off and left me to deal with everything alone without bothering to check on us or pay any kind of child support. Until very recently. And, if you'll remember, I was two years younger than you and going to school full time when I got pregnant."

"I know," he acknowledged with a solemn nod.

"I had to quit school. It took me until just a few years ago to finish my program and become certified as an OT. That entire time in between, I struggled with working two and sometimes three part-time jobs just to feed us and keep a roof over our heads while raising her by myself."

He winced a little but she didn't see any reason to spare him the details. Why should she? She wanted him to have a clue about what she and Ella had gone through because of him.

Her pulse beat faster, anger pumping through her bloodstream. This confrontation had been a decade in the making. She wasn't going to cause a scene, for both their sakes, but she also wasn't going to make any of this easy on him. He didn't deserve to have Ella in his life now.

"And I also never went after you for any kind of support," she continued. "I could have. You know I could have, and I'd have gotten it, too. I could have ruined your life for what you did, but I didn't." She could ruin it now, if she chose, and he knew it. "And do you know why? Because I recognized that Ella and I were better off without you. I recognized that you were a toxin, and I wanted you out of our lives for good."

Evan let out a breath, all but squirming in his chair, the sun still blinding him. "I know, and I get it. I've got no defense for what I did. And now that I'm a father again and I see all the work that goes into raising a child, all the little milestones I missed with Ella…" He met her eyes, and to his credit he didn't look away.

"You feel guilty now."

"Yes. I did all along, but even more so now." He lifted his hands. "All I can say is, I'm sorry, Tiana. For leaving you both like that, and for making you do all the hardest work in the world in raising her by yourself."

His apology surprised her. It seemed so sincere. But he'd fooled her before, and other men had since too. "Thank you for that."

He gave a slight nod. "How is she, anyway? Does she have a father figure in her life?"

"No." How was she? She was a gorgeous, bright and kind little girl who was always seeking the approval and attention of the men around her. Unconsciously trying to heal the wound of her father leaving her.

Tiana had learned all of that when she'd taken Ella to an old college friend in Seattle who had a child psychology practice for therapy after the horrific incident with Brian. More than any of the rest of it, that knowledge broke her heart. "And to answer the first question, she's fine. She's well-adjusted, gets good grades and has a real way with animals." In spite of everything. Ella was a miracle.

Evan sighed almost in relief at her answer and sat back. "I appreciate that you were willing to do the mediation and do this without involving lawyers too much. And if it makes you feel any better, I have no intention of seeking partial custody. I don't want to try and take Ella away from you. That's not what this is about."

His words should have eased her deepest fears but instead they stirred them, making them shove against the lid of the box she'd stuffed them in before entering the restaurant. "That's good. Because I would fight you until my dying breath to make sure that never happened."

He shook his head, a wry smile tugging at his mouth, and she'd be lying if she didn't admit to feeling a subtle pang. He'd been her first love. Her first everything. And then he'd shattered her whole world. "You're a lot tougher than you used to be."

He had no idea. "I've had to be tough."

"Yeah, I guess you would have." His eyes held something that seemed a lot like respect, and that surprised her too. "All I'm asking for is a chance. If Ella wants to meet me, then I'd like to meet her. Introduce myself. Get to know each other a little. Talk over the phone every so often so we stay in touch. And maybe one day if she was comfortable she'd want to come to California—" Tiana opened her mouth to protest but he cut her off with an upraised hand and a firm look. "Maybe one day. I'm not saying anytime soon."

Not until hell freezes over. But it wasn't her decision, was it? Once this initial visit happened, it would open a virtual Pandora's box of possible repercussions. What if Ella wanted to be with him instead? What if one day, when she was old enough, Ella decided she wanted to move to California to be close to him? Or worse, move in with him?

Fear congealed her insides, her stomach muscles cramping.

She was already fifty steps ahead, worrying about things that might never happen. Her anxiety was expert at it. "When do you see this meeting happening?"

"The sooner the better. I was hoping to see her before I fly home this weekend. The court liaison is free this Saturday, if that works."

So soon? "Where would you meet?" She didn't want him coming to her house. It had to be on neutral ground.

"Wherever Ella's most comfortable."

It was what Ella wanted, so she had to find a way to

make peace with it. "Fine. But you should know, Ella's been through a lot already in her short life. If you do anything to hurt her or try to take her away, I'll do whatever it takes to make sure you never see her again." She didn't care if it made her seem like a cold, raging bitch. She didn't give a shit what he thought of her—her only concern was for Ella. "Are we clear?"

He held her gaze for a few heartbeats, taken off guard. "Yeah. We're clear."

"Text me if it's a go for Saturday." She started to rise.

Evan shot a hand out across the table to grasp her wrist. "Can't you stay and eat? I was hoping we could..." He gave a nervous laugh, seemed at a loss of what else to say.

She raised an eyebrow, incredulous. "What? Be friends?" Her acid tone let him know that was never going to happen.

"That we could not be enemies at least," he said slowly.

She pulled free of his hand and straightened. "Whether or not we're enemies depends entirely on you," she said, then dropped a five-dollar bill on the table beside her untouched coffee and strode for the door.

By the time she got to her car the shakes had settled in. She shut her door and gripped the wheel, glad he couldn't see how much this had rattled her.

Closing her eyes, she took slow, deep breaths until the worst of it had passed. She hated that Evan had once again become part of their lives, but there was no help for it. All she could do now was support her daughter and hope that the secret fear of losing Ella turned out to be unfounded.

****

Evan stayed and ate alone, though he took Tiana's empty seat to escape the blinding sun hitting him right in the eyeballs. The meeting hadn't gone at all as he'd envisioned—or hoped.

The woman he'd just met with was hard to reconcile with the one he'd once known, except physically. She was still as beautiful as ever, still dressed in her long, bohemian-style clothes. But there was a hardness to her now. A blade-sharp, cold edge that had sliced him where he sat, just from meeting her eyes.

Had he caused that? Or had something or someone else caused it? Maybe he'd started it, and someone else had finished it.

It hadn't been easy to sit there and face her after all this time. He knew she hated his guts, and he didn't blame her. From all appearances and from what his lawyer had dug up on her, she seemed like a good mother. What had she told Ella about him? Had she poisoned their daughter against him over the years? He would find out the answer to that soon enough.

He left the restaurant deep in thought, and frustrated. While he hadn't expected Tiana to be more than civil, deep down he'd hoped they could move past everything and at least try to have a cordial relationship from now on, for Ella's sake. But she wasn't even giving him a chance to show that he'd changed.

He was more than okay with paying Tiana all the support he owed to her. His music career was finally starting to take off and he'd always felt like a deadbeat not paying any kind of support.

The sun had completely disappeared behind an impenetrable blanket of slate-gray clouds when he walked outside. He'd become so used to SoCal's dry, warm climate, he felt downright chilly in just his suit jacket as he walked to his rental car.

Parked two rows over, he spotted the manila envelope stuck beneath one of the windshield wipers. It had his name on the front.

Frowning, he pulled it free and glanced around. Had Tiana left it for him? Some kind of legal threat?

Once behind the wheel he pulled it open to check the contents. Ella Fitzgerald was written on top of the first page, followed by a list of paragraphs.

He pulled the papers out, confused. But the moment he began scanning the contents, he knew it hadn't been Tiana.

What he read stunned him.

Background information about Tiana and Ella. Various incidents over the past few years that she must have gone to great lengths to hide, because his lawyer hadn't mentioned any of it. What the hell? Was any of this true?

He kept reading, his alarm growing.

A gasp shot out of his mouth when he got to the bottom of the first page. "*Child* molester?" he blurted and flipped the page, horror bursting through him as he kept reading. Tiana had allowed Ella to be alone with a sexual predator for long periods of time? The asshole had jerked off in front of her? "What the hell…?"

Ella's been through a lot already in her short life.

Tiana had said that. Surely to Christ she hadn't meant *this*?

It was unbelievable. He glanced around again, shaken. Who had left this for him? No friend of Tiana's, so they must have followed him.

That concern paled in comparison to the envelope's contents. All this time he'd thought Tiana had been a wonderful mother to their daughter. Now he wasn't so sure. Is that partially why Tiana had been so defensive earlier? Was she afraid he'd known all of this and would try to take legal action against her?

Jesus. If what he'd just read was true, if Ella was in danger living with her mother, then maybe she was better off—safer—with him.

He tucked the papers away and set the envelope on the

seat, beyond disturbed. He would send everything to his lawyer as soon as he got back to the hotel, see if they could find out if any of this was true.

Evan hoped it was all lies. But if it wasn't, he might have to take action to protect Ella. If he subsequently decided to pursue custody at any point, he now might have the ammo he needed to make it happen.

Chapter Six

Tiana left the hospital the following night after completing a session with an elderly patient recovering from a debilitating stroke. On her way to the parking lot she checked her phone and found a message from Lizzie.

We're at Beckett and Sierra's with a litter of orphaned kittens. Ella in her glory. Walter, not so much.

Tiana chuckled and walked to her car parked out back. Poor Walter. And poor *her*, because now Ella would be all over her in her ceaseless campaign to get a pet. She'd wanted a dog originally, but Tiana would bet that her daughter would settle for a kitten as of today.

On my way, she sent back, looking forward to getting home and spending time with her two favorite people.

The constant rain that seemed to have gone on forever this spring had finally stopped. Warm sunshine shone down between gaps in the clearing cloud cover, glinting off the newly emerging green leaves in the trees overhead. Birdsong filled the air.

Her mood lifted. Even with the constant weight of her troubles pressing on her, she'd made a conscious decision not to let them rule her life. Aunt Lizzie had taught her many valuable things over the years, but one of the most important lessons was this: *She* was responsible for her own happiness. No one else.

It was true, and something Tiana had learned time and time again after every failed relationship ended. Whenever she became overwhelmed by the things life seemed to enjoy constantly throwing at her, one of the things that helped the most was stopping and taking note of everything she had to be thankful for. Counting her blessings centered her, reminded her what was truly important. And, without a doubt, the most incredible blessing of her life was Ella.

On the drive home she geared up for the conversation she had to have with her daughter that night. There'd been no word yet from Brian's lawyer about whether he was going to take the plea bargain or not. And if Ella didn't object, she would meet with her father on Saturday morning with a court liaison present.

If she wanted no part of it—and if she was honest, part of Tiana still didn't want the meeting to happen—then Tiana would cancel and let the lawyers work it out, while Ella talked to a judge.

A rainbow stretched across the cloud-strewn sky above the rolling ocean as she came into Crimson Point. More people were out enjoying the break in the weather, walking along the damp sand with their children or dogs. A few kites fluttered in the sky over the beach and birds zipped down to the water.

Beckett and Sierra's heritage Victorian home looked like something out of a magazine as she pulled up, the sunlight glinting off the windows in the multicolor-painted turret and the carefully tended garden bursting to life in vivid shades of green and chartreuse.

Her mood dimmed a little when she saw Aidan's SUV parked behind Beckett's truck in the driveway, a fresh anxiety creeping in. While she didn't dread seeing him exactly, the thought of apologizing to his face for the suspicious and borderline hostile way she'd treated him almost made her break out in hives.

She drove home, parked in her driveway and walked back up the lane. The side door was unlocked but she tapped on the wooden frame of the screen door on the side porch before entering. Voices carried from the kitchen so she slipped off her shoes and headed through the cozy living room toward it.

She found Beckett and Sierra in the kitchen mixing up what had to be kitten formula.

They looked up when she neared the kitchen doorway. "Hey," Sierra said in a hushed tone, a tired smile on her face. "Ella's in the laundry room with Lizzie and Aidan. Poor mama cat was hit by a car last night. She left seven kittens behind, so it's all hands on deck right now."

Aww. "I have it on good authority that Ella's in her element. I'll see if I can lend a hand."

"Sure. There are extra syringes and formula back there. They'll show you what to do."

Ella's whispered chatter reached her when she neared the laundry room door. She popped her head inside to find Lizzie feeding her own kitten, and Ella…

Her heart tripped over itself when she took in the sight before her.

Aidan held a tiny black and white kitten to his broad chest, cradling it there in his big hand while Ella carefully fed it with a syringe, a studious frown on her face. The half-smile on Aidan's as he oversaw the operation was so full of easy affection it made her insides flutter.

No. No fluttering.

But could anyone blame her? Seeing such a big, powerful man cradling the helpless little thing against his broad chest made her smile. If more men knew how much women melted at the sight of a guy taking care of an animal, the shelters would never be short of male volunteers.

"Hi, you're just in time," Lizzie said.

Ella and Aidan looked over, a big smile breaking over her daughter's face. "We're feeding kittens!"

"I see that." She met Aidan's gaze, suffering another flutter at the pure male interest and appreciation in his expression. Seeing a good-looking man holding a kitten was adorable. Seeing Aidan cuddling one to his well-muscled chest to assist her daughter was something far more visceral.

She pushed aside the tingle of alarm that thought brought and smiled at them. "They're so tiny."

"They're hungry wee things, but haven't quite got the hang of the syringes yet," he said, the lilting cadence of that sexy Scottish burr rolling over her like an invisible caress. Best accent *ever*.

"Can I help?" she asked, willing her heart to resume its normal rhythm. He exerted a magnetic force on her even while she wanted to pull away.

"Sure, there are two more over there with Walter," Ella told her, nodding toward the corner before going back to feeding her kitten.

Tiana looked over and barely held in a laugh. Walter was lying flat on the rug in the corner, looking like someone had let the air out of him. His ears and tongue were spread out along the rug, one tiny black kitten burrowed into the side of his neck and an orange one trying to crawl up his head. He stayed perfectly still, only his eyes moving to look up at her.

Save me, his expression said, yet he didn't move a muscle.

"Awww." She grinned and pulled out her phone to take a picture before kneeling down to pet him. "You are such a good boy, Walter," she whispered, stroking his back gently. She got a slight tail thump for her efforts.

"He's so good with the kittens," Ella said behind her. "It's like he knows they need him. He just lies there and lets them crawl all over him. Bravo Zulu, Walter."

"Bravo what?"

"It means well done. It's a Navy term," she explained with a casual shrug.

Tiana looked at Aidan, who was fighting a smile. "Your influence, I'm guessing?"

His eyes sparkled. "Aye. Your wee lass catches on quick."

Okay, it was pretty damn cute. "Walter appears to be the perfect foster dad. They must miss their mama terribly." Why was life so damn mean sometimes?

"I know, it's so sad. But they'll be okay, because we'll look after them."

Tiana shared a smile with Lizzie over the "we" comment and snuck some pictures of Ella while she worked. She may even have included Aidan in one or two of the shots as well. So she could send them to Lizzie after.

Riiiight. Like you're going to delete them after?

She cleared her throat, unwilling to examine her motives. "Which one should I feed first?"

"Either of them."

"Okay." She bent and scooped up the orange one trying to summit Walter's head. "Are you hungry, little man? Let's fix that." She got her own syringe and filled it with formula, then sat on the bench next to Lizzie and began feeding him, drop by drop. Most of it dribbled down his chin but some of it went down, and his tiny little mewls tore at her insides.

"Aren't they adorable, Mama?" Ella said.

Oh yeah, she knew exactly where this was going. "So adorable they make my uterus ache."

She met Aidan's gaze when he chuckled and couldn't help smiling back, that telltale flutter low in her abdomen stirring its own warning. Now that she'd decided he wasn't the enemy, he posed even more of a threat to her in some ways. The man was sexy as all hell, and he was interested. But he was leaving soon, so even if she hit her head and did a one-eighty where men were concerned, she still wouldn't get involved with him.

Once all the kittens were fed they fell asleep except for the black-and-white one Ella had fed. The pure joy on her daughter's face as she played with it was beautiful to see. Her little girl had such a kind and loving heart in spite of everything she'd gone through. Tiana gave it thirty seconds after they left for Ella to start in on her about adopting one.

"How about some coffee?" Beckett said from the doorway, hands in his pockets as he watched them all.

"That sounds great," Lizzie answered and stood, catching Tiana's arm before she could follow Aidan out of the room. "He's so good with her, Tia," she whispered. "As in, unreal. Your radar's definitely busted beyond repair, because that hot—and single, by the way, because I checked—hunk of a man is a genuinely nice guy who adores your daughter." She gave Tiana a push. "Now go ask him for a walk and apologize."

"Jeez, will you give me a minute?" She'd planned to apologize and didn't need any prompting.

"No." Another push. "You'll thank me later. Take your coffee to go, or I'll stay mad at you the rest of my visit."

It was an idle threat, but Tiana didn't argue. So when she and Aidan both had a mug of coffee in hand, she approached him to ask softly, "Can we take a short walk?"

He studied her in surprise for a second, then nodded. "Of course."

Outside the clouds had parted more, allowing floods of sunshine to come pouring through. It glimmered off the cresting waves below the cliff, the soothing rush of the ocean soft in the background. The views from the cliff were incredible. She and Ella loved looking for the orcas, humpbacks and grey whales that migrated along the coast.

She turned toward Aidan as he came down the steps. "Should we walk to the beach this time?"

"Aye, if you like." He shortened his strides to keep pace with her as they walked along the side of Beckett and Sierra's property to a trail that wound down the cliff side to the beach.

"I owe you an apology," she told him without mincing words.

He frowned slightly, being nice. "For?"

"For being curt and…kind of hostile with you before."

"Ah. Apology accepted, then. But if I might ask—why the sudden change of heart? Was it the kittens?"

She huffed a laugh and put aside her pride. "Well, they didn't hurt your cause. Mostly I realized that I was misdirecting my anger at you, when really it should be aimed at myself."

He lowered his mug to stare at her, his expression curious. The sun gleamed on his short, dark auburn hair, bringing out fiery streaks of red. The scruff on his jaw and cheeks glinted with red-gold highlights. "And why's that?"

Tiana hesitated. She had her reasons—good ones, in her mind—but she didn't like the idea of letting him see that much of her ugly past. "I had a…difficult upbringing when I was young. Long story short, I was only able to leave my family behind because Lizzie gave me a safe place to land."

"She seems like a good person."

"She's the *best*. Anyway, I lived with her until I could support myself. Then I met Ella's father, and that's a whole other story."

He stayed silent, waiting for her to continue.

She took a bracing sip of coffee. "The hard truth is, I haven't always made good decisions about relationships. Or men in general." She glanced over, found him watching her with that quiet, steady stare. It was unnerving and comforting at the same time.

"If it helps, I haven't either," he said after a few beats.

That surprised her. He seemed so supremely confident in himself and everything he did. He'd have no shortage of female attention. "No? Do you mean the relationships, or men?"

"Relationships," he confirmed, the hint of a smile tugging at his mouth.

His lower lip was fuller than the top. Sexy and utterly kissable. She imagined sucking on it. Gliding her tongue across it and then slipping inside…

"I'll tell you mine if you tell me yours," he said, jerking her from her thoughts.

She covered her awkwardness with a soft laugh. "Maybe one day." She cleared her throat, looked down at the waves as she and Aidan crested the top of the path and began the descent down the hillside. "I'm guessing you heard what happened last summer with Ella?"

"No."

She glanced at him in surprise, raising her eyebrows. "No?"

He shook his head. "About what?"

She was sure he would have heard from Beckett or Jase by now. Or maybe Noah.

She pushed out a hard breath. "There was a guy I was dating. I thought he was perfect. Worse than that, I trusted him with Ella and left them alone together when I shouldn't have."

"What happened?" he asked, frowning.

Telling him made her squirm. "He tried to molest her."

Aidan stopped so fast it was like someone had nailed his boots to the ground. "What?" he rasped out, his tone low and dangerous.

She only had the nerve to meet his eyes for a second before she lowered her gaze to study her sand-covered shoes, guilt writhing inside her. "Things had been building for a few weeks, but I didn't see it. Didn't notice how withdrawn she'd become, or clue in when she wanted to hang out at Beckett's house after school rather than coming home when Brian was there."

"What did he do?" His tone and expression were ominous.

"He broke into the bathroom when she was in the tub. Undid his pants and..." Her throat tightened. She cleared it, swallowed and forced herself to keep going. "Masturbated in front of her."

A low hiss came from between Aidan's teeth, and when she found the courage to look up his expression had shifted from horror to absolute rage.

"He threatened to hurt me if she told anyone," she finished.

"Jesus Christ," he muttered, his jaw flexing as he shook his head.

She nodded. "I had no idea anything was going on." That's the part she couldn't forgive herself for. "Ella finally told Beckett and Sierra one night. Beckett went straight to my house to confront Brian. When I got home from work Brian was in the back of Noah's cruiser with a busted nose. I couldn't believe it. Didn't want to believe it. The worst part is, it was my fault."

"No." He bent to set his mug down, then straightened to take her by the upper arms, his gaze firm on hers. "You're not to blame for what that piece of shite did."

"Yes, I am." Her voice caught slightly. She tormented herself with it daily. Hourly.

"Nae, lass." He squeezed her shoulders, his touch warm and comforting, and she was even sorrier that she'd treated him so poorly before. "You couldn't have known if Ella didn't say anything."

She inhaled a deep breath. "The trial is pending. If he won't take the plea deal the State offered, then it means

Ella will have to testify in a trial. And there are other victims. He's done it before. Noah told me last week. They were even younger than Ella."

Aidan shook his head. "Christ, I had no idea any of this was going on."

"I'm actually glad about that. It's not a pretty story. And now Ella's father has suddenly decided he wants to have visitation rights. Ella wants to meet him this coming weekend and I don't have a choice in the matter, so that's another thing we're dealing with right now." The silver lining was that the visits would probably be few and far between, since Evan lived in another state.

"I'm so sorry. No wonder you hated my guts."

Her eyes darted up to meet his, and she caught the teasing light there. She smiled weakly. "Well, now you know the worst of it. But I was wrong to be a bitch to you, and I'm sorry. You've been nothing but wonderful to Ella." He still hadn't let go of her, and she had the strongest urge to curl up against his broad, muscled chest. To hide there while his powerful arms came around her and shut the rest of the world out for just a few minutes.

"Stop apologizing. I've already forgiven you, so let that go now."

She relaxed and stayed silent for a long moment. "Any chance your story's going to make me feel better after all that?"

His warm brown eyes lit with the edge of a smile. "It might, but compared to that it's not so terrible after all."

"Yeah. Perspective's a bitch sometimes, isn't it?"

"'Tis." He released her arms, leaving cold spots where his hands had just been, and bent to retrieve his mug. "Do you want to keep walking?"

She glanced out at the expansive view of the sea, feeling as though a slight weight had been lifted from her shoulders. "Yes."

"Then let's crack on. And I hope Brian enjoys being

molested in prison once he gets there."

She smiled at his savage tone, liking him more and more with each passing minute. Good thing he was leaving soon.

"Also, I think you should brace yourself for the onslaught of begging that's about to happen." He slanted her a look. "Ella has her heart set on taking that black-and-white kitten home once it's old enough."

That made her laugh, and it felt so damn good. "Oh, God, I knew it."

His answering smile captivated her and she had to tear her gaze away. If she hadn't sworn to herself to avoid getting involved with anyone, she might have been sorely tempted to try Aidan MacIntyre on for size.

As predicted, Ella pounced on her the moment they hit the lane on the walk home. "Pleeeease, Mama? I've already named him Bruce. Mac and I were trying to think up names, and he said Robert the Bruce was the first king of Scotland."

"Did he?" She'd have to thank Aidan for his "help" next time she saw him. And actually, she was kind of looking forward to seeing him again.

"Yes, and cats are way less work than dogs. We don't have to walk him or even let him outside to do his business, because he'll use a litter box."

"And who's going to clean that?"

"I will."

Uh huh. For the first day or two, then it would fall to Tiana. "Ella, we've got a lot going on right now without adding a kitten to the mix." She sighed at the look on Ella's face. She'd have to have a heart of stone not to be moved by her daughter's devastated expression. "I'll think about it, okay?"

"But he needs a home. You don't want him winding up at the shelter like Walter did, do you?"

Ah, the old guilt trip routine. Tiana exchanged a secret

grin with Lizzie. "Sweetie, I promise to think about it. In the meantime, I want to see you taking care of all the kittens whenever you have free time. Miss Sierra's got her hands full with them and a full time job, and needs the help. If you put in the work, that will help your cause when it comes time to find the kittens homes."

Her face lit up and her bright blue eyes widened, probably because it was the first time Tiana hadn't shut the whole pet campaign effort down flat, and had set out a specific task Ella could do to help earn her right to be a cat owner. "Oh, I will!" She practically skipped on the rest of the walk back.

After bath time Ella asked Lizzie to read to her a story. Tiana cleaned up the kitchen, thinking about Aidan. What did he think of her now that he knew? She wouldn't blame him if it changed his opinion of her. It had certainly made her think less of herself.

"Okay, she's ready," Lizzie announced as she came down the hallway in one of Tiana's robes. "I'll make the popcorn and have the movie ready to go when you're done tucking her in."

This was their last night together, and Tiana couldn't help but be sad about that. Being around Lizzie was like being bathed in sunshine. When she left, their world would be a little colder and grayer. "Great, thanks. Mint chocolate chip's in the freezer, by the way."

"This is why you're my favorite niece."

Ella was waiting for her when she walked into her daughter's bedroom, her damp blond hair fanning out across her pillow. "You ready for bed?" Tiana asked with a smile, sitting on the edge of the mattress to stroke a lock of hair back from Ella's soft cheek.

Ella nodded, but the silent way her daughter watched her set off warning bells in Tiana's head. "Something wrong?" she asked.

Ella looked away, fidgeting with her hands.

Crap, what was it? Had something else bad happened? "Baby, if something's wrong, you can tell me."

Those summer sky eyes slowly came back to hers. "Are you mad at me?"

She blinked, taken aback. "What? Why would I be mad at you?"

"For wanting to meet my dad."

Her insides stilled and her heart twisted. *Ohhh...*"No, honey, I'm not mad."

Ella searched her eyes, as if unconvinced. And Tiana realized her daughter felt guilty. Guilty for wanting to meet Evan.

That wasn't okay.

"Ella, I'm not mad, I promise. If you want to see your dad and get to know him, it's okay. Really."

"It's just… I've wondered about him. What he's like. All the other kids in my class have dads. Except for one, who has two moms. They think it's weird that I don't even know mine."

A swift pain hit her in the chest. She'd known Ella was missing a father figure in her life. But she'd never realized how deep it was. How big a wound it had made in her daughter's soul to never have a father around. It explained why she was so attached to Beckett and Aidan, however. "Do they make fun of you?"

She shrugged, the motion stiff. "A few of them. But I don't care, because they're stupid for being mean and I don't want to be their friend anyway."

Tiana wanted to cheer. "I'd say that's a good decision. You're so wise for your age, you know that?" She took Ella's hand, laced their fingers together and put on a smile to hide her own insecurities, the deeply buried fear that Ella would fall in love with Evan and find Tiana lacking thereafter.

Or that one day, Tiana might lose her because of it.

Those were her issues, however. They should never

touch Ella. She had to make sure they didn't.

"You'll meet your dad on Saturday with the lady from the court, and you can decide what you want to do after that." She paused. "He's matured a lot since I knew him, and become a much better person. I think you'll like him," she added, the words burning her throat and putting a quiver in the center of her gut. "I'm not going to love you any less for wanting to spend time with him. There's nothing you could ever do that would make me stop loving you."

A pleased smile spread over Ella's face. "I know."

The answer squeezed Tiana's heart. That Ella felt secure in the knowledge that she would always have unconditional love from her. That was a gift beyond measure.

"Love you," Tiana murmured, bending to kiss Ella's forehead before snapping off the light. "Sleep tight."

"Don't let the bedbugs bite."

"I won't."

She shut the door and walked down the hall to join Lizzie on the couch for a movie, determined to enjoy their remaining time together, but her mind was already racing ahead to what would happen in the future with Evan and the possible trial with Brian. Even though all of that was mostly outside of her control, she couldn't help but worry.

All the men in their lives had hurt them by leaving, or worse. Ella had suffered the most.

Tiana had vowed to protect her against any more pain, but that was impossible. And there was nothing she could do to protect her daughter from the hurt she'd suffer if Aidan left Crimson Point for good and never returned from Scotland.

Chapter Seven

After finishing up the final inspection of a newly remodeled craftsman-style house the company had just completed, Aidan drove to the dune buggy rental place that afternoon to meet up with the guys. He still hadn't told Beckett the news that he might not be able to return at the end of his upcoming contracting stint. He'd tried twice over the past two days and both times Beckett had been busy with something else.

Aidan couldn't put it off any longer. He had to tell him today.

All that aside, he called his mum back home in Edinburgh and talked to her for a bit before walking into the garage feeling pretty pleased with himself.

"Your father's driving me crazy being underfoot all the time. I tidy something up, turn around, and he's made another mess. It's like having a child in the house again, I swear. I wish he'd take up golf again," his mum said over the phone. It was almost eleven at night back in Edinburgh, so his dad was fast asleep. Aidan and his mum were the nighthawks in the family.

"Best give him a list of things to do before you both drive each other mad," Aidan advised.

"Aye. And it had best be a long one."

"Good luck." Jase was already inside the rental place. He burst out laughing when he saw Aidan, it confirmed that he'd made the right decision about the face paint. "Listen, mum, I'm here now. Gotta go."

"All right, dear. Have a good time. Love you."

"Love you too. Say hi to dad."

"What the hell is that?" Jase demanded with a grin as Aidan ended the call.

"My war paint," he replied, sauntering past him to the counter to get a helmet and goggles. Before heading here he'd painted his face blue and added a white St. Andrew's cross over it for good measure. Scottish pride was never out of style, even here in Oregon.

Beckett walked out of the back with Noah and stopped dead, his mouth twitching as he fought a smile. "Gone Braveheart on us, huh, Mac?"

"Aye. You bastards can shoot me full of paintballs, but you'll never take my freedom."

The other three all snickered. Then something moved behind Beckett's ankles, drawing Aidan's attention. He started laughing. "You brought Walter?"

"Walter is a dune buggy maniac. I couldn't leave him at home, and besides, he needs a break. Those kittens have been crawling all over him for days and he just puts up with it. They even keep trying to nurse from him. Poor guy."

Aidan winced in sympathy. "That's just wrong."

"Yeah, I owe him big time." Beckett bent to scratch the dog's long ears.

Aidan shook his head at the dog's outfit. "You got him a helmet and goggles?" The helmet had a dog skull on the front, and the crossbones beneath it looked like they were made of doggy biscuits.

"Doggles. He loves 'em. Wait 'til you hear him when we start ripping around out there." His hard face split into a proud smile. It was almost startling, to see Beckett smile. He did it more frequently now. Sierra was a godsend for him.

Aidan shook his head again then clapped his hands together once. "Awright, big man. Show me to my war machine."

Four dune buggies were all lined up outside waiting for them. The owner came over to give his standard safety speech, took one look at their bored expressions and stopped. "I'm totally wasting my breath here, aren't I?"

"Totally," Beckett agreed, slapping him on the back. "We promise not to roll them. Right, boys?"

Everyone answered in the affirmative. But Aidan had his fingers crossed behind his back. He was here to win, plain and simple. If a little roll over was required now and then to accomplish that, then so be it.

After a few pictures together, they all chose their weapons, gathered ammo and strapped into their vehicles. "Fair warning, I'm not taking it easy on any of you bastards," Aidan warned. "Except for you, Walter. I'll abide by the Geneva Convention and consider you a non-combatant for this."

The dog was already strapped into the back of Beckett's buggy with a special harness, his mouth open in a kind of grin, his long tongue lolling out of the side of his toothless mouth.

"I'm coming for you, Mac," Jase warned from his right. He'd healed up well from his surgery after losing part of his liver and small intestine to a bullet back in the fall. Right now he had his war face on.

"I'll be waiting, wee man," Aidan said, and fired up his engine. He pumped a fist in the air and let out a whoop as he hit the accelerator, tearing down the trail after Beckett. The wind whipped through the edges of his helmet, the ceaseless roar of the ocean growing louder as they approached the dunes.

God, it was breathtaking. The sun was out, making the

endless expanse of sandy hills sparkle like mounds of brown sugar. Nearer the water it was a darker, damp strip.

Beckett led the way across the ocean of sand, presumably knowing where he was going. They reached the top of a steep dune and spread out all in a row, their front wheels resting on the crest, with a steep drop before them.

"You boys ready?" Beckett yelled over the wind and noise of the engines.

Aidan grinned at him, then looked to his right, pointing a warning at Jase, and Noah beyond him. "Prepare to die."

Jase held up a middle finger, his grin visible from behind the face shield on his helmet.

"You wish, you wee bastard," Aidan called back.

Beckett shot down the hill. Aidan hit the gas and followed, plunging down the back side of the tall dune. A piercing howl sounded, startling him, and it took him a second to realize it was Walter. Grinning, he chased after Beckett, just Walter's nose visible over the back of the seat because he had his head tipped back, still howling away like a lunatic.

Laughing, Aidan cut to the left and shot up the next dune, angling to cut Beckett off. But Beckett was ready for it and veered away at the last moment. Aidan tried again, caught the faintest flash of movement as Beckett raised his arm, weapon in his grip.

Pop, pop, pop.

Aidan ducked as three paintballs slammed into his windscreen. "Oh, it's like that, is it? Awright, big man." He swung to the right, reached for his own weapon and cut hard right again to swerve around in front of Beckett to return fire.

Pop, pop.

One round hit Beckett's hood, but the other hit the doorframe, splattering Beckett's shoulder with paint.

Aidan cackled and let out a war whoop. "First blood!"

Pop, pop, pop, pop.

Paintballs slammed into his buggy, seemingly out of nowhere. Christ, he was taking fire from all sides now.

He ducked, barely missed being hit in the side of the head as a ball zinged past and splatted on the inside of the roll bar. "Weaver, you wee bastard!" he yelled at Jase and cranked the wheel to the side, unwilling to let that go unanswered.

Damn, it was fun.

They chased each other all over the dunes for the better part of an hour, shooting until they ran out of ammo. By the end of the battle Aidan had two shots to the body, Beckett had one, and Noah and Jase were shot to hell.

"I'll lie and tell Molly you died bravely," Aidan shouted to Jase when they paused near the base of a dune to grin at one another.

"Screw you, Mac." He took off, spraying up a tall rooster tail of sand with his back tires, right through Aidan's open door.

Laughing, Aidan followed, heading for the ocean. Together all four of them played a wet and sandy version of aggressive bumper buggy, dipping in and out of the waterline as they raced down the damp, compact sand, cutting each other off, crashing into each other and generally acting like lunatics.

Aidan hadn't had this much fun in forever.

By the time they brought the buggies back to the rental garage, the owner was waiting out front. He shook his head, his shoulders heaving with a sigh when he saw the state of the vehicles. But they hadn't rolled any of them, and all the buggies were still in one piece, so no real harm done.

Beckett collected extra money to cover the cost of fixing the dents and paint, then gave it to the owner, a buddy of his. On the way back to Crimson Point they stopped at a nearby bar for a beer, then drove back to Beckett and Sierra's for a cookout. Walter was out cold by the time they arrived, exhausted from his dune buggy excursion, so Beckett carried him inside.

"Oh my God, what did you do to him?" Sierra asked when she met them at the door.

"I've never seen an animal have that much fun," Aidan told her. "The kittens can all nurse on him at once now and he won't feel a blessed thing."

Poppy was there too, along with Molly and the baby. Aidan took Savannah while Molly filled her plate, tucking her into the crook of his arm.

Sierra smiled at him and shook her head. "I can't believe how comfortable you are with her. Most men I know freak if you wave a baby in their direction."

He gave an easy shrug. "I guess I got used to it with my nieces when they were small. Though it's hard to remember them being this tiny." Savannah gazed up at him with solemn, dark brown eyes. Her father's eyes.

Aidan had served with Carter when their units did joint operations overseas, and liked him. But although Savannah wasn't Jase's by blood, he was that wee lass's father in every way that mattered.

"It took me a while before I trusted myself not to drop her," Jase said, sliding a burger onto Molly's plate.

"It's pretty much the same as holding a rugby ball," Aidan told him. He'd decided to wait to tell Beckett about the work visa after dinner, when everyone else left. "You just tuck it into you good and close and make sure you don't drop it."

Everyone was seated on the back porch eating burgers and the salad Sierra dished out onto their plates when Aidan caught the sound of an excited little voice coming around the side of the house. Smiling, he stood and walked over to Molly, Savannah in his arms.

Ella appeared at the end of the porch, her face lighting up when she saw him. "Mac! I came to help feed my—I mean, all the kittens."

He smothered a laugh. "That's a good lass. They're sleeping on Walter. He's all worn out from his dune buggy field trip this afternoon."

She eyed him in consternation. "Why is your face blue?"

"It's my war paint. The Scottish flag." He grinned at her expression, but the smile froze when her mother suddenly appeared around the corner. "Tiana. Hi." The sight of her was like a punch to the solar plexus. Now that she'd lowered her guard and decided they could be friends he wanted way more. He wanted all of her, for the time he had left here.

She stopped too, apparently surprised to see him. Or maybe because his face was blue or because he was holding Savannah, he couldn't be sure. But her smile was genuine, and it made his heart thud against his ribs. "Hi. Nice face."

"Thank you." He handed Savannah over to Molly.

"Sorry to interrupt," she said to Beckett and Sierra. "I didn't realize you had company. Ella got your text about the kittens and begged me to bring her right over."

"No, don't be silly," Sierra said, crossing the porch to beckon her up the steps. "We've got plenty of burgers and sides. You guys hungry?"

"I'm not hungry," Ella blurted, already through the porch door and on her way to the laundry room.

"Shocking," Tiana said with a laugh, and for a moment, Aidan couldn't move. Or breathe.

He'd never seen her laugh before. Not like this, so easy and carefree. It lit up her face and eyes, transformed her from attractive to stunning, and for the life of him he couldn't look away.

A wave of possessiveness hit him, so strong he had to fight the urge to walk over to her and wrap a proprietary arm around her shoulders. Or kiss her until she melted and plastered that trim, curvy body against his. He was six-three, so the top of her head came just to his chin.

Instead he followed her and Sierra over to the table on the back patio where Sierra had all the food set up, and helped himself to more salad. "Where's Lizzie?" he asked Tiana.

"She took my camera and walked into town to snap some pictures before she heads to the airport. She's flying out tonight—cab picks her up at six—and has got it in her mind to make up a calendar with pictures from her trip."

"I'll be sorry to see her go."

"Oh, us too, believe me." Her eyes were so sad, he wanted to hug her and kiss it away.

"Is your car fixed yet?" Sierra asked her, sliding a cheeseburger onto a bun for her.

"No, they had to order in some parts and they won't be in until tomorrow. That's another reason why I had the courtesy driver bring us here. It's a school holiday tomorrow and Ella's been invited to a birthday party-slash-sleepover up the coast. I've got an appointment with a family lawyer in Portland at eleven in the morning. The rental car place in town is closed for some reason. Any chance I could trouble you or Beckett for a ride to the closest one in the morning?"

"I'm going into Portland tomorrow too," Aidan interjected.

Tiana looked over at him in surprise. "You are?"

"I've got an appointment with an immigration lawyer." He was still holding out hope that something could be done to allow him to come back and work here in the fall. "Anyway, I'd be happy to drive you both. If you're comfortable with it," he added. Truce or no, he didn't want to push too hard and make her retreat when he was just starting to make progress. As things stood he had just over two weeks left here. He wanted to spend all of it with her.

Her smile was soft but it pierced his heart like a bullet.

She was slow to trust due to things in her past, but he sensed he was beginning to win her over. That made it all the sweeter. "You're sure?"

"Of course." He'd love to spend more time with her and Ella, and this way he was helping them too. Maybe that would earn her trust even more. He wanted that. He wanted *her*. To make her smile. Laugh.

To make her come, while crying out his name.

"Well then, we'd love that. Thank you."

He smiled back, anxious to move the needle from her tolerating him to needing him. Nothing less would do. "I'm looking forward to it."

What he wasn't looking forward to was the conversation he'd been putting off for the past few days. Once everyone had left, once it was only him, Beckett and Sierra, he helped clear the last of the dishes.

Beckett eyed him. "Something on your mind, Mac?"

"You wash, I'll dry," he said.

Sierra took the hint. "Great, I'll go see to the kittens."

Beckett washed the first bowl and handed it to him. "So? You gonna tell me?"

"The appeal on my work visa was denied. Unless a miracle happens, I won't be able to work in the States again after my contract job is over."

Beckett looked away and grabbed the next dish. "I was afraid that's what you were gonna tell me."

"I'm meeting with my lawyer in the morning. Hoping he'll be able to get the ball rolling on something else. Maybe permanent residency or something."

"I'd hate like hell to lose you. You're an integral part of my company. And I'm not just saying that because I'm the boss."

He didn't want to go. "And you like having me around to keep you entertained with my stellar personality?"

The hint of a smile tugged at Beckett's hard mouth. "It's never boring with you around, I'll grant you that."

He reached over and clapped a strong hand on Aidan's back. "Let's hope your lawyer has an ace up his sleeve. If there's anything I can do on my end, just name it. I want you to come back here to stay when this next contract's up."

Aidan thought of the friends he had here. Then he thought of Tiana and the prospect of never seeing her again and his insides tightened. "Thanks. That makes two of us."

Chapter Eight

"Have a great time, sweetie." On the birthday girl's doorstep Tiana hugged Ella goodbye then pressed her cell phone into her daughter's hand. "It's fully charged. I've put Aidan's number in there as Mac. Call or text us anytime, okay? We'll head straight back from Portland after our appointments. And you can always contact Beckett and Sierra too, if need be."

"What about Mr. Noah and Miss Poppy? Or Mr. Jase and Miss Molly?"

"Them too." And wasn't it wonderful to have a trusted circle of friends they could turn to?

Ella nodded, a big smile on her face. She'd been asking for a phone for almost as long as she'd been asking for a pet, so having a cell phone for a whole twenty-four hours was pretty exciting for her. "Bye."

"Love you. I'll be here to pick you up in the morning."

"Okay. Love you too," Ella called, already heading for the open front door where the birthday girl waited with her mom. Tiana waved at them, waited for the door to shut, then turned back for Aidan's SUV.

Her tummy flipped when she opened her door and

climbed in, the interior holding the scent of clean, masculine spice. Aidan was male perfection in jeans and a dress shirt that hugged every muscular line of his chest and shoulders. It made her imagine what he'd look like shirtless. All those sculpted muscles flowing into each other. All that warm, smooth skin to explore.

"Good to go?" he asked.

"Yes." She buckled up, a tiny bit nervous about being alone with Aidan for the next two hours, and two hours more after her appointment on the way back to the coast. She'd offered to pay for gas but he wouldn't hear of it.

"She seemed excited."

"Yes. She doesn't get to have many sleepovers, but I know this mom pretty well, so…" She rubbed her hands over her thighs, the denim of her jeans soft beneath her palms. "I'm trying to loosen the reins a little bit, but with everything that's happened it's tough for me."

"I can understand that. It's great that you recognize it and are trying, though." He turned onto the main road that would take them to the highway. "How does she feel about meeting her dad tomorrow?"

"A little nervous, but mostly excited." The opposite of Tiana.

He nodded. "And what about you?" he asked, slanting her a look.

"I'm…dealing with it," she said with a slight laugh.

His answering smile sent a wave of longing through her. "Good on you."

"You must think I'm a neurotic freak after everything I've told you."

"No, I think you're a loving, protective mother who wants to make sure Ella doesn't get hurt again."

His words pierced her protective armor, landing a bull's eye in the soft, defenseless place inside her that she did her best to hide from the rest of the world. He got it. He really got it. "That's exactly it," she said softly, astounded by his perception.

She looked out her window, unprepared for how it felt to be understood by this attractive man she barely knew. It shook her deep inside, made her feel simultaneously vulnerable and respected.

When she risked a glance at him again, her pulse quickened as she took in the strong lines of his profile, the quiet confidence and authority he radiated. A lot like Beckett and Jase. But she'd never wanted to stroke her hand through Beckett's or Jase's hair, or climb into their laps to kiss them senseless.

She mentally shook herself. "You met Beckett and Jase in Afghanistan, right?" She should have asked him ages ago.

"Aye. Our units worked together on missions from time to time."

"How long were you in the military?"

He nodded. "For fourteen glorious years."

"Army?"

A smile tugged at his mouth. "No. Royal Marines. Four-Five Commando, based in Arbroath."

"Oh." She'd have to look them up when she got home. She wanted to know more about Aidan's background. "Were you an officer?"

"Captain."

Oh yeah, she could easily picture him in command. That was sexy. Picturing him in his uniform was as well. And imagining how that command and control thing might translate into the bedroom with him filled her head with all kinds of tantalizing possibilities. *Yum.* "You guys must have gotten to know each other really well, considering the conditions you were in together."

"Aye. They're good lads."

"They are." Lord, the man fascinated her. And she'd decided that allowing herself to indulge in a little fantasizing was harmless considering he was leaving soon, and she had no intention of acting on it. "Okay, I've got a million more questions, but it's a long drive and I don't want to make you regret taking me with you."

He glanced over, the male interest in his eyes unmistakable, and made her heart beat faster, her body warming at the thought of being the center of his focus. "Not possible. Ask away."

Oh, she would be in a world of trouble if he ever made a move. Because she didn't think she'd be able to resist him. "Okay. What about the story you didn't tell me about that day we walked to the beach?"

He winced. "You would start with that."

"If it's too personal—"

"You're awright, fair's fair." He rolled his shoulders. "All right, short version. I thought I'd found the woman of my dreams. Ginny. She was from Glasgow and I met her when I was home on leave from Afghanistan. We moved in together. We'd talked about getting married and I'd planned to pop the question when I got back at the end of my last tour. Only when I got home, she'd moved out and left a note saying she'd found someone else. Someone more exciting that she didn't have to wait around for to be with."

Tiana gaped at him, astonished. "That's *awful*."

He nodded, a sardonic smile curving his lips. His incredibly kissable lips. "Aye, it wasn't a fun experience."

"She seriously moved out and broke up with you with a *note*?" She couldn't fathom it.

"She did."

"That's cold."

"It was, though in hindsight I suppose it wasn't a complete surprise. I knew something wasn't right between us. She'd been pulling away, in contact with me less and less while I was gone." He shrugged. "I guess I just didn't want to face what was happening."

Ginny had left him while he'd been at *war*, and every

day over there could have been his last. God.

"I guess I thought it was just the strain of separation during the deployment. I'd heard other blokes talk about it with their wives and girlfriends. But I thought we could fix it once I got home."

Tiana shook her head, scowling. "I don't like her."

Aidan's chuckle stirred her insides. "I'm over it now. She did me a favor after all, didn't she? Left me before we'd made any promises, instead of afterward."

"I guess." Tiana still didn't like her. Breaking up with him was one thing, but the way Ginny had gone about it was cowardly and cruel. "What did you do?"

"I got on with it. After my service was up I took a military contracting job based in Florida."

"Wow, I would never have guessed we had that part in common," she said after a moment. "Being abandoned."

He turned his head to look at her, reached out to squeeze her shoulder in a show of support. "But we're both better off for it, aren't we?"

True. "Yeah, I guess we are."

The rest of the drive to Portland passed far too quickly. "Are you close to your family?" she asked as they pulled into town.

"Aye. Speak to my mum and dad every week at least. My sister and the girls not as much, but fairly often."

She didn't offer any insight about her own family.

He was telling her funny stories about his family when they reached her lawyer's office a few minutes later. Aidan parked along the curb out front. "My appointment's a few blocks down and shouldn't take long. Wait upstairs for me and I'll meet you there when I'm done."

"All right."

"Good luck."

"Thanks." She shot him a grin. "You too." It was a relief to get out of the SUV, because the longer she spent with him, the more tempted she became to kiss him.

Up on the seventh floor, she found that her lawyer was fifteen minutes behind. He finally brought her into his office, a corner unit with a sweeping view of the downtown core and the river, and seated her in front of his wide desk. "I'm afraid I've got some bad news."

The hope she'd been holding onto deflated like a popped balloon. "Oh, no. What?" What now?

"Ella's father is looking into possible child endangerment charges against you."

Her eyes flew wide, her insides turning to ice. "What?" she whispered, aghast.

"His lawyer sent notice this morning." He flipped through a printed document sitting in front of him. "There's information here about several of your previous relationships. Apparently one man was arrested for drunk driving with Ella in the backseat?"

Tiana cringed. She'd been at work late and had asked Ross to pick Ella up from afterschool care. She'd had no idea he'd been drinking at an office party that afternoon. Of course, she hadn't realized yet that he was an alcoholic. "Yes," she said softly.

He frowned as he kept reading. "There's also mention of possible molestation by your previous boyfriend last year."

The blood drained from her face in a prickling rush, then flooded back in, making her skin burn. *Oh, shit...*

"And something about an incident with a cougar in the summer?" He looked up at her.

Her heart raced, thudding against her ribcage. How had Evan found out? "The cougar was stalking us. We live near a wooded area. It could have happened to anyone." Luckily Poppy had seen it, run to get a rifle and killed the animal before it could attack.

The lawyer nodded and went back to scanning the papers. "And then there are also some things listed here about your background. Incidents concerning you and your parents when you were younger. Nothing I can see that would pertain to your relationship with Ella, but…"

A hot, stinging rush hit the backs of her eyes, warning that tears were imminent. Evan was trying to paint her as unfit. Using her past pain to hurt her far worse than anything she'd ever been through. Why would he do this? He'd said he wasn't going after custody.

"This is crazy. I would never intentionally put Ella in any kind of danger." Her voice sounded so shaky. "He can't use this against me, can he? Especially when he's the one who abandoned his daughter when she was a baby?"

"That depends on what evidence he uncovers, and what the judge thinks of it. The ongoing issue of Brian is the most concerning to me."

Her anxiety spiked. She'd hoped to keep that and the looming trial separate from the issue with Evan. Now it looked like that was impossible.

"Yes," she whispered, feeling ill. Even if it wasn't her fault that Brian had been a child predator, even if she'd severed ties with him and immediately pressed charges the night the truth had come to light…she was still responsible. She'd left Ella alone with him on countless occasions. Had never guessed what was really happening.

She collapsed back in her chair, unable to comprehend this new twist. Evan had seemed so sincere and almost amiable during their meeting. She'd wanted to believe him. Believe that he wouldn't be a threat.

Her mind raced. Why would he do this? And how had he found out? Was someone helping him? "So what do I do?"

"We'll mitigate as much of this as we can," he said, making notes on a legal pad. "He's trying to smear your reputation and fitness as a mother. But try not to worry, because I've got your back, and he's been a deadbeat, absentee father Ella's whole life. This is probably just scare tactics on his part to see how we react."

"What are we going to do?"

"Prove beyond a shadow of a doubt that you're the far better parent and guardian for Ella. Which you are, and any judge will see that. And I'm sure that your ex hasn't been an angel, given his industry, so we'll dig into his life and use whatever we can find. You've already said that your closest friends will act as character witnesses if need be. Then there's Ella's teacher and dance teacher, and your aunt Lizzie." He reached across the desk to cover her hand with his and gave her a reassuring smile. "Honestly, don't worry. I've seen so many cases like this, and yours is strong. It's going to be fine."

Tiana walked out into the waiting room in a daze to wait for Aidan, her worst fear staring her hard in the face. If Evan proved she was an unfit mother in court…

She shook her head, struggling to hang on to her composure. *I won't let them take Ella away from me. I won't lose her.*

I can't.

Chapter Nine

Aidan hoped Tiana was having better luck at her appointment, because his was turning to shite.

He ran a hand over his face and sat back into his chair with a sigh of combined frustration and disappointment. "There's nothing else that can be done?"

"Other than start the paperwork to apply for a green card, unfortunately, no," his lawyer said.

"So that's it, then. As of April 25th, I can no longer work in the States."

"Correct."

Bugger. Now what?

"I'm sorry, Aidan. I know how much you wanted to come back to live and work here."

"Aye." What would he do in the UK? His family was there, yes, but he didn't want to be a security contractor for the rest of his life. He'd had his heart set on moving back to Crimson Point.

"Do you want to go ahead and start the other paperwork?"

"Please. Any chance at all that we can somehow fast track it? Get a decision by September?"

He shook his head, a faint smile on his face. "No.

We'll make your application as strong as we possibly can, but there are no guarantees."

All right. Move on. "Let's get started."

On the way to pick up Tiana he ran through his options. None of them were appealing.

Looking forward to the distraction of Tiana's company, he found a parking spot a ways away from the building her lawyer was in and went up to get her. He walked into the office, took one look at Tiana's face as he entered and knew instantly that something awful had happened.

He gave her a smile when she looked up and saw him, wanting to get her out of there so he could ask her about it. Her in distress triggered all his protectiveness. "Hey there. Ready to go?"

She nodded slowly and pushed to her feet, face pale, her expression almost haunted. He waited until they were out in the hall alone together before asking. "What's wrong?" he murmured as he walked with her toward the elevator.

"It's Evan," she answered after a moment. "When we met at the restaurant he seemed so sincere about only wanting to meet Ella, and not seeking any kind of custody. But he was lying through his damn teeth again because my lawyer just informed me he's going to try to use certain...incidents from my past to prove I'm an unfit mother and file for custody."

Well, shite. "That's insane. Anyone who knows you knows what a fantastic mother you are. He'll never prove you're unfit, no matter what he tells the court."

She didn't answer, but the worried frown and the way she chewed at her bottom lip told him how upset she was. She was all in her head still, thinking about what the lawyer had said and what Evan was planning.

"If it comes to it, you've got plenty of friends to testify on your behalf—including the sheriff." She looked so distraught that he had to try and comfort her, and risked slipping an arm around her shoulders and tucked her into his side. She didn't pull away, and that in itself spoke volumes. He liked the feel of her there. Liked being able to pull her close and offer reassurance and protection. "Beckett and Sierra will defend you. And so will I."

She tilted her head to look up at him. "You barely know me. And I was pretty much a bitch to you until recently."

He knew enough to know she was unlike any woman he'd ever known. "Because you were being protective of your daughter. And you," he added, hugging her into him. Her softness melded to his harder frame, some of the stiffness leaving her body.

"Can you not be so nice to me right now? I'm trying really hard to keep it together."

He squeezed her shoulder, barely resisting the urge to kiss her. The woman distracted the hell out of him. She was on his mind constantly. "All right. Would you prefer sarcastic arse, or straight up numpty?

Her lips twitched. "Numpty? Is that even a word?"

"Aye, of course it's a word, and a bloody good one. It means idiot."

"Hmm, I think I'll go with sarcastic ass."

"My specialty, unless you count being a bit of a snoop." He shrugged. "I can't help it."

He was heartened to see the slight smile forming on her luscious lips. Since he was tempted to take her face in his hands and kiss that lingering sadness away, he reined in the impulse and hit the call button for the elevator.

While they waited for it to arrive, he rubbed his hand up and down her upper arm, glad for the excuse to touch her. "Evan doesn't stand a chance if he pushes this. It'll turn out all right in the end, you'll see. He abandoned his own daughter. Any judge with half a brain won't look kindly on that."

She blew out a breath. "I hope so. I can't lose her. She's everything to me."

His heart squeezed. "There, you see? That sounds like the exact opposite of someone who could be called an inept mother."

The bell dinged and the doors slowly slid open. The elevator was empty so he gestured for Tiana to precede him and hit the button for the lobby.

"How did your meeting go?" she asked as the doors slid shut behind them.

He could see she was still upset, so he appreciated even more that she'd asked. "Not the news I'd been hoping for, honestly. The appeal was denied. So it seems I might not be returning to the States after this contracting job after all." That left him scrambling to revise his future plans and wrap up his life in Oregon before he left, just in case he couldn't work here again. Worse, it also meant he might not have a chance with Tiana now.

"Oh no, I'm so sorry. Did they at least tell you what else you could try—" She broke off, glanced around as the floor of the elevator seemed to sway beneath them.

Aidan widened his stance for balance and grabbed hold of her arm to steady her. The elevator shuddered, a quiet clanking noise coming from above them.

The swaying intensified. Tiana gasped and gripped his arm, wobbling while the elevator began to swing from side to side. The car suddenly ground to a halt, the clanking noise from above growing louder. The entire thing rattled, shuddering around them, then an ominous, low rumbling filled the air.

Earthquake.

Aidan pushed Tiana back into a corner and leaned into her, wrapping one arm around her waist while he braced his free hand on the wall to keep them steady. She didn't say a word, just dug her hands into his shoulders and held on.

The rumbling grew louder and the swaying motion turned into a violent jarring back and forth. Bits of debris crashed down on the roof of the elevator and the lights flickered.

Then the power went out, plunging them into the darkness. And still the shaking continued.

Shite. It was a bad one.

He stayed where he was, keeping Tiana trapped in the corner and sheltered as best he could. They had just passed the fifth floor when the shaking started. If the cable snapped, they had a long drop and there was nothing he could do to protect her when they hit bottom.

She was rigid against him, her fingers curled into the fabric of his shirt. He pressed his cheek to her hair and held on, counting out the seconds. Over a minute now, and they were still swinging back and forth, the walls of the elevator hitting the sides of the shaft with jarring thuds, the scrape of metal rending the air.

More debris crashed down on the roof. Tiana flinched when something big slammed into the metal above their heads but she didn't make a sound.

Aidan held her tighter. He counted to ninety-seven before the shaking began to ease. His pulse was elevated when they finally came to a stop.

For several seconds neither of them moved. Easing the pressure of his arm around her, he stroked his hand over her rigid back. "You okay?"

She gave a tight nod, her silky, apple-scented hair soft against his cheek. "You?"

"Aye." With one last pass down the length of her back he released her and stepped back. She went with him, seemed to belatedly realize her fingers were clutching at his shirt.

She let go. "Sorry."

"Nothing to be sorry for." He glanced around. A faint trace of light was coming through the slit between the doors. He tried the emergency button on the panel. Nothing happened.

"That felt pretty bad. Can I use your phone? I need to check in with Ella."

"Sure." He swiped in the code and handed it to her, continued to look around as she made the call. The call button wasn't working either. Nothing on the panel was lit. If the building had a backup generator, either it wasn't on yet or it had been knocked out by the quake as well.

"There's no signal." Her voice was tight.

"We're probably just too deep in the building." Or the towers could be down.

"What if there's a tsunami?" she said, and he could hear the stress in her voice. "Ella's staying in an inundation zone."

"If there is one the alarm will sound and the adults will evacuate them." It was cold comfort, even to him, but he needed to make her stay calm because there was nothing they could do for Ella at the moment.

"Oh, God..."

"She's going to be okay." Based on the severity and duration of the quake, lord knew what kind of damage they'd find once they got out of this elevator. Best he could do at the moment was keep Tiana safe and get out of here so she could contact her daughter.

He tried several other buttons on the control panel, and got nothing. "We're on our own for the time being," he said, and pressed his fingers into the seam between the two doors to release the magnetic latching mechanism. Tiana aimed the light from his phone toward him so he could see.

He pulled the doors apart, shoving them open with brute force. A crumbled brick wall greeted him. The next floor was well below them. Bits of brick and mortar rained down in the tight gap between the elevator and the wall, warning him to keep his head inside.

"Can we get to the next floor?" Tiana asked.

"No." He paused as sounds reached him through the walls. Voices. Clipped and urgent, and the thud of footsteps using what he presumed was the stairwell as people tried to evacuate.

Then he smelled it.

Smoke.

Ah, shite.

Tiana sucked in a breath. "Aidan…"

"Aye, I smell it. I'm getting us out of here right now." Stretching his arms high over his head, he felt around for another exit.

THE BUILDING WAS ON FIRE. And they were trapped in here.

Tiana swallowed her terror, aiming the light from Aidan's phone toward the elevator roof as he jumped up and slammed his palms against the ceiling. She'd lived in the Pacific Northwest for years and was well aware that it was at extreme risk for a large earthquake. But experiencing one firsthand was something else entirely.

The car shook as his weight landed. She didn't bother asking what he was doing; it was clear he had a plan. The quake had been scary enough, but not knowing whether Ella was okay, and that an even greater threat might be rushing toward her daughter in the form of an unstoppable and deadly wall of water, was terrifying.

Hurry, hurry, she urged Aidan, her heart pounding in her throat. They needed to get out before the smoke got them. She was desperate to get out of the building so she could contact Ella—if the cell towers were still working. Not being there to protect her daughter was like a blade twisting in her chest.

Aidan jumped again, grunted as his hand made contact with something in the ceiling, then a heavy object rattled across the roof and clattered down the shaft. A small amount of light from the elevator shaft filtered down through a gap in a panel he'd opened.

He jumped one more time, slamming the panel aside and dislodging more debris. Above her she could just make out the shape of cables disappearing up into the darkness. The scent of the smoke grew stronger.

"Right. Let's get out of here," Aidan muttered.

Before she could say anything he'd jumped up to grab the sides of the opening. She watched in amazement as he hoisted his upper body through it, then levered himself out of sight.

His hand appeared a second later, reaching for her through the opening. "Give me your hand."

She shoved his phone into her purse and lifted her arms up. Warm, incredibly strong hands locked around her right wrist. She clamped on with both hands.

"On three, you're going to jump, and then I'll pull you up."

"Okay," she answered shakily, adjusting her grip. Her hands were cold and already growing damp.

"One. Two. *Three.*"

She jumped, automatically tightening all her muscles as he began to pull her upward. The sheer amount of strength he displayed astounded her as he drew her up until her head cleared the opening.

"Grab the top with your left hand," he told her, his voice strained. She let go of his arm with her left hand and slapped her palm down on top of the roof, pushing upward while he kept pulling on her other arm.

They were both breathing harder when he got her through the panel. She crouched on top of it uncertainly, afraid to move. "All right?" he asked.

The smoke was thicker here. Enough to irritate her eyes and throat. "Yes."

"Sit tight. I'm going to open the doors above us and get us out the same way."

"Okay." Having just witnessed his athletic ability, she had no doubt he could do it.

He rose to his full height and stretched out his arms to grasp the seam between the closed doors above them. More smoke flowed into the shaft as he pried them apart and looked through the gap. "I don't see any flames, but right now this is our only way out. We'll have to chance it."

"All right." She sounded way calmer than she actually was.

Aidan levered himself up onto the floor above, then knelt and reached down for her. This time she could see his face a little. "Ready?"

"Yes." She reached up for his forearm, locked her hands around the steely muscles there. "On three?"

"Aye." He counted down, let out a low groan as he pulled her upward, until she could scramble through the opening on her hands and knees. There was no one else on this part of the floor but the smoke was heavy in the air. Acrid enough to sting her eyes.

"We're going to have to crawl to the stairs," Aidan told her. "Stay low and hug the wall. Follow me."

She did as he said, the side of her left hip brushing the wall, her right sliding against Aidan's as they crawled. Keeping her head low, she took shallow breaths while her pulse hammered in her throat. She jumped when debris fell from the ceiling mere feet in front of them, crashing to the floor with a thud. More smoke poured through the hole.

"Keep going. Don't stop." Aidan led her around it.

Hard bits of debris bit into her knees and palms as she crawled but she kept going, her sole focus on escaping. Ella needed her. Might be in terrible danger.

She could hear other people now. Running somewhere close up ahead.

"I see the door."

Tiana stayed right next to Aidan as they closed the distance to the stairwell. He laid a hand on the door first to check for heat, then opened it. "No flames," he told her. "Smoke's not as bad in here." He grabbed her hand and pulled her through it, then lifted her to her feet.

The air was clearer. She drew a deeper breath, trying to get her bearings in the sudden chaos. People were rushing down the concrete steps below and above them.

Aidan pushed her back against the door as a herd of humanity came thundering down the steps toward them. As soon as it was clear he tugged her forward. "Keep your arm around me," he ordered, and started down the steps.

Tiana slung an arm around his waist from behind and tucked her fingers into one of his belt loops. His fingers closed around her wrist to anchor her and held on as they descended.

Below them a door banged open. More people spilled out into the stairwell. Someone was sobbing. The back of Tiana's neck prickled as the sudden rise in panic from below hit her. Aidan slowed, turned a corner on the stairs and came to a stop. She peered over the railing.

People were pouring through the open doorway on the next floor down. Thick, black smoke billowed out of the opening, and she caught the flicker of flames somewhere in the hallway.

She coughed and put a hand over her nose and mouth as the rising wall of smoke hit her. It burned her eyes, nose and throat, so thick and black it blotted out what was happening down the stairs. She pressed closer to Aidan, terrified. Thank God he was with her, because he made her feel a lot safer than if she'd been alone.

Through a fleeting gap in the smoke two people emerged through the doorway below carrying someone. A sharp, terror-stricken cry rent the air, and it was like a match on tinder.

Panic erupted. People started pushing and shoving,

yelling and shouting as they swirled in a chaotic mass around and below Tiana and Aidan, each fighting to get down the steps.

Tiana sucked in a breath, her skin shrinking as she saw people fall and get swallowed up under the stampede of panicked people trying to escape. Oh, God, they were trampling each other in their terror.

A woman's thin scream echoed upward as she fell beneath the onslaught. The tightly packed crowd rushed right over top of her, crushing her into the concrete steps.

Beneath her forearm, Aidan's stomach muscles contracted sharply. He reached back to lock an arm around her, holding her in place against his back. She pressed her face into his shirt and closed her eyes, having no intention of moving.

The door below banged shut. Several groups pushed past them, jostling them against the railing. Aidan held her fast, waiting for the frightened mass below to thin out a bit. Finally Tiana opened her eyes and peered around Aidan.

Through the clearing smoke, she could see the trampled woman lying facedown on the steps, struggling to get to her hands and knees. "Help," she moaned, reaching a hand out blindly to the crowd rushing past her.

It twisted Tiana's heart. "We have to get to her."

"Aye. Come on." Aidan started down the steps.

Someone crashed into Tiana from behind, sending her slamming into Aidan's back. He didn't budge, immediately steadying her, then pulling her after him.

Her knees wobbled as the soles of her wedges hit each step. Someone had finally stopped to help the injured woman to her feet, only to get shoved aside and carried away on the tide of bodies streaming down the stairs.

Aidan reached the woman, his huge frame forming a protective shield as he bent and hoisted her upright. "Tiana, come to her right side," he commanded over the noise and confusion.

She rushed to obey, reaching for the woman's right arm as she came up alongside her. Looping the woman's arm across her shoulders, Tiana hurried down the steps while Aidan guarded the victim's exposed side.

The woman was crying pitifully, the side of her face streaked with blood. The smell of it turned Tiana's stomach.

"It's okay, we're getting you out of here," Tiana said to her. The woman didn't respond, hanging in their grip like a rag doll as they carried her down the stairs as fast as they could.

Tiana lost count of how many flights they descended. The smoke kept clearing as they neared the bottom and the crowd began to thin out. Debris littered the lobby floor. Groups of people were gathered around on the sidewalk out front of the building. Some people were covered in gray dust. Others were bleeding.

Together they helped carry the injured woman outside, staying close to the building. Pieces of it littered the street, and more might fall yet.

Two firemen were setting up what looked like a triage station near the entrance. Tiana helped Aidan bring the woman over to them and carefully eased her to the ground. Her bleeding head, face and shoulders were covered in a fine gray dust, her eyes wide and blank with shock.

"You're safe now," Tiana told her while Aidan spoke briefly to the firemen. "You're going to be okay."

"Angela!"

Tiana glanced over her shoulder as two men burst from the crowd assembled near the front doors and came running toward them. One of them was her lawyer. The men knelt in front of Angela, taking her hands and speaking to her urgently.

"Is she a friend of yours?" Tiana asked her lawyer.

"She's my assistant," he answered, pausing to meet Tiana's gaze. "Thank you for helping her."

Aidan arrived and set a protective arm around her shoulders. "Come on. I'm parked about a block from here."

She followed him down the sidewalk, a new wave of dread slamming into her when she couldn't get a signal on his phone. The level of damage from the quake became more apparent with each step they took.

Tiana gazed around in horror. The downtown area looked like something out of an apocalypse movie. Piles of brick and other rubble littered the streets. Smoke rose in clouds over the rooftops, filling the sky, and flames burst through windows in the buildings they passed.

People and cars jammed the roads and sidewalks, clogging them in every direction. Some people were running. Others were stumbling along, clothes torn, bleeding. Frightened, urgent voices swirled around her, distant sirens an eerie wail in the background.

Ella. Was she okay?

"I'm parked over this way," Aidan said, pulling her around the corner to the right.

Half a block down the street, that terrible, now-familiar rumbling noise started up again.

Tiana swallowed a cry as the ground began to undulate beneath them, like they were standing on the deck of a ship at sea.

She froze and grabbed Aidan around the waist. He whirled and crushed her to his chest, pushing her flat against the wall of the closest building beneath a slight overhang in the roof. "I've got you. I've got you," he said against her ear, his solid body forming a protective cage around her.

She squeezed her eyes shut and hung onto him as the world shook and rattled all around them.

The ground thudded with each impact as more rubble

tumbled down from the buildings. People were yelling. Screaming. Glass shattered and hit the pavement with a crystalline tinkle that sent a primal shiver up her spine. Distant explosions ripped through the air, pulsing against her eardrums and chest.

Something large rushed past them as it fell, so fast it created a breeze. She screamed when a huge chunk of building hit the ground, hard enough to buckle the sidewalk beneath their feet.

"It's all right. I've got you," Aidan repeated, his voice calm amidst the terror.

Her lungs were as tight as her muscles when the shaking finally stopped. She lifted her head from Aidan's chest, her heartbeat throbbing in her ears.

"Hurry," he said urgently, grabbing her hand and running down the ruined sidewalk.

Tiana stumbled after him, her legs like marshmallow. Debris kept raining down in the street. More fires had broken out, flames and smoke pouring from shattered windows in the buildings they passed.

Through a veil of smoke, she spotted Aidan's SUV up ahead. It had some debris on it, but the windshield was only slightly cracked and it looked like it was still functional. He yanked the passenger door open for her. She climbed into the seat, slammed the door shut and locked it, her whole body trembling.

Shit, oh, shit... Was it over, or was there more coming?

Aidan jumped in behind the wheel a moment later. "Give me my phone."

There was no message from Ella as she handed it over. "There's still no signal." They couldn't get a call out or receive one.

"Aye. Cell towers must be down." He turned on the SUV's radio.

Tiana pushed past the fear to listen. What was happening? Was Ella okay? *Please, God, let her be okay.*

Aidan handed her back his phone. “Keep trying.” He tuned to a news station and together they waited, silent and tense.

“The U.S. Geological Survey confirms that an eight-point-two quake has hit the Portland area this afternoon at twelve-twenty-three local time,” the radio announcer said. “A tsunami warning has been issued for the entire coastal region.”

The bottom of Tiana’s stomach fell out. *No.*

“Officials have ordered an immediate, mandatory evacuation to higher ground…”

Tiana made a strangled sound and clapped a hand over her mouth, terror forking through her. *My baby. My BABY!*

Aidan cursed and curved his hands around her shoulders, turning her and pulling her to his chest. He held her there, his arms locked around her. “She’s going to be okay, lass. She’s going to be okay.”

Her throat closed up as tears flooded her eyes. They were trapped here on this side of the Willamette River while a lethal wave of water was rushing at her daughter, and there wasn’t a goddamn thing Tiana could do to protect her.

Chapter Ten

Molly sighed in relief as she sank onto the living room couch and stretched out on her back. She grabbed the throw blanket from the back of it and pulled it over herself, glancing at her watch.

It was almost twelve-thirty. She'd just put Savannah down for her afternoon nap. If all went well, Molly had at least an hour to sleep, and since Jase was at work, she planned to take full advantage of a quiet house.

She jerked awake just as she began to drift off, the sensation of swaying tricking her subconscious into thinking she was falling. But she actually was moving.

Her eyes snapped open. She lay perfectly still, staring up at the chandelier in the middle of the living room ceiling. It was swaying. Wobbling back and forth.

A low rumble filled the air, then the whole house started shaking.

Savannah.

She threw the blanket off, her heart rocketing into her throat as she vaulted off the couch and tore for the stairs. The floor rolled beneath her feet as she reached the upper landing and raced for Savannah's room.

Throwing the door open, she ran for the crib, grabbed her sleeping daughter and hugged her close as she looked around for shelter. Books and toys fell off the shelves in the bookcase. There was nothing big enough for her to fit under so she ran for the guest room next door and crawled under the desk to ride out the shaking.

She held Savannah close and huddled under cover, fear lashing at her. Thuds sounded from somewhere in the house. Drawers and cabinet doors in the guest room banged open and shut. The shaking went on and on. She shut her eyes and pressed her face to the back of Savannah's head, willing the sharp edge of panic away.

At last the shaking eased and everything seemed to settle. Her heart continued to clatter against her ribs as she opened her eyes and glanced around. The damage didn't seem too bad, but was it over? She'd never been through a quake before.

Only when she was reasonably sure it was over did she crawl back out from under the desk and go downstairs. Broken dishes and glasses littered the kitchen floor and a few lamps had fallen off tables in the living room.

She bypassed it all, heading straight for the mudroom to bundle Savannah up, put on her own coat, grabbed the packed diaper bag she always kept by the door, and went outside. There was no smoke and she didn't smell gas, but there was no way she was going back in there until she knew it was safe.

Her fingers shook as she pulled out her cell and dialed Jase. A beeping noise filled her ear. She checked the phone, swore when she saw there was no service and started down the driveway to see if she could get a signal closer to the road. The sky was leaden with thick clouds and a cool wind was blowing off the water, but it wasn't raining yet.

At the road she checked her phone again. Still nothing.

"Dammit." She looked back toward the house. Maybe she'd just risk going into the garage to put Savannah in the car and drive her into town to meet Jase at his office.

If he wasn't there, she could go to Beckett and Sierra's, or Poppy and Noah's.

Plan in mind, she walked back up the driveway. No sooner had she reached the front porch than the ground began to rumble and undulate again.

She ran to the middle of the lawn well away from any trees or power lines that might fall, and watched anxiously as everything around her seemed to sway. By the time the shaking stopped she was done. Clutching her still sleeping daughter to her, she marched for the road. She'd walk into town, screw risking going inside for the car.

Partway up the street, she stopped when a white pickup barreled around the corner.

"*Jase.*" Thank God. The instant she saw him she knew everything would be okay. She let out a deep breath, sagged in relief as he sped toward her and pulled to the curb.

He jumped out, his face a mask of worry as he scanned them both, already reaching for them. "Are you guys okay?" His arms closed around her tight, cradling her and two-month-old Savannah to his hard chest. The baby woke and started fussing.

"We're fine. Just scared witless. I tried to call you but there's no service." She leaned into him, wrapped her free arm around his waist. "What about you, are you okay?"

"Yeah." He pulled back to check them both again, as if he didn't believe they were actually okay. "Is the house damaged?"

"Some things fell over and we lost a lot of dishes. But I didn't smell gas or smoke and the structure seemed okay when I left."

"Thank God." He kissed her and let go, his expression concerned. "They've issued a tsunami warning."

"No…"

"Everyone's evacuating the inundation zone right now, all along Front Street and the waterfront."

Fear clutched at her heart. Poppy's shop and Sierra's vet clinic were right in the middle of Front Street. "What about Poppy and Sierra—"

"They got out. I passed them on the way out. I saw Noah's patrol car parked there, though. He's down there right now." He ushered her to the truck, opened the back door so she could put Savannah in her car seat.

She hated Noah or any of their friends being in harm's way, but as sheriff, it was his job. "Was Beckett or Aidan with you when it hit?" she asked as she buckled their daughter into the seat. Because sure as hell, they would both be heading down to Front Street to help Noah.

"No. Beck was at home with Sierra. Up there on the cliff they're safe from the tsunami. I'm taking you over there and then going to help Noah."

She grabbed his arm. "Jase—"

"I'm going, Moll. I can't leave them, and we have to help as many people get out as we can."

Dread coiled like a snake in the pit of her stomach as she got into the front as Jase went around to get behind the wheel. Arguing with him about this wouldn't do any good. He'd been a soldier—an elite one—most of his life. He and the others had the skill set that might help others survive. Beckett, Noah and Aidan were his brothers and he would be at their sides through whatever threat they faced, even a lethal wall of water rushing toward the town.

"What about Aidan?" she asked.

"He took Tiana into Portland this morning. I heard on the radio on the way here that the quake originated there." He looked over at her, his aqua eyes worried as he put the truck in gear. "They were right in the epicenter when it hit."

****

Because he was halfway through a twenty-four pack

of beer when the shaking started, it took Brian a few seconds to realize what was happening.

As soon as it registered to his befuddled senses that they were having an earthquake, he leapt up off the couch and raced across the room to crawl under his kitchen table, holding onto a sturdy wooden leg while the world shook around him. He wasn't sure if it was the quake or the beer, but the floor seemed to roll under him like a wave.

He stayed there for what felt like an hour while dishes fell out of the cupboards and shattered on the floor. A few pictures fell off the walls, and several pieces of unsecured furniture toppled over with loud crashes. The whole house seemed to groan as the wooden frame wobbled and shook on its foundation.

Even when everything stopped he didn't move, remaining under cover until his heart came down out of his throat. In the stillness it was suddenly, eerily quiet.

He climbed cautiously out from beneath the table and glanced around at the damage. He had one hell of a mess to clean up but he was unhurt, and while he hadn't been through an earthquake before, that one had seemed pretty bad.

The power must have gone out because all the lights were off. He would have no heat, no light for who knew how long—

He sucked in a breath as it hit him.

The power was out.

A prickle of heat raced over his skin.

He looked down at the bulge below the hem of his right jean leg. The electronic monitor they'd locked on him only had enough battery for 40 hours, max. If the power was out and the quake had been bad enough, the entire system might be down.

Movement caught his attention through the kitchen window. Over the back fence his neighbors were in their backyard, gesturing at their house and talking loudly amongst themselves.

He wandered down the hall to his front door to get a better look. Several paintings were lying smashed on the floor but when he opened the door the outer structure of his house seemed to still be intact. He couldn't say the same for other homes on his street, however.

A few chimneys had toppled over, and a few of the brick homes had sustained visible damage, large cracks fracturing their exteriors. People ran out of one three houses down, shouting, drawing the attention of others as they gestured and pointed toward the roof where smoke boiled out from under the eaves.

Several neighbors had their cell phones out. "...can't get a signal," one man said next door.

"Looks like the quake knocked out the cell towers and power," the guy he was talking to said.

That was music to Brian's ears.

He rushed back to the kitchen, intent on his task. All the drawers and cupboards were in various states of disarray, their contents strewn across the tile floor. He rummaged through a pile from one drawer and seized a roll of tinfoil.

After wrapping a length of it over the ankle monitor to try and jam the signal in case the system was somehow still working, he hurried to his bedroom, ignoring the mess as he shoved clothes and other items into a backpack.

From his safe he grabbed the two thousand in cash he always kept there for just such an emergency. One final stop by the catastrophe in the pantry to grab water and food, and he waded through the mess in the garage, shoving it all out of the way so he could get his car out.

With the power out he had to manually open the rolling garage door, but no one paid him any attention as he backed his car out and hurried back to shut the garage door. Excitement bordering on euphoria surged through his bloodstream as he drove out of his damaged neighborhood. He spotted several other fires on his way toward the highway. The first responders were going to be busy for the next while.

He wasn't sure where he was going; he just wanted to get far, far away from here. Get the ankle monitor off. Escape.

A loud wail started up from somewhere nearby, startling him. His heart jumped into his throat but after a few seconds he realized it was the tsunami warning system and not the cops chasing him. He swore and turned around, speeding back toward the other end of town where the high ground was. Where Tiana and Ella lived, safe from any approaching waves.

They'd never even know I was coming.

The thought came out of nowhere, a tiny whisper that grew in strength with each passing moment.

It was their fault his life was ruined. Yet theirs went on as though nothing had happened. They were both free to do whatever they wanted while he was judged everywhere he went and treated like an animal, his every move tracked. It wasn't fair. They should have to suffer too.

I could make them suffer.

The thought was way too appealing to ignore. The pandemonium happening right now would give him the perfect cover. No one would expect him to show up at her place, let alone do anything.

He could get his revenge and then take off, disappear from the area forever while everything was in a state of chaos. Change his appearance, use cash only until he could establish a new identity so they couldn't trace him. As long as he could get the damn tracking device off.

A solid, unshakable calm stole through him, making him smile. Oh yes, this was happening.

Emergency vehicles sped past him as he drove to the high side of Crimson Point, away from any danger of flooding. The house Tiana rented at the end of Salt Spray Lane was at a lower elevation from her psycho neighbor who'd punched him, but still high enough to be far out of the tsunami inundation zone.

Instead of using the lane where someone might spot him he drove around to the other side of the woods that bordered it. Leaving his backpack in the trunk, he picked his way through the forest, his pulse picking up speed with every step.

He paused just inside the trees when the lane came into view, staying behind some underbrush to camouflage himself. Tiana's car was gone.

Dammit, where was she? Picking up her brat?

Using the trees for cover until the last moment, he darted out to run behind the garage. The power was out here too because when he peeked in the kitchen window he saw the same kind of mess from his own house, and the digital clock on the microwave wasn't working.

There was also no sound coming from inside. No urgent voices or rushing feet. And there was no way in hell Tiana would keep Ella inside such an old house after a powerful earthquake like that.

He glanced toward the lane. Had she raced off to get Ella? Or had they maybe gone up to the neighbor's place?

He broke into the back door of the garage and went straight to where the toolbox used to be. It had fallen on the concrete floor along with Ella's bike and other sporting equipment.

He pulled a screwdriver and a pair of industrial shears out of it, then set to cutting the fucking ankle monitor off him. There were other things he could use in here for a weapon, and bottles of hard liquor he planned to use to keep this buzz going. By the time the people checking the monitor received a tampering signal or figured out he was missing, he would be long gone.

His ankle bled sluggishly from the shallow nicks he'd

made while cutting the thing off him. He limped from the garage and hugged the band of forest all the way to the cliff's edge. For a moment he stood there staring out at the rolling waves, wondering if one of them marked the tsunami coming toward the town.

Then he reared his arm back and launched the monitor into the air, watching it hurtle toward the violent ocean below.

He was free. All he had to do now was figure out where to hide.

When Tiana returned, he would dish out the payback she deserved. Then he'd be on his way to a brand new life, vindicated and free once more.

Chapter Eleven

Tiana held Aidan's phone to her ear, praying. *Please go through, please go through.*

The call wouldn't connect.

"Anything?" Aidan asked her from the driver's seat of his SUV. They hadn't gone anywhere because the roads were all choked with debris and traffic but she felt safer in here than outside and she was warmer, too.

"No." She'd been trying for the past two hours and service was still down. It might be for days, and every minute she couldn't contact Ella filled her with despair and helplessness.

Radio reports said that two tsunami waves had hit the area. The first had come up the river and taken out a few bridges. The second had been smaller and had impacted the coastal region to the north and south. No damage or casualty reports were being broadcast.

Tiana was desperate to hear from Ella. She trusted the mother who was looking after her, but what if the house had been badly damaged in the quake or tsunami? What if Ella had been hurt? It made her sick to her stomach.

She tried sending another text, hoping service would be restored and her message would get through, then set the phone in her lap with a frustrated sigh.

Even hours after the initial quake, everything was in chaos. Fires from broken gas lines dotted the downtown core. All the routes out of the city were blocked. Landslides had closed off roads and bridges.

All around them, snarled traffic stretched out in every direction as far as the eye could see. People had abandoned their vehicles in the middle of the road, worsening the congestion and making it virtually impossible for emergency crews to reach victims and fight the fires.

"We're not moving out of here for a long time yet," Aidan said, still parked along the curb behind a large mound of debris. Several more, smaller aftershocks had hit the city. Fire and medical crews were overwhelmed, spread thin and unable to get in or out.

Tiana felt awful for the people suffering with no way to get help. "How much gas do we have left?" There was a gas station two blocks south, but with the power out it wasn't operational and they couldn't get to it even if it had been.

"Half a tank."

Enough to get them back to the coast once the roads opened up, but not if they sat idling in traffic for hours waiting.

It started to rain, fat drops splatting against the windshield and roof. The precipitation would make the landslide situation worse. She swallowed the lump in her throat and didn't complain. There was no point, and Aidan didn't like being stuck here any more than she did.

"You getting hungry?" he asked her.

"A little." She was starving, having only had a cup of coffee before leaving the house at six and a protein bar an hour ago, but her worry over Ella eclipsed everything else. Twice she'd considered walking out of the city to see if she could hitchhike back to the coast. But staying with Aidan was smarter, and safer.

"I've got some water in my emergency kit, but the protein bars were it for food." He glanced over at her. "It'll be dark soon. I've got some cash on me. I could see if anything's open in the vicinity, maybe find us something to eat. We're in for a long night. Possibly a few of them."

The prospect of not getting to Ella for days yet almost pushed her to tears. She didn't want to move from the SUV, but sitting here alone might be dangerous as night fell. When people got desperate they did terrible things.

"I'll come with you. Here." She handed him back his phone. They'd charged it fully using the SUV's battery but they had to be smart and conserve whatever power was left in it. The last thing they needed was to have a dead battery when the roads finally opened again.

They got out and Aidan locked up. "Hopefully it'll still be here when we get back," he joked, but Tiana couldn't summon the effort to smile as she pulled her hood up and zipped her jacket all the way to the top. He took her hand, lacing his fingers through hers, and she was glad for the contact and the calm, assertive energy he gave off. "Stay close."

She planned to be his shadow.

It felt like they were rats in a maze as they tried to navigate a path through the tangled mess around them. The first four streets they came to were blocked off in either direction. Every time they found a clear route, they'd hit another obstruction soon after and have to double back, looking for another way out. People huddled together in groups around bus stops and in doorways to keep dry, their faces pinched with worry.

They must have wandered for close to an hour before they spotted a lineup of people two blocks away down an alley.

"Come on," Aidan said, leading her down half a block before turning into another alley. Debris had fallen from the buildings on either side, forcing them to climb over some piles of brick and shattered glass. Her wedges weren't meant for climbing but when she slipped Aidan was there to steady her.

When they finally reached the next main street they came to the lineup. At the far end stood a small supermarket with its lights on. Police officers guarded the entrance and stood along the lineup to preserve order. "Cash only," they said at intervals to the newcomers. "Debit and credit card system is down."

Tiana was just glad they would be able to get food. It took the better part of another hour for her and Aidan to enter the store, and by then a lot of the shelves were empty. People were getting impatient, snarling at one another and pushing as tempers frayed.

"Peanut butter and crackers sound good to you?" Aidan asked her.

"Yes. I'll see if I can get us some fruit, too, and meet you at the checkout."

They split up to forage through the store. She could feel the tension building inside it as frustrated people got tired of waiting in line at the checkout. Arguments broke out as some learned too late that the store was accepting cash only and were forced to leave empty-handed.

More officers were stationed throughout the store. Tiana hurried to the ravaged produce section and grabbed a few, mostly green bananas, a couple of apples and two bags of nuts before going to find Aidan.

Partway down the aisle, she came to an immediate halt when she saw two men in a heated argument with a policeman. Shouting about not being able to pay because they didn't have cash.

"I've got two toddlers and my wife back at the car, and we live over an hour from here. There's no way we're getting out of the city for a day or two at least. We don't have any supplies and my kids are hungry. What am I supposed to do, huh? I can't get cash because none of the bank machines are working."

More people began to gather around the spectacle, calling out in support of the frustrated father. The cop shook his head and held up his hands, trying to maintain some personal space as a crowd formed around him.

Dread coiled in the pit of her stomach like a snake, ready to strike. Tiana took a step back and started to turn around. Grunts and cries broke out behind her. The father and another man were fighting the cop.

It was as though a shockwave of panic electrified the crowd.

People started pushing and shoving to get to the shelves. Tiana could all but taste the desperation in the air as she whirled. It fueled the underlying fear and anger, added to the chaos as more and more people began rushing through the store to grab whatever they could from the shelves.

She dropped her groceries and shoved her way through a mass of people trapping her, heading for the exit while she scanned anxiously for Aidan. People were already running for the doors, trying to steal whatever food they'd grabbed. Police barred the way, shouting warnings.

Ahead of her a knot of men raced at one officer. He drew his weapon.

She skidded to a halt, her lungs constricting.

"Tiana!"

She whirled in time to see Aidan barreling toward her, gasped as he grabbed her wrist and yanked her in the opposite direction just as the first shot rang out. She swallowed a cry as screams erupted around her. People ducked and hit the floor, sheltering children. More fights broke out as the fear level skyrocketed.

As Aidan pulled her along in his wake, a man to her right reached into his waistband and drew a pistol.

A cry locked in her throat but before it could escape

Aidan grabbed her around the waist and took her down to the floor.

She barely had time to get her hands out to catch herself before she smashed into the floor. Pain shot out from her hipbones, knees and elbows. She started to scramble to her hands and knees but Aidan was already rolling them, tumbling her over and over as he wedged them behind cover into a small space behind a display table.

He pinned her there with his body, his arms wrapped tight around her, one hand on the back of her head to press her face into his shoulder. Tiana put her palms to his chest and lay there, afraid to move, her heart hammering as more gunshots shattered the air. People were running all around them, trampling boxes and cans in their haste to find safety.

She squeezed her eyes shut and pressed her lips together to keep from making a sound as the volume of fire increased around them. Painful, terrified screams erupted all over. "Aidan," she whispered shakily, terrified.

The hand on her head tangled in her hair. He turned them, placing her mostly beneath him, only inches separating their faces. She stared up at him, barely able to make out the shape of his face, her entire body pulled taut with fear.

A heartbeat later, warm, firm lips covered hers.

She jolted, her hands automatically flying to his shoulders to push him away. But he didn't move.

His hand cradled the back of her head, his lips moving across hers with slow, firm intent, snapping her out of the panic and unlocking her lungs. His clean masculine scent surrounded her, and with his warm weight on top of her, her body unconsciously recognized that she was safe—that he had placed himself between her and any harm to shield her.

Her heart gave a hard, painful throb, then settled into a less frantic rhythm and she stopped resisting. He had her. Wouldn't let anything happen to her. And she wanted to escape from this madness.

By degrees, the fear, the chaos in the background began to fade a little beneath the weight of the warm, powerful body atop her, the scrape of his stubble on her face and the pressure of his lips on hers.

He gentled the kiss, drawing it out for another few heartbeats. His fingers rubbed along her scalp, sending a hot thrill deep into her abdomen in spite of the danger just beyond their hideaway. She curled her fingers around his shoulders, flexing them into the muscle there, and momentarily returned the kiss.

When he raised his head a few seconds later she felt dazed, her brain stuttering as it struggled to come back to the here and now. He felt so solid poised on top of her, the unmistakable ridge of his erection trapped between them.

Beyond their refuge, the shooting had stopped. There was no more screaming or yelling.

Aidan stayed where he was for endless minutes, unmoving, his breathing calm and even while her pulse tripped at what had just happened. She might have thought he'd kissed her just to distract her or snap her out of her fear, except he'd kept kissing her even after he'd accomplished that. And that hard ridge pressed against her abdomen was all too real.

Finally he lowered his head again, the subtle prickle of his stubble against her cheek shooting a stab of need deep into her belly. "You okay, lass?" His low, accented voice was like an erotic caress to her heightened senses.

She managed a nod and he nuzzled her temple. Ugly reality intruded. One they had to face.

"Good," he whispered. "Then let's get moving."

Chapter Twelve

Aidan remained on high alert as he eased Tiana off him and inched out of their shelter to survey the scene. It was quiet, the cops rushing to secure the scene.

Immediately he spotted two wounded people nearby, between the end of the aisle and the exit. One was a cop. Another cop was already kneeling beside him. In the background three men in handcuffs were being hauled toward the front of the building. All the other shoppers were being held inside the store.

He turned back for Tiana and held out a hand. "Have you got any first aid training?" As an occupational therapist she would have years of medical-based training, but he wasn't sure about the first aid part.

"Yes." She climbed out beside him and glanced around, a gasp leaving her when she saw the wounded men on the floor. "Oh, God." Without waiting for him she rushed toward them, earning another measure of his respect.

Even from fifty feet away Aidan could tell that the man closest to them—the cop—was critical. The wounded civilian was moving a little, lying curled up on his side.

As Tiana knelt beside the wounded cop Aidan did the

same on the man's other side. "I'm a Royal Marine, and she's an occupational therapist," he told the assisting cop. "We'll stay with him while you secure the building if you want."

The cop scrutinized him a moment, then glanced back down at his buddy, clearly torn. But the situation in here could flare up again at any moment and it needed to be brought under control. He nodded once, jaw tight. "Thanks. I'll be back as soon as I can. His name's Mark. He's got two kids."

"Got it."

"Mark, I gotta secure the scene, but I'll be right back. Okay, brother? I'll be right back." He squeezed Mark's shoulder then got up and hurried off to help his fellow officers secure the place, leaving Aidan and Tiana to care for his wounded brother in blue.

With ambulance and fire crews already overwhelmed, these victims wouldn't be transported to the hospital for a long damn time. He and Tiana would have to do what they could to stop the bleeding and try to stabilize Mark.

Mark had been shot high up on the right side of his back. He was lying on his stomach, conscious but barely. "He's breathing okay." Tiana reached for Mark's hand. "We're going to help you," she told him, her voice calm even though her expression was pinched with worry.

She was handling the shock well. Better than most civilians would have. Aidan swept his gaze around and spotted the pharmacy at the back of the store. The cops had their hands full for the moment, and Mark needed immediate care. "Let's turn him over, then I'm gonna go collect some supplies," he told Tiana.

She was still holding Mark's hand. "What if he's got a spinal injury?"

"We won't move him from here, just turn him over so we can assess him better."

Together they carefully rolled him onto his back. Mark

was still breathing on his own, his airway clear. The front of his shirt was soaked with blood, the bullet having exited the front of his shoulder next to the edge of his bulletproof vest. A few inches to the left and the round would have hit the protective plate instead of flesh.

"I need something to stop the bleeding," Tiana said, looking around.

Aidan peeled off the cop's vest and opened his button-down shirt to expose the T-shirt beneath. Grasping the neckline, he tore it right down the center. After removing it from Mark he wadded it up and handed it to Tiana. "Put direct pressure on his shoulder. I'll be right back."

She nodded and leaned over the cop, using her body weight to press down on the T-shirt without hesitation.

Good lass.

Aidan squeezed her shoulder and ran for the pharmacy section of the store to grab things. Gauze pads, bandages, gloves, pain killers, disinfectant spray, tweezers. Anything and everything that might help.

He found a pharmacist hiding in the back and made her get him IV supplies and bags of saline. She was clearly terrified, still in shock, and he had to bark at her a few times to get her to snap out of it.

He jogged back to Tiana with all the supplies. It wasn't anywhere near close to what they needed to provide adequate care for Mark, but it was better than nothing, and it would buy him some time.

When Aidan arrived, the same cop from before was assisting Tiana with Mark. He looked up at Aidan. Mark's feet had been propped up on a stack of boxes. "We've called for a medevac, but it's gonna be a while," he said to Aidan.

"Aye." He set the armful of supplies down. "I'm going to start an IV. All I've got is saline, but it's better than nothing."

"The chopper is en route. They're going to see if they

can land in the parking lot, but if not, they'll hoist him out."

"Good. Let's get some fluids into him," Aidan said.

Tiana looked up at him, her eyes worried as she pressed the wadded-up, blood-soaked shirt to the exit wound in Mark's shoulder. "His breathing's worse and his pulse is slower. I elevated his legs to try and slow the blood loss, but…"

"You did well." He gloved up, knelt next to Mark and set about getting the IV into a vein in his arm. The cop was unconscious, his face gray, but he was still breathing. Increasing his blood volume would give him a fighting chance at least.

They shoved a stack of gauze pads beneath Mark where the entry wound was, letting his weight and gravity put pressure on it, then covered him with an emergency Mylar blanket to try and conserve his body heat. "All right, that's the best we can do for him," Aidan said. "Let's check on the other guy."

Tiana brushed some hair back from Mark's forehead. "Keep fighting," she said softly, and rose to help the next man.

Another cop was helping the second patient. Unlike Mark, this man was alert and hanging on well enough, hit high up in the thigh. The bullet or fragment appeared to have missed the femoral artery, as it wasn't spurting.

The assisting cop had removed his own shirt to press to the wound. Aidan gave him gloves, bandages, gauze and another Mylar blanket. Both men thanked them for their help.

Aidan stood and stripped off his gloves, speaking to Tiana. He wanted to get her the hell out of here and back to his vehicle. "We should go, lass."

"Okay." She peeled off her gloves, but her hands were stained with blood. He grabbed a container of bleach wipes from the shelf and pulled out a few for her, helping her clean up.

He scrutinized her as they walked toward the front of the store. She was pale and quiet. Too quiet.

He stopped a few paces up the aisle to wrap his hand around her nape, bringing her pretty, mismatched gaze up to his. “You okay?” She’d handled herself incredibly well throughout everything. But there was no way she’d ever faced something like this before. It had to have shaken her.

She gave a slight nod. “Think so.”

He squeezed gently, gave her a reassuring smile. “You were brilliant.” He was damn impressed at the way she’d stepped up and handled herself. A lot of people went to pieces during a crisis or at the sight of blood. But Tiana Fitzgerald was made of far sterner stuff than that.

A weak smile curved her lips, but faded quickly. “I wish I could have done more.”

“We did all we could.” Now it was time for him to take care of her.

He released her nape and lowered his hand to find hers, linking their fingers together. “Let’s grab another jar of peanut butter and get out of here, hmm?”

Only a few shoppers remained inside the store, all gathered near the exit. Everyone was subdued, their shock at the outbreak of violence clear on their faces. Aidan paid in cash for the few items they brought to the checkout. Store security at the door checked their items against the bill as they left.

Outside, he wrapped an arm around Tiana’s shoulders and kept her close on the way back to his vehicle. It was still raining and already getting dark, fires from the burning buildings lighting up the sky. The roads were just as congested as before but the overall atmosphere of chaos seemed to have died down.

He checked his phone. “No messages or calls,” he told her, because she was understandably desperate for news from Ella.

Tiana was silent throughout the return walk. She let out an audible sigh when his SUV came into view. "It's still there."

"Wheels and all, how about that." There weren't many people in the streets anymore. Anyone in the immediate vicinity had either found other places to gather or were trying to make their way out of the city on foot.

He scanned their surroundings as they approached the SUV, staying vigilant. Disasters had a way of bringing out the worst in humans, as they'd just witnessed in the store. He'd seen it far too many times over the course of his military career to drop his guard now.

A few shadowy figures stood near the adjacent building as they reached his vehicle. Heading for the passenger side, Aidan kept an eye on the man closest to them, about twenty meters away. He unlocked the SUV and opened the front passenger door for Tiana.

He caught the faint scuff of footsteps behind him an instant before Tiana gasped and whirled to face that direction. "*Aidan*."

Instantly he spun around, shoving her behind him as he faced the threat. The man held a pistol aimed at Aidan's head, stopping mere feet away. "Gimme the keys," he snapped.

Anger punched through him. Not only because this bastard was threatening him, but because Tiana was behind him and had already been through too damn much.

Fuck this.

Aidan lunged, his hand flashing out lightning quick. He grabbed the arsehole's wrist, wrenching it down and back, stripping the weapon away with the other.

The guy jerked in shock with a startled sound and tried to pull back but Aidan had already clamped his free hand around the back of the bastard's neck. Without warning he slammed his forehead into the other man's, ignoring the shock of pain as he reared his leg back and drove his knee up into the guy's bollocks at the same time.

The dobber crumpled like a cheap tent, holding his bawbag and screaming.

"Get the fuck outta here," Aidan snarled at him, shoving him with his foot for good measure.

Moving fast, he pushed Tiana into the SUV and slammed her door shut. "Lock it," he ordered, and hustled around to the driver's side. He put the pistol on the floorboard, fired up the engine and pulled away from the curb. The streets were a mess but he wasn't staying there, a sitting target for whatever lowlife decided to try and take the SUV next.

Tiana didn't say a word as he navigated through the tangled mess of streets. He made it two blocks over before he had to stop because a construction crew was using heavy machinery to try and clear the intersection of debris.

"You're bleeding," she said when he turned off the engine.

He touched his forehead, wiped at the blood dripping down his nose. "It's nothing. He got the worst of it."

"You headbutted him," she said, incredulous.

"Aye. We call it a Glaswegian Kiss."

She didn't smile or seem the least bit amused by the term. Instead she undid her seatbelt and leaned over the front seats to rummage through the emergency kit on the floor in the back. "You moved so fast, I still can't believe it. I've only ever seen things like that in the movies." She turned back to him, her expression full of concern as she used an antiseptic wipe to clean away the blood. "This is going to sting."

"It's all right." He clenched his back teeth together at the burn as she cleaned the cut, warmed by her concern. She had a big heart. Aidan wanted to win it.

She squinted at it. "I can't tell if you need stitches or

not."

"I'm fine. Head wounds always bleed a lot. I've got a thick skull."

Looking doubtful, she pinched the edges shut and put a butterfly bandage over it. "Want me to press on it for a while?"

"I'll be fine."

"Okay, then take two of these at least." She handed him two pain tablets.

He made a face. "I don't need them."

"Please take them. For me."

He couldn't refuse her when she said it so nicely. And she'd been through enough tonight without worrying more about him. So he took them with a bit of water from one of the packs from the kit.

The construction equipment was making good progress on clearing the mess, but they weren't finishing anytime soon, and who knew how many more obstructions there were up ahead. "I'm not sure when we'll be able to get out of here."

"We'll just have to make the best of things then."

"Aye." He was thankful she was taking this in stride. She was understandably still worried about Ella, but learning that the tsunami had been minor seemed to have eased her anxiety some.

He reached back to grab the blankets he kept in the kit. They needed to conserve all the remaining fuel for when it was time to begin the drive out of the city, so he didn't turn on the vehicle and use the heater. Instead he tucked one blanket around her, draped the other over himself, then reached out to cup her chin in his hand. "Okay?"

She gave him a smile. "Yes. Thanks."

He wanted to do a whole lot more than wrap her in a blanket, but he sensed that kissing her again so soon might make her slam a wall back up between them. "Let's see if there's an update." He switched on the radio and set to work spreading peanut butter on crackers for them both.

The news was grim. The Tillikum Crossing and Sellwood Bridges were out. The Portland Spirit, tugs and other river craft were now being pressed into service as ferries to shuttle passengers and vehicles across the water to one of only two remaining routes out of the city that hadn't been damaged by the quakes or landslides. Again, they reiterated that the tsunami had done minimal damage to the coastal region.

Tiana breathed a sigh of relief and leaned her head back to close her eyes. "That's the first real good news I've had all day."

He studied her profile, illuminated in the glow of the temporary lighting the road crews had set up. He'd already wanted her before, but now… What they'd been through together today had intensified that by a thousand. She was caring and sweet, brave and incredibly strong. And sexy. He'd never wanted a woman as much as he wanted her.

He drew his fingers through her silky red waves. Her eyes popped open, shifting to his. The air in the vehicle turned thick and heavy, the memory of that stolen kiss amidst the flying bullets hanging between them.

She searched his eyes. "Did you kiss me just to distract me?" she whispered.

"At first." He stroked her hair, slid his thumb across her cheekbone. He'd have given anything to be back in Crimson Point right now, with Ella safe in her bed so he could get Tiana naked in hers. "But I've been wanting to kiss you for a damn long time."

Her pupils dilated, her eyes darkening as her tempting lips parted slightly.

On a silent groan, Aidan cupped the side of her face with one hand, leaned over and kissed her. She turned toward him, leaning into the kiss, her fingers pushing into his hair.

He relearned the shape of her lips, slid his tongue across them before delving inside to stroke gently. Her soft moan sent all his blood racing to his groin. She twined her tongue with his, stroking and caressing, pressing closer.

He was so revved up, his head swimming with her scent and taste, that any more of this and he'd have her laid out on the back seat and be pushing inside her.

With a low growl he sucked at her lower lip, licked it one last time and ended the kiss, hauling her up and across the console to settle her between his thighs. The feel of her hip pressed against his erection was sweet torture as he wrapped his arms around her and hugged her close. "You're incredible, you know that?"

"No, you are."

He nuzzled the fall of her hair away to kiss the side of her neck, smiling as she shivered lightly. "Still cold?"

"No." She cuddled closer, the curve of her breasts nestled against his chest. "Getting hotter every second."

Damn. "You're not into exhibitionism by chance, are you?"

Her head came up, a shocked look on her face, then she laughed. "Sorry, no. Though you do tempt a girl."

He groaned and kissed her again, wishing he could strip her naked and roll her under him, explore every inch of her with his hands and mouth. Hold her still while she moaned and begged and came undone against his tongue. Then he would settle between her thighs and sink into her, savor every second of being deep inside her body as he lost himself in her.

His heart squeezed when she pulled his head down to kiss the bandage on his forehead, then the tip of his nose. "I gotta say, Aidan. I think Ginny was nuts to leave you."

He grinned, pleased she thought so highly of him. And that the mention of Ginny's name and the memories it brought didn't hurt the way they once had. She'd broken his heart. Had made him doubt himself and relationships for a long time. With Tiana here, all that was a distant memory. "Aye?"

"Yes." She shook her head. "I don't know what she was thinking."

"I do. She was lonely and bored. I was gone for long stretches. She wanted excitement, adventure. And I'd had enough of that for three lifetimes by the time my final tour ended." He ran his fingers through her hair, enjoying the soft length of it, imagining what it would feel like trailing over his bare skin. "When I got home all I wanted was peace and quiet and calm. Time with her and my family."

"Of course. Why didn't she understand that?"

"Because she wasn't the right one for me." It had taken him far too long to realize that. He'd allowed her to shake his confidence and make him swear off relationships afterward. Although now it seemed as if he'd simply been waiting to meet Tiana.

"You've got that right." She sounded almost outraged.

He had so many questions for her. And with them alone and time to kill, there was no better time to ask them than now. "What about your family? You never told me about them. Just that you left Idaho and went to live with Lizzie." He nudged her. "You know I can't help being nosy when it comes to you."

Rather than stiffen or pull away, she actually leaned into him more and settled her head on his shoulder. "Promise not to hold whatever I say against me?"

"Aye. I would never do that."

She was quiet a moment, toying with the neckline of his shirt, her breath warm on his neck. "My parents were really conservative. And strict. Their families were the same way. Lots of rules, few freedoms for me, and we went to church every Wednesday and Sunday. But over time it became more than that. Religion started to take over their lives, and mine with it. We went to church almost every day. Then they moved to an even more conservative church. That's when things started to turn bad."

Aidan ran a hand up and down her spine as she spoke, not wanting to interrupt her.

"The church and its members isolated themselves from the rest of the town we lived in. My parents moved to a town hours away up in the mountains to be part of a new church. They became… Well, there's really no other word to describe it other than zealots. It was old-school hellfire and brimstone. Women weren't allowed to work outside of their home. They were to keep the house, look after their man and raise children. The leader even started to advocate polygamy."

Aidan's hand paused, tension growing in his muscles. "Did your parents pressure you to do that?"

"Not at first. But in the end, yes. Lizzie had already broken away. She was cut off, excommunicated from the church and everyone in it. I missed her so much. She was the only one who understood me. And when I found out my parents had agreed to marry me off at age seventeen to a man who already had two wives, I freaked."

Jesus. He was so glad Tiana had escaped that life. What the hell had her parents been thinking? "Understandable. How did you get out?"

"I packed my things, snuck out in the middle of the night and hiked down to a logging road. A trucker stopped and drove me into the closest town. Luckily nothing happened to me. I contacted Lizzie the next morning. She paid for my bus ticket to Seattle, and I moved in with her there. She helped me get on my feet, but then I met Evan, and… Well, you know the rest."

He was stunned into silence for a few moments. "Wow, that's… Not at all what I expected to hear." He hugged her closer, rubbing his cheek against her hair. "I'm so sorry you went through all that." No wonder she didn't trust men.

"It wasn't easy, I'll admit that, but all of it made me who I am. And I got Ella out of the deal, so it was more than worth it."

That made him smile. "Aye. And I'm proud of who you are. You're a survivor."

"Yeah." There was pride in her voice. "I am."

Content to hold her like this, Aidan tucked her closer and kissed her temple. "Can you sleep a bit?"

"Do you think Ella's safe?"

"Aye. I know she is."

"Okay. Then I'll try."

Eventually they dozed off together, waking early in the morning as the sky turned pearl gray when another minor aftershock rumbled through the ground. He smoothed a hand down her back and kissed the top of her head. "Just a little one," he murmured.

"Hmmm." She sat up, slid off his lap and moved to the passenger side to check his phone. "Still nothing."

Aidan curled his fingers around her hand, brought it to his lips for a kiss. "We'll see her soon, I promise."

It took another three hours for the construction crew to clear the rubble blocking the road ahead. Once they did Aidan and a few other cars eased past the restriction and began their trek out of the downtown area.

They finally reached the river just before noon, then waited hours longer to catch a makeshift ferry across. Since there was only one open route out of the city in the vicinity, the drive out was excruciatingly slow.

Out of pure frustration, at one point he put the vehicle into four-wheel-drive, turned off the road and headed across a farmer's field to reach a rural access road. Traffic was jammed there too, forcing them to a crawl for the next fifteen miles until an intersection opened up other options.

"God, I wish we were in a bulldozer or a tank so we

could just plow through everyone," Tiana grumbled, surprising a laugh out of him.

"At least we're moving. At this rate we'll be back in Crimson Point by nightfall."

She opened her mouth to say something but gasped and grabbed for his phone when it started ringing. "It's Ella!" she cried, and answered. "Ella?"

He glanced over in time to see her squeeze her eyes shut, her face twisting with a mother's agony, and for one instant his heart plummeted, fearing the worst. Then a tremulous smile wobbled on her lips and she met Aidan's gaze as she responded to whatever was said on the other end. "We're coming, baby. We're on the way to get you right now."

Chapter Thirteen

Due to landslides, downed power lines and other damaged infrastructure, it took them until two that afternoon to bypass the worst of the damage and make their way toward the coast. More than seven hours after getting out of Portland.

"We'll be running on fumes soon," Aidan said to her as they waited in the endless traffic lining the two-lane highway. "We need a petrol station."

She stifled a groan of disappointment and frustration. "I think there's one up ahead, but it's still a few miles from here."

"Well, if we run out of fuel before then, you can steer and I'll push." He gave her a grin. "We'll still move faster than this."

She gave a soft laugh to placate his attempt at lightening the mood, but her heart wasn't in it. It was back on the coast with Ella, and having to endure yet another delay in getting to her was beyond frustrating.

The next few miles passed with agonizing slowness. With only a few routes open, traffic was in total gridlock. "I hate motorcycles, but God, I'd kill to be on the back of one right now. We could cut through all of this and be there to pick up Ella in two hours."

Aidan reached across to take her hand from her lap. "I know, lass. We'll get there."

It took the two hours it should have taken total to come within sight of the gas station. "Oh my God, is this the lineup for gas?" she blurted.

"Looks like."

She was ready to jump out of the vehicle and start walking. She kept her mouth shut, because complaining wasn't going to do anything but make this worse.

When they were within twenty cars from the station, an attendant came out to post a sign saying they were out of fuel.

Tiana groaned and slumped down in her seat, covering her face.

"I'll find out what's going on," Aidan said, and got out of the SUV.

Tiana braced her elbow on the window frame and put her head in her hand, fighting back tears. Ella was waiting for her. Probably watching out the window right now, and they were God only knew how many hours from getting there.

She sat up when Aidan came back, cutting a strong, sexy figure as he moved through the line of parked vehicles. "They've another tanker lorry on the way," he said as he got back behind the wheel. "Should be here within the next hour or two."

Better than being stuck here for the next day or two.

They were silent for a few minutes. Then Tiana pushed up the console between them and slid across into his lap. Aidan groaned and cuddled her close, the warmth and strength of his arms reassuring. "Not much longer," he whispered to her.

She hugged him tight. "Thank you for being with me."

"Thank you for being so brave."

She hadn't been, really, not compared to him. She appreciated the compliment though.

The fuel tanker arrived just over two hours later. It took another forty minutes to fill the reservoir and get the lineup moving. Finally it was their turn at the pump. They had enough cash left for two-thirds of a tank. It was enough to get them to Ella and then home.

"Finally," Tiana breathed as they pulled out of the station, sending a text to Ella.

"Traffic's picking up, too."

It was. Now that the congestion of the service station was behind them, they were picking up speed.

Another two-and-a-half hours later, they were almost there.

"I can't wait to wrap my arms around her," Tiana said, her pulse quickening as they neared the town where Ella had stayed overnight. During the drive she'd also texted Lizzie to let her know they were all okay, and Aidan had called his parents back in Edinburgh.

Listening to the obvious affection in his voice as he spoke to them was endearing, and also highlighted the absence of Tiana's parents in her own life. But she didn't regret leaving and cutting them out of her life.

Aidan squeezed her hand, making her look over at him. He'd been holding her hand since they'd left the service station.

She didn't want him to let go. Didn't know how she was going to let him go after this.

Everything they had been through had torn down the remaining walls between them. She couldn't keep him at arm's length anymore and didn't want to. Even if it meant having her heart broken, she couldn't walk away now. She wanted to have all of him, even if it was only for a few weeks more—but given what she'd been through, getting involved was probably another bad decision.

"I think it'll be mutual," he said. "You've both had quite a scare."

"Yes." The goose egg on his forehead had gone down

a little but now a bruise was spreading out from the bandage she'd put on it. She couldn't tell if the shadows beneath his eyes were from fatigue or if they were turning black because of the knock to his head. She'd dozed on and off through the night but he'd been awake the entire time, keeping watch. "Aidan."

He looked over, and the impact of that warm brown gaze sent a wave of yearning through her. "Aye?"

Shit, she hadn't anticipated this shift. But it was already too late, she was already emotionally attached, in a far more intense way than she had been with anyone before him. The man had literally put himself between her and all the danger they'd faced, both human and natural. He would have protected her with his life if necessary. How could she not yearn for him with every fiber of her being?

"Thank you," she murmured. It seemed woefully inadequate in light of all he'd done. "I have no idea what I'd have done without you since yesterday morning." It had been less than thirty-six hours, and yet it felt like an eternity.

He focused back on the road. "You'd have done whatever needed to be done to stay safe and get back to Ella quick as you could." His tone rang with conviction.

His lack of ego about what he'd done only made him more heroic to her. "When exactly are you going back to Scotland?"

He was silent for a second. "The twenty-eighth."

Just over two weeks from now. Shit, what a mess. The timing sucked and she was still gun-shy, but giving up her chance to be with him even temporarily might turn out to be one of her biggest regrets later.

Twenty minutes later they reached the town Ella was staying in. The beige, two-story house looked okay from the outside but the entire area was without power also.

Aidan had barely stopped the SUV in the driveway

when the front door burst open and Ella came flying out, her hair streaming behind her in a golden banner. "*Mom*!" she cried, racing toward them.

Tiana scrambled out and ran to her, grabbing Ella around the back to lift her off her feet and hug her so, *so* tight there in the middle of the driveway. "Hey, sweetheart," she choked out, her throat so tight she almost strangled on the words. But she was also smiling so wide her cheeks hurt.

Hearing over the phone that Ella was okay was one thing. Being able to see her and hold her made it real. "Oh, God, I'm so glad to see you."

Ella didn't answer, her little arms squeezing the back of Tiana's neck fiercely. A tiny sob shook her thin frame.

"It's okay now," Tiana whispered, closing her eyes as she inhaled her daughter's familiar scent. Every atom in her body relaxed, the tide of relief flooding through her entire body. "Everything's okay."

A vehicle door shut behind them. Ella lifted her head to peer over Tiana's shoulder. "Mac!" She pushed at Tiana's shoulders.

Tiana lowered her to her feet and let her go, all tangled up inside as Ella sprinted for Aidan. His grin would have melted the coldest of hearts, and the way he caught Ella when she launched herself at him, wrapping her up in those big arms for a bear hug…

He unknowingly won another chunk of her reluctant heart.

"She's been waiting by the front window since you talked to her first thing this morning."

Tiana turned to face the birthday girl's mother, who was walking toward her with a smile, carrying Ella's pink backpack. "I'm just so relieved."

"I can imagine." The woman handed over the overnight bag.

"Thank you so much for taking such good care of her."

"No, not at all. I'd heard girls' slumber parties can get a little nuts, but that was a level of crazy I was not prepared for."

Tiana laughed and drew her into a hug. "I owe you."

"No, you don't. You'd have done the same for Danielle if she'd been at your place."

"Yes." She stepped back. "Did you sustain much damage?"

"Mostly just broken things inside. Still waiting for the power to come back on. I heard the highway to Crimson Point is blocked by a rockslide. You guys'll have to backtrack inland and go around from the south to get there."

"Thanks." Although she didn't care how long it took them to get home now that they had Ella back safe and sound.

Her daughter was still clinging to Aidan like a little monkey when she headed for the SUV. "Highway's out south of here. We'll have to go inland and around."

"All right." He kissed the top of Ella's head. "You ready to go home, wee lass?"

The smile Ella gave him squeezed Tiana's chest in an invisible vise.

Oh, man. Aidan was going to break both their hearts when he left.

Thanks to more destruction from Mother Nature's fury, they didn't reach Crimson Point until just before sunset. "Doesn't look like the tsunami did much damage," Tiana commented from the back seat as they drove along Front Street. She'd stayed in the back with her arm around Ella the entire way here, unwilling to let her daughter go.

"Naw. Beckett said the largest wave was just over five feet high. The Sea Hag was flooded a little. Everything else just got shaken up."

The power was out here as well, and based on the way the roads were at the moment, it could be a few days or more before the town had electricity again.

"Is our house still okay?" Ella asked. She'd slept off and on during the drive back. When she'd been awake, she'd chattered away with them, asking about what had happened in Portland, and wondering whether the kittens were okay. Tiana and Aidan had both omitted all the violence and chaos they'd seen.

"Aye, lass. Beckett took a look at it. Some things inside fell over and there are a couple of cracks in the foundation, but nothing too serious. Everything can be fixed."

"So can I sleep in my bedroom tonight?"

"We'll see," Tiana said, hugging her into her side. "We're going to drop you off at Beckett and Sierra's to help with the kittens for a while so Aidan and I can make sure the house is safe."

"Okay." She frowned as she stared out her window. "You know how sometimes animals can sense earthquakes before they happen? I wonder if Walter knew and tried to warn them."

Tiana shared a smile with Aidan in the rearview mirror. "We'll have to ask Beckett and Sierra when we get there."

Ella called out to Sierra the second she was out of the SUV and headed for the stately Victorian's front door, where Beckett and Sierra were both waiting. "Are Walter and the kittens okay?"

"They're great," Sierra called back.

Aidan walked her and Tiana up to the house, shook hands with Beckett and talked outside with him for a minute while Ella hurried inside to see the animals. "Did you guys have much damage?" Tiana asked Sierra when they reached the kitchen.

"Nothing major. Lost some dishes and a couple pieces of furniture and three of the stained glass windows need to be replaced. But we weren't hurt and the house is still standing, so I'm counting my lucky stars."

"Yes."

"You both look like you could use a shower and a change of clothes," Sierra said, taking in their blood-stained shirts and jeans. "We've got some hot water thanks to the generator."

Tiana groaned. "I would kill for a shower and a tooth-brush."

"No murder necessary. Come with me." Sierra led her upstairs to the guest bathroom. "We don't have much hot water, so wash your hair first, fast, just in case it runs out," she advised.

"I'll be quick. I don't want to use it all up before Aidan has his shower."

Sierra got her a spare toothbrush, a top and a pair of jeans. "They might be a bit big on you."

"That's fine, I don't mind. Thanks."

"Welcome. When you're done we'll have something to eat."

Tiana washed her hair and scrubbed herself clean in the shower as fast as she could, toweled off, then brushed her teeth. The cordless blow dryer was under the sink. With clean, dry hair and fresh clothes, she felt like a new woman.

Aidan was in the kitchen eating a sandwich when she got downstairs. "Shower's all yours," she told him, her insides heating at the way his eyes tracked over her body. Sierra's jeans were a little big on her but the top was actually tight across the bust.

"I put some clothes on the counter for you," Sierra told him.

"Thanks. Be down in a bit," he said, his gaze lingering on Tiana as a smile tugged at his mouth. And all she could think about was him standing naked in the shower as the water ran over his long, hard body.

She ate with Beckett and Sierra, talking about the earthquake while Ella was preoccupied with the kittens and Walter in the laundry room. "Until yesterday I didn't even know there was a fault line in Portland." Portland Hills, and it ran right through the middle of the city. That's why the damage had been so severe there, and mostly limited there as well.

"We're damn lucky it wasn't the Cascadia fault that gave way. That's the one scientists have been warning everyone about for years," Beckett said in between bites of his sandwich. "The damage from an upthrust quake on that fault would have been way more widespread, and the resulting tsunami would have wiped out most of the coast."

It chilled Tiana to think about it. "What we had was bad enough, but it sure makes me want to do even more to be prepared for the Big One." She took a sip of her iced tea. "Aidan said he got texts from Noah and Jase saying everyone was okay. Have you seen them?"

"Yes. Their places sustained some minor damage, but nothing serious."

"Molly must have been so scared, going through that with an infant." There was nothing more terrifying than the thought of something happening to your child.

"They're all okay, thankfully."

She turned toward the stairs when Aidan came down dressed in a fresh pair of jeans and a plaid, flannel shirt with the sleeves rolled up to his elbows.

Her mouth went dry at the sight of him, her body vividly remembering the feel of his hard weight on top of her during the shooting. Protecting and shielding her. The way his hands had felt in her hair. His mouth covering hers.

"I'm going over to my place to grab a generator, then come right back to pick you up," he said to her.

"Oh. Sure." She gave him a smile, her gaze lingering on him as he left through the door off the kitchen.

"So what happened to you guys?" Sierra asked, slinging an arm around her waist and leading her to the couch in the living room where they could talk alone. Several garbage bags and boxes full of broken dishes sat near the wall, brooms and dustpans beside them.

"Boy, where to begin?"

Sierra's deep blue eyes widened as Tiana recounted the events of the past day-and-a-half. "They were shooting at each other in the store?" she asked in horror.

"Yes. I don't know if that cop made it." Then she told her friend about the armed mugger waiting for them at the truck. She frowned. "Aidan didn't tell Beckett all of this?"

She grunted. "He might have. But my husband is seriously like a human vault. I have to pry things out of him with a crowbar and explosives most of the time."

Tiana had come to appreciate his tight-lipped tendencies with respect to what had happened with Brian and Ella. "Well, anyway, Aidan disarmed the guy, headbutted him and kneed him in the nuts. Dropped him like a bad habit right there in the middle of the street."

"Oh, *that's* how he cut his forehead? I thought it was from something falling during the quake."

"Nope." She shook her head. "When that guy came out of nowhere holding a gun, I was too scared to move and everything happened so fast. Aidan was like an action hero in a movie."

Sierra's smile was full of fondness. "Ah, yeah. These guys can sure handle themselves when things go sideways." She sighed, waggled her eyebrows. "Sexy, right?"

No point in denying it. "At the time I was too scared to feel anything else. But after I had time to process it, yes."

"You definitely deserve wine. Feel like helping feed a kitten or two? I'll pour us a glass."

"Love to."

She helped feed two kittens and chatted with Sierra while waiting for Aidan to come back. Hard to believe how much she'd come to trust and rely on him in the past thirty-six hours.

She'd gone from being wary to trusting him with her life in that short space of time, from feeling a bit awkward around him to wanting to tear his clothes off. It was more than a little jarring. But there was no denying it.

She spotted Aidan pull into the driveway through the laundry room window. Having broken in the quake, Beckett had covered it with plastic. "Aidan's here. You stay here and help Miss Sierra, all right? I'll come back to get you once we've cleaned up and made sure it's safe to go home," she said to Ella. "If it gets too late, you're going to sleep over here."

"Okay." Her daughter didn't even look up from feeding the little black and white kitten. Bruce. "Isn't he the most adorable thing, Mom?"

Tiana withheld a chuckle, glad to see Ella was once again on the pet campaign trail. "He's pretty cute, all right. Bye, sweetheart. Love you big." She kissed the top of Ella's head, said goodbye to Beckett and Sierra and headed outside, excitement and nerves skittering through her at the prospect of being alone with Aidan again.

"Is your place okay?" Tiana asked as she got into his vehicle. He'd changed into a T-shirt. The fabric hugged his muscular chest and shoulders in the most delicious way.

"Mostly. I'll be needing new dishes and some glass for a few windows. The supports for the carport collapsed. Noah's already been in contact with the insurance adjustor. They'll come out to assess the damage soon as they can. He and Poppy said to say hello. They're both doing fine, and saw Jase, Molly and the baby earlier. None of them were hurt."

"Thank God. And you're welcome to stay with us until everything's fixed. I mean, provided our place is safe enough," she added, flushing.

"Thanks, I appreciate that." The heated look he slanted

her sent a flurry of tingles racing over her skin.

She found herself holding her breath as they neared the bungalow she and Ella had called home for the past year and a bit. It had been built in the sixties and needed some upgrades to bring it into the twenty-first century, but it was cozy and…home.

The sun was sinking toward the ocean, enveloping the front of the house in shadow. She got the flashlight from Aidan's glove compartment and scanned the darkening exterior anxiously as they got out of the SUV. "Can I go in?"

"Aye, Beckett's already checked to make sure the structure's sound. It's safe."

The front door creaked a little as she swung it open, bracing herself for what she would find inside. Even from the entryway it was evident that there'd been a major earthquake.

In the kitchen, all the cupboards and drawers were open by varying degrees. Her heart sank a little at the sight of all the broken glass and dishes strewn across the floor but she shook herself because all of that could be replaced.

A bookshelf had fallen over in the living room. The painting Lizzie had given her as a college grad gift lay facedown on the rug in front of the couch, glass fragments glittering in the beam of the flashlight. Framed photos from the mantel lay strewn on the floor.

She made her way through the rest of the rooms, taking quick inventory of the damage. The bathroom was a mess. Her bedroom had the same kind of damage as everything else. And in Ella's room…

She sucked in a breath when she saw the armoire lying across Ella's bed. "Oh, God." Ella routinely spent free time on the weekends lying across her bed, reading. She put a hand to her chest, feeling sick at the thought of what would have happened if they'd been home when the quake hit.

Footsteps crunched on glass out in the hall. She didn't turn around as Aidan came up behind her. "Beckett's bringing us some extension cords so we can hook up the generator," he said, coming to stand beside her. He glanced around, then frowned at her. "What's wrong?"

"The armoire. I'd meant to anchor it properly into the wall. But I kept putting it off."

His warm hand settled on her shoulder. "She's all right, lass."

Tiana nodded, drew in a shaky breath, his touch easing her inner turbulence. "Yes." She cleared her throat. "Is Beckett on his way now?"

"Aye."

"Then I'll get started cleaning up." She got the broom from the utility closet and started in the kitchen while the guys got the generator hooked up.

"And Aidan said, let there be light," he announced from outside the kitchen window.

Seconds later the sound of an engine fired up, and light flooded the kitchen. "Wow, look at that," she called out.

"I know, I'm a miracle worker." He came inside and immediately began helping her with the cleanup. It went way faster with the two of them working.

Partway through they both froze when another aftershock hit. Aidan wrapped an arm around her and pulled her into him but it was minor and only lasted a few seconds.

"God, I hate those," she said, willing her heart to climb down from her throat.

They put the kitchen back together as much as possible and moved on to the bedrooms. First Tiana's, then Ella's. Aidan muscled the armoire off the bed and moved it across the room where it couldn't hurt Ella if it fell again. "I'll anchor it tomorrow," he promised.

"Thank you." It was so incredible to have him here to help.

She paused in the midst of picking up a row of fallen books when she spotted Ella's favorite stuffed toy lying on the carpet. The little gray elephant had been crushed by the armoire. Its trunk was permanently bent, its face flattened.

The sight of it shook her, serving as another reminder that it could have been Ella crushed beneath the weight of the armoire. Every last charge against her as a mother piled up in her head. Things Evan might try to use against her to get custody of their daughter.

She didn't realize she'd made a sound until Aidan's hands closed around her waist from behind. The heat of him bathed her spine, helping to chase away some of the ice inside her. "It's my job to keep her safe," she blurted, tears flooding her eyes. "And yet every time I turn around, I've done something else to put her in danger."

Aidan made a low sound and spun her around to face him, taking her face in his hands. "You're talking nonsense because you're tired."

"No, I'm not. If we'd been home when it hit, she might be dead right now."

"Lass." He pulled her to his chest and hugged her tight, his cheek resting against the side of her hair. "She's fine, and up at Beckett's place right now. She's *fine*."

She nodded, still holding the elephant to her chest. It scared her to think of how close she was to losing control. Of losing full custody of Ella.

Of losing control over herself.

Her emotions were stretched too thin and Aidan was far too tempting, too close, everything about him making her want to throw caution aside and live in the here and now. Take what was right in front of her.

She struggled to contain everything. Not let him see how much she wanted and needed him. How terrified she was of being hurt again. Although from a legal standpoint, there was no crime in dating someone—and if the courts looked into Aidan, he was a stand-up, respectable former Royal Marine.

Being with him shouldn't hurt her if Evan pursued custody, and they'd been through so much together over the last two days. Their ordeal and the way he'd protected her had forged a bond unlike any she'd ever experienced.

"I…I should probably take this up to her, to help her not be scared," she said. "It's her favorite—Lizzie gave it to her the day she was born. She can't sleep without it, I can't believe she left it behind…" She was babbling, couldn't seem to stop.

Aidan reached between them to gently pry the toy from her clenched fingers. "Look at me." His tone was like a velvet caress, weakening her battered defenses.

Tiana closed her eyes, anxiety and need and arousal all battling for supremacy inside her.

She was afraid to look at him. Because once she did, there was no stopping this. And if she took this next step with him, she wouldn't be fine.

In fact, deep down she was certain that she would never be the same again.

So you're willing to let him walk away?

No. She wasn't. Not after everything they'd been through. Not after all he'd done for her and Ella.

She turned around, ready to risk it all.

Chapter Fourteen

The molten hunger in his eyes sent a torrent of heat rushing through her body even as her old fears bubbled to the surface again. "Aidan..." she murmured, dropping her gaze to his chest.

She'd done it. Given her unspoken consent. Now her heart was trying to pound its way out of her chest.

His hand came up to stroke her hair away from her face. She leaned into his touch, craving more. Craving this wonderful, incredible man that for some reason wanted her in spite of all her imperfections.

Her heart beat an erratic rhythm against her ribs. She'd never experienced anything like this before. Not with this level of intensity. This was...something she'd only read about before. Was it because of everything they'd gone through together? Because she'd relied on him for survival?

His fingers stroked against her scalp in a drugging caress that had her eyelids drooping. "What are you so afraid of?"

She looked up at him again. God, he was beautiful. And strong. And brave.

He was also going to rip her heart out when he left.

It wasn't easy to voice her insecurities aloud, but she

felt comfortable with him. Close to him in a way she'd never felt with another man. "Of making another mistake. Of getting my heart broken again," she whispered.

He cupped the side of her face to run his thumb over her cheekbone. "I'll not hurt you, lass."

Her insides squeezed at the tenderness in his voice, the yearning in his eyes. No, he wouldn't hurt her intentionally. "But you're leaving soon. In another few weeks." That was going to leave a scar, no matter how gently the cut was made.

"Aye," he agreed, his gaze locked with hers. "But I'm here now."

His words reverberated in the deepest recesses of her heart. He was right here in front of her, and he wanted her.

Any other arguments she had stored up vanished in the space of a single heartbeat. Before she could think herself out of it, she gave free rein to the need pulsing inside her, took his face in her hands and pulled him down to her waiting lips.

Aidan made a rough sound in the back of his throat and caught her around the hips, hoisting her in the air and turning them. Her back pressed against the wall and then the hot, hard length of him pinned her there, his hands spearing into her hair while his tongue delved into her mouth.

She wrapped her legs around him, rubbing the hot ache between her thighs along the ridge of his denim-covered erection. Now that she'd temporarily pushed aside the worry and guilt, she was free to give full rein to her need and focus on nothing but sensation. He felt incredible and smelled of clean, male spice. She couldn't get close enough. Couldn't touch enough of him.

He rubbed his hips against her in slow, sensual circles, the counter pressure she provided making the throb in her core worse. She tipped her head to the side when his mouth slid over her jaw to her neck, the prickle of his whiskers sending chills across her skin.

More. More. She wanted to escape everything else and just experience this. Being with Aidan, a man no others could ever compare to.

The hot stroke of his tongue made her gasp and tighten her hold on his shoulders, the taut muscles there flexing beneath her fingers. One big hand slid down to her shoulder, following the curve of her ribcage until his palm came up to cradle her breast. He squeezed gently, slid his thumb across the straining nipple.

She moaned and strained in his hold, pushing into his hand. "Want to see you," she managed, her fingers impatiently tugging at his shirt. She wanted to memorize everything about him so she could always remember it in the lonely months ahead.

"Aye." Aidan released her only long enough to peel the soft fabric over his head, his hips still wedged between her thighs to hold her in place, and tossed the shirt aside.

She had only a second to witness the incredible view of his powerful chest and stomach before his mouth was back on hers, stealing her ability to think or breathe. Instead she made do with mapping all the muscular dips and hollows by touch, trailing her hands over his smooth skin, caressing with her fingertips while she rocked into his erection.

He gave a throttled groan and wrapped his arms around her bottom, lifting and turning to carry her down the hall. Her bedroom was dark by comparison, only the light coming from the kitchen and a tiny bit of moonlight allowing her to see his shape as he yanked the covers down and set her in the middle of the bed. She scrambled up onto her elbows and peeled her top off, tossing it aside before undoing her jeans and shimmying out of them.

He helped drag them down her hips, his sharply indrawn breath slicing through the room when he realized she was bare beneath the denim. "Ah, lass," he said thickly, stripping the jeans down and off her legs.

The bed dipped as he came down on top of her again, his hands sliding beneath her back to undo her bra. Tiana arched to help him, her breathing erratic as he pulled the flimsy lace off her, exposing her breasts to his gaze.

Aidan. She was about to feel *his* hands on her. *His* mouth. *His* body.

Another low sound came out of him as he cupped her in both hands, the heat of his stare tingling along her skin. He kissed her once hard on the mouth, sucking at her lower lip for a moment, then skimmed his lips down the column of her neck and nuzzling the valley of her breasts, that delicate prickle of his whiskers sending another wave of heat punching through her.

A soft, throaty cry came from her when his tongue swept over a taut nipple, followed by the perfect heat of his mouth as his lips closed around her.

She writhed beneath him, glorying in the sensation of being pinned by this big, sexy man who seemed to take pleasure in making her feel good. Her fingers crept from his shoulders and up his neck to bury in his hair, holding him to her as she demanded more. So much more with him.

Sensation zinged through her, coalescing in the hot glow between her splayed thighs. He was hard against the inside of her thigh, and she wanted him naked too. A sense of vulnerability began to rise but she shoved it aside. They'd been through so much together. He'd taken care of her in the worst of circumstances. There was no reason to feel vulnerable now.

Still, her hands were unsteady when she ran them down his ribs to push at his waistband. He got the message, lifting up enough to allow her to undo the button and zipper and push them down, his mouth still busy at her breasts, as though he couldn't pull himself away from them.

Finally she was able to reach into his underwear and

close her hand around his rigid length. He froze, a long, low groan rolling from his throat. He pushed into her grip, nice and slow, and her insides clenched at the thought of finally being able to have him inside her. For him to fill her, take away this empty ache and end the terrible need he'd created.

She twisted to the side to reach for the top drawer of her bedside table, gasping when his teeth scraped against her sensitive nipple. Somehow she managed to get the drawer open and grab a condom from the box but he took it from her and set it aside, his powerful hands now closing around her hips as he released her breast and eased lower.

A low, soft growl came from him as he nuzzled her belly, his fingers digging into her flesh. "I want my mouth between your legs," he said in a low, dark voice.

Oh, God... She was so worked up the image was enough to melt her brain.

Beyond the power of speech, she grabbed fistfuls of his hair and parted her thighs for him. His stubble scraped along the tops of one thigh down to her knee, then back up the tender inside, making her gasp as a million nerve endings shot to painful life.

"Ah, God, you're so wet," he growled, his hands moving to her thighs now, pushing them outward to make room for himself.

Panting, Tiana lifted her head in time to see the breadth of his powerful shoulders wedged between her open legs, his head moving toward her center—

He settled his mouth over her core, gave her a slow, sucking kiss that had her arching off the bed and biting her lip as every muscle in her body went rigid. He held her fast, taking his time with slow sweeps of his hot, smooth tongue over her folds, making the swollen bud of her clit pulse, waiting, waiting for the moment he touched her where she craved him most.

She let out a half-sob when his tongue stroked the side of it. Tender and slow, as though he was determined to take his time. She adored him for it. "Aidan," she choked out, gripping his hair tighter. "Ohh…"

"Mmmm," he murmured and began licking her, slow and soft and steady, pausing only to slide his tongue into her.

She whimpered, let go of him to reach up and cup her breasts, squeezing and rolling her nipples while he pleasured her. And when he slid a finger into her, his tongue caressing so tender and sweet, the edge of orgasm shimmered at the edge of her consciousness.

Yes. Please. There.

"Are you close, lass?"

She hadn't realized she'd spoken aloud. But oh, that low, sexy accented voice. "Yes," she gasped out. "Hurry."

He gave her folds one last lingering kiss, then sat up to shove his jeans and underwear off. Tiana sat up, finding the condom packet with one hand. She tore it open and reached for him. Aidan was on his knees in front of her, the moonlight allowing her to see every sculpted line of his torso and the thick, length of his erection waiting for her.

She got to her knees in front of him, wrapped her fingers around the hot flesh. He hissed in a breath, one hand sliding into her hair as he watched her roll the condom down him. She pumped him with her hand, enjoying the feel of him and his reaction.

The hand in her hair tightened, pulled her head back. She let out a startled gasp, staring up at him in the slight moonlight. His face was taut with need, his magnificent chest rising and falling with each uneven breath.

His mouth came down on hers, the hand in her hair clenching as he bore her down onto her back. "Touch yourself," he ordered in a rough voice, his tongue plunging between her lips as the scalding length of his erection settled along her folds.

He rocked his hips gently, sliding his cock over her most sensitive flesh. She moaned and cupped her breasts, reveling in his low growl as she played with her nipples.

Heat and pressure built between her legs. "Aidan," she whispered. So good. So good with him.

"Now stroke your clit," he commanded, coming up on his forearms to look down between their bodies.

She slipped a hand between her thighs, moaned at the sweet, honeyed pleasure as she caressed the swollen bud at the top of her sex. He rumbled in approval and flexed his hips, lodging the thick, hot head of him inside her.

Her breath halted, released on a plaintive cry as he worked himself deeper with slow pressure, the spot he caressed magnifying the pleasure of her fingers on her clit.

"Aye, just like that," he whispered, watching her face now as he worked himself in and out of her.

She was only able to gaze into his eyes for a moment before hers slid closed, his motion and rhythm along with her own touch pushing her right to the brink. It was so good. So perfect. Better than she'd ever experienced.

"Make me come," she blurted, mindless with the need for release.

In answer he surged deeper, faster, groaning deep in his chest.

Tiana's whole body clenched as the first wave hit. She cried out, locking one hand on his hip to keep him where she needed him, rocking and rubbing as the orgasm burst upon her.

A low, almost feral growl emitted from him. He drove into her harder, faster. She gasped for breath as her release ebbed, slid the hand between her legs up to wrap around his shoulders, holding him close, moving with him. She'd never felt anything half so intimate as being locked with him as he sought his own release, her own body sated and relaxed, everything focused on him now.

His muscles bunched beneath her hands and his breathing grew shallow. "Tiana," he moaned, burying his face into the curve of her neck.

She kissed the top of his shoulder, cradled him tight, her hands coming up to his cheeks to turn his face so she could take his mouth with hers. He drove deep into her and shuddered, groaning into her mouth as he came, his tongue twined with hers.

Finally, his huge body relaxed. Seemed to melt as his weight came down on top of her, pinning her to the bed. She slowed the kiss, drawing it out, loving the feel of his weight pinning her, knowing she'd made him feel as good as she had a few moments ago.

Even better, he seemed to be in no hurry to pull out of her and roll away, instead stroking her hair as their lips clung together. She stroked her fingers through his hair, down to trail over his sweat-dampened shoulders and the muscular length of his back.

With one final groan, he ended the kiss and lifted his head to look down at her. In the soft moonlight his slow smile was so gorgeous it made her whole chest ache. "My bonnie, red-haired lass," he whispered, as if she was the most precious thing in the world to him.

A sweet sting lanced her chest. She'd never felt so adored. Or been so sure that her heart would never recover from him.

****

They stayed in bed together for almost an hour longer before getting up and dressed. Tiana stayed behind to keep cleaning up when Aidan walked up the lane to get Ella.

When they returned—hand-in-hand, Tiana noticed—her little girl looked around at the piles of debris they'd bagged up at the kitchen door. "Do we have any dishes left?"

"Paper and plastic ones," Tiana answered.

"Oh. Well, that'll work." With that Ella sauntered off to check her bedroom.

"She took that well," she said to Aidan, who was taking off his boots.

"She's glad to be home. Tried talking me into letting her bring Bruce here for the night but I held fast."

She grinned, knowing firsthand how persuasive Ella could be, especially when she turned on the pleading blue eyes bit. "Good for you."

He straightened and put his hands on his hips, looking completely edible standing there in all his strong, masculine glory. It was even worse now that she knew what he felt and tasted like. Knew what he could make her heart and body feel. "What do you need help with next?"

She loved that he wanted to keep helping. "It can wait until tomorrow. Aren't you exhausted?"

He shook his head. "I'm okay."

The man had been up all night keeping watch over her. He had to be dead on his feet, even if he wouldn't admit it. "Go get some sleep."

His eyes held a sensual gleam. "Where do you want me?"

"In my bed." She wasn't putting him on the couch, and Ella's bed was too small for him.

A tiny gasp drew her attention to the wall that met the hallway. Ella's face appeared around it, her eyes alight. "Is Mac sleeping over?"

She hid a wince, wishing Ella hadn't overheard that. In light of her past relationships, it probably wasn't a good idea for Ella to be seeing yet another man stay in her mother's bed. "Yes, he's tired, and his place hasn't been cleaned up yet."

"Yay!"

Tiana covered a grin. *Okay then.* Apparently she had

nothing to feel guilty about, wanting Aidan to sleep in her bed. "And it's bedtime for you too, young lady. Let's go." She took Ella by the shoulders, turned her around and herded her toward her bedroom.

"Can we make him pancakes in the morning?"

"If the power's back on by then."

"Can't we use the barbecue? That's what Mr. Beckett's been doing."

"We'll see." She pulled back the covers and took the stuffed elephant from the bedside table. "His trunk got hurt in the earthquake. I put a band-aid on it."

"Ohhh…" Ella cradled the toy to her with such care, it melted Tiana. "Poor thing. I'll take care of him."

"I know you will, sweetheart." Tiana tucked her in, kissed her forehead and paused to gaze down at her. Thankful for each and every blessing she had, and especially that Ella was okay. "I love you. Glad to have you home safe."

"Me too." She looked up, her face worried. "I missed the meeting with my dad today. Will I still get to see him?"

Tiana kept her expression neutral. He'd texted several times to check on Ella but Tiana hadn't responded yet. She would, though. "I'll call him in the morning to see if he's still available. With the earthquake, I'm sure all the flights were delayed or cancelled."

"Okay. Night, Mama."

"Night, baby."

Aidan was waiting for her in the hall. "All good?"

"Yes." She went to him, wrapped her arms around his waist and tipped her head back to kiss him. It was almost surreal to have him here. To be able to touch and kiss and enjoy him. "Want me to tuck you in too?"

He lifted a dark auburn eyebrow. "Is that a trick question?"

She laughed. "I already tired you out enough for one

day. I'm just going to tidy up a few more things, then I'll join you."

"All right." He gave her a slow, thorough kiss, swatted her butt, then disappeared into the master bedroom.

She spent the better part of an hour putting things back in their rightful place, including the books from the shelves in the living room and the pictures on the mantel. Twenty minutes in she paused at the sound of little feet leaving Ella's bedroom, but then the door shut again and all was quiet.

Tiana finished in the living room and then went back to tackle the kitchen, thinking about Aidan and her daughter, of how lucky she was to have them in her life. Things could have turned out so much worse considering all that had happened, and without Aidan, they might have. Now Ella was home tucked into her bed, all cozy and safe, and Tiana had a delicious and protective hunk of a Scotsman sleeping in her bed.

He had showed her how to shut off the generator earlier. She switched it off and used the faint moonlight coming through the windows to find her way down the hall to her room. But when she opened the door she stopped, her heart turning inside out.

Aidan was on his side facing toward the door, fast asleep. And Ella was cuddled up against his chest, one thick arm over her waist. He was still dressed, she could see his shirt.

Unbidden, a jolt of alarm streaked through her regardless.

On the heels of that initial, knee-jerk reaction, anger and guilt hit her. Her throat thickened and a rush of tears pricked the backs of her eyes, filling her with a desperate, bittersweet ache.

Aidan would *never* harm Ella. He was incredible and would lay his life down before letting anything happen to either of them. Tiana had never imagined finding a man like him, and yet there was still a part of her that froze up at the sight of Ella in the bed with him.

It wasn't that Tiana didn't trust him; she did. The quake had triggered all her protective maternal instincts all over again. They were still on overdrive, and the need to watch over her daughter tore at her.

Too tired to think about it any longer, she crossed to the bed and gently eased Ella away from Aidan before climbing up to place herself between him and her daughter. Being sandwiched by the two of them filled her with the most powerful sense of peace and safety. Aidan was warm and solid behind her. A perfect match to his personality.

She was falling so hard for him even though she'd tried not to. But not falling was impossible after the way he'd proven himself and earned her trust.

Unfortunately for her, now that she'd finally gotten it right where a romantic relationship was concerned, he was leaving for Scotland in two weeks. He might never come back, and they hadn't talked about the future because it was too soon. A whirlwind romance might be all she could have with him.

She'd had one before, but this time was totally different. This time, it wasn't enough. She wanted more.

And this time, it would be a thousand times more painful when it ended. Because she wanted everything with Aidan.

Chapter Fifteen

Aidan jerked awake when someone crawled over him. He got a face full of blond hair as Ella clambered to the side of the bed, dressed in her pajamas.

"There's no power yet," came a husky whisper on his other side. Tiana came up on one elbow to push her hair away from her face, morning sunlight coming through the window above the bed making the fiery waves glow.

"It's okay," Ella answered, sounding as wide-awake as though she'd been up for hours. "I'm going up to help Miss Sierra with the kittens. She said I could come first thing in the morning and get something to eat, too."

Aidan glanced at his watch. It was only six-thirty. "I'll walk you up," he offered.

"No, that's okay, I'm going to ride my bike."

Tiana sat up. "I'll go with you."

Ella rolled her eyes. "Mo-o-o-om."

"No. Let's go." Tiana got up and herded her daughter down the hall to the guest bathroom, then popped her head back in to speak to him. "I'm going to run her up there and be right back. Don't move."

Ooh, that sounded promising. "All right."

She flashed him a wicked smile. "Be back in a jiffy."

He didn't know what a jiffy was, but he'd wait there all damn day if it meant the possibility of having Tiana alone in this bed again.

The hurried patter of excited feet raced down the hall a minute later, then the front door shut.

Aidan got up and found a spare toothbrush to use, then climbed back in bed, excited as a little kid waiting for a surprise.

The front door opened and shut. Soft, measured steps came down the hall. Then Tiana slipped into the room, grinned and rushed over to stretch out beside him.

He wrapped his arms around her and pulled her close. "Morning."

"Morning." Her soft smile wrapped around him, her different-colored eyes bright, that adorable scattering of freckles across her nose and cheeks giving her a fairy-like look. Not a drop of makeup on, and she was even more beautiful to him for it. "Sleep okay next to the human egg-beater?"

He grinned. Human eggbeater was the perfect way to describe Ella in her sleep. She'd kneed him in the kidney once, and nearly hit him between the legs if he hadn't blocked it just in time. "Not bad. At least I wasn't cold."

"That's good." She sighed, but it was contented, not sad. "I know it's only a thirty-second walk up to Beckett and Sierra's, but with everything that's happened I've turned into a real helicopter parent these past few months. I'm trying to loosen the apron strings a little, give her more freedom and independence. But not right now."

He stroked his fingers through her hair. "Not an easy thing, is it?"

"No," she admitted with a wry smile. "But me backing off a bit is best for both of us. She needs it to help build her confidence, and to know I trust her."

"You'll both get there." Aidan let the quiet surround

them for a moment, gliding his fingers over her nape, enjoying the way she sighed and tipped her head to the side to allow him better access.

His head was full of thoughts and emotions. He'd never imagined he would spend last night with Tiana and Ella curled up next to him. Like he was part of their family.

That made him protective, and territorial as hell. He already wasn't sure how he could walk away from them, but there was no getting out of his contract now. He'd have to fight for them. Figure out a way to come back to them. Because they were both under his skin and in his heart now.

"So. What shall we do to pass the time now that we're all alone?"

A sensual female smile curved her pretty pink lips. "I have an idea." She leaned down to kiss his forehead, right next to the bandage, and pushed at his shoulder. "Get naked and lie on your stomach."

Now this promised to be interesting.

He pulled his T-shirt over his head, tossed it aside and got rid of his jeans and underwear, distracted by the sight of Tiana doing the same. He groaned deep in his throat at the sight of all that smooth, creamy skin revealed to his avid gaze. It had been too dark in here last night for him to see her properly.

But when he reached for her she smacked his hand and pointed at the bed. "On your stomach."

Grumbling a token protest he did as she said, unable to stop himself from reaching out to run a hand down her back when she sat up and undid her bra.

She glanced at him over her shoulder with a teasing smile, slipped the bra off and then leaned over to grab something from inside the nightstand, giving him a perfect view of her rounded arse. He curved his hand over one perfect globe, barely had time to enjoy the feel of it before she swung back around, and then his tongue got stuck to the roof of his mouth.

Her breasts were round and full and topped with tight pink nipples. She smacked his hand as he reached for one. "Lie still," she admonished, and scooted down his side.

He settled his cheek against the pillow, unsure what she had in her hand because he'd been too distracted by the sight of her breasts in full daylight. Then she swung a soft, smooth thigh over his arse to straddle him and he stopped thinking altogether.

A cap popped open. She rubbed her hands together, then stroked her palms from the base of his spine all the way to his shoulders, leaning into him with her weight.

He gave a low, grumbling groan, his eyes falling closed as his sore muscles sighed in ecstasy. A fragrant, clean scent filled the air as she gave his back the most heavenly rubdown.

"Too hard?" she murmured.

"God, no." It felt incredible. Heavenly to lie here and simply receive the pleasure of her touch.

He kept his eyes closed, drifting on a tide of warm arousal as her hands worked their magic. Then the motion of her hands changed. She curled them around the tops of his shoulders and shifted her position, her hips wriggling as she settled into place.

His eyes shot open moments later when a soft, decadent moan filled the air. It took him a second to realize she was rocking against him, rubbing over a spot near the base of his spine, using the oil she'd just spread across his skin as lubricant.

And enjoying the everloving hell out of it.

He sucked in a breath, his semi-hard dick going to full mast in a single heartbeat. "What are you doing back there?" he managed, fighting to lie still.

"Enjoying our massage," she whispered back, moaning again as she rubbed and rocked, her fingers flexing into the muscles across his shoulders.

His whole body went rigid, arousal punching through him. "Can I turn over now?" He wanted to so bad. Flip over to cup and suck her breasts, then haul her upward to straddle his face so he could give her a massage of his own. With his tongue.

"No." She gasped, sliding against him in tiny, slow circles that were driving him mad. "Stay still."

It was insanely hot to lie there while she used him to get off, but frustrating too, because he couldn't see it or touch her. And he was so damn hard he hurt.

More moans. Turning throatier. Almost whimpers.

Jesus, she was trying to kill him.

"Want me to come like this, or with you inside me?" she panted out.

He didn't even have to think about it, his cock surging against the mattress. "Me inside you."

"Okay. Turn over."

He was already moving, the air shoving from his lungs when he finally saw her. Her mismatched eyes were heavy-lidded, her cheeks flushed with arousal. Her nipples were tight little points he wanted to suck on, and below the tidy triangle of red-gold hair between her thighs, her folds were flushed and glistening.

"Oh, hell, Tiana," he breathed, grabbing her hips as he sat up and buried his face in her neck.

She pushed at his shoulders again. "I gave you permission to turn over. Not sit up."

He growled in protest, cupped her breasts in his hands and sucked on one perfect nipple while he squeezed the other, earning a gratifying mewl from her before he gave in to her pushing and lay flat on his back.

She was on him in an instant, her mouth on the side of his neck. Burying a hand in her hair, he slid the other down the curve of her spine to her arse to dip a finger into her from behind, growling when he felt how slick she was.

But she wriggled out of his grip, her mouth moving down his chest, his belly. Her fingers closed around his aching cock, making his hips arch. Pleasure ripped up his spine, and the way she looked up at him with those dilated, mismatched eyes as her tongue trailed along the line of hair beneath his navel made him swallow hard.

Holding him tight in her slippery fist, she stroked him and bent her head, giving him a glimpse of her pink tongue as it stole out to lick at the swollen head.

"Aw, Christ," he whispered, clenching his fingers in her hair. His pulse hammered in his ears, his whole body pulling tight.

She licked him again, parted her lips, then took him into her hot, wet mouth.

A low, ragged groan tore from him. His eyes closed at the raw pleasure of it but he forced them open, not willing to miss a moment of this incredibly sensual woman as she sucked him off. She teased him with her tongue, sucked him like a lollipop, that incredibly unique stare locked with his.

His heart almost exploded.

With firm pressure on her hair he used his hand to guide her, another bolt of lust surging through him at the way her eyes heated. He could barely breathe, didn't care, drowning in the raw pleasure she gave so generously. But it was too good. He was already addicted to her. There was no way to get her out of his system now.

"If you're planning to make use of that for yourself, you'd best stop right now," he ground out, his voice rough.

She released him for a moment, touched her tongue to the exquisitely sensitive ridge on the underside of the crown. "In a minute."

He drew in a sharp breath as she took him back in her mouth, sucking harder. "Stop," he warned, giving her hair a tug.

She murmured and pulled off him, quickly shifting to straddle him as she tore open the condom packet and rolled it down him. Then she reached down to grasp the base of his shaft and planted one hand on his chest. Staring down into his eyes, she slowly sank down onto him.

Tight, wet heat engulfed him. Aidan tensed and made a deep sound of pleasure at the back of his throat, his hands closing over her curvy hips. She sighed, her eyelids drooping, and reached down to rub the rosy bud of her clit in slow circles.

God in heaven. It was so insanely hot that she wasn't shy about her body or what felt good for her.

He tugged her forward, splayed one hand across the middle of her back to bring her breasts to face level and sucked one hard nipple into his mouth. She made a soft mewling noise and kept rocking, her fingers busy between her legs. "I'm close," she gasped out.

Lost in sensation, Aidan sucked on one breast, then the other while the pleasure of being clenched inside her burned like fire. Her moans grew louder, then breathless, and her core squeezed around him.

"Aye," he managed, rubbing his tongue across her nipple.

Her back bowed, her cries of release surrounding him as she shattered. Her core milked him, and her enjoyment of his body shoved him over the edge. He shouted as his own orgasm hit, wringing him out from head to toe.

They sat wrapped around each other, clinging while they returned to earth. She hummed and kissed the top of his head. "That was so good," she whispered, still a little out of breath.

Good? Bloody fant*astic*. Last night had been intense, but now she was part of him. He would never be able to get enough of her.

He dreaded leaving her and Ella in two weeks' time. Couldn't bear the prospect of not having them in his life if he couldn't get an extension on his US work visa. What the hell would he do then? He had to find a way to come back to them.

He drew Tiana down to lie atop him and pulled the covers over them, stroking his hands over the length of her back. She was so soft everywhere, like a kitten. "Can you go back to sleep?"

"Mmm, yes." She snuggled into him, her cheek resting in the side of his neck.

They both jolted awake sometime later at the sound of the front door closing with a slam.

"I'm back," Ella called out, her footsteps hurrying toward them.

"Shite," he breathed as Tiana leaped up and started pulling her clothes on. He caught her eye as he did the same, hopping awkwardly when he almost tripped getting his second foot into his jeans.

She laughed as she did hers up. "Bet this has never happened to you before, huh?"

He grinned and tugged his shirt over his head, managing to be decent a split second before a knock came on the master bedroom door.

"Are you guys awake?" Ella said as she shoved the door open.

"Aye," he answered, a little startled. What was the point in knocking if she was just going to throw the door open? "You finished feeding the kittens already?" He stood there pretending nothing out of the ordinary had been going on, and that he hadn't just been stark naked with her mother ten seconds ago.

"Yes." She frowned. "Your shirt's on backwards."

Somehow he kept a straight face. "Is it? Thanks, I'll fix it."

"Can we make pancakes? We can do them on the barbecue like Mr. Beckett did."

He raised an eyebrow at Tiana. “Do we have the makings for pancakes?”

“They’re nothing like Miss Poppy’s. She makes the best ones, from scratch, but ours comes in a box,” Ella informed him. “We’ve got bottles of water in the garage we can mix into it.”

His lips twitched. “All right, pancakes from a box it is.”

“Okay, I’ll go get everything ready.” Ella spun around and disappeared back down the hallway.

Just then a beeping sound came from the kitchen and the furnace kicked on.

“The power came back on!” Ella yelled.

Aidan laughed and righted his shirt. “I love that wee lass.”

When Tiana started for the door he caught her by the elbow and tugged her to him for a full body hug. “Get back under the covers,” he ordered. “You’re getting breakfast in bed, lassie.”

She blinked up at him. “Really?”

“Aye.”

A startled smile spread across her face. “Okay, then. I—” She stopped as her cell phone rang on the dresser. She picked it up and answered, watching him. “Hi, Noah. You guys okay?”

Her face tightened at whatever the sheriff said next.

“Oh,” she murmured, a frown puckering her forehead. “That’s… Yes. Thanks for calling to let me know.”

“Something wrong?” he asked when she lowered the phone.

Her eyes were troubled. “Brian’s missing. And they found his ankle monitor below us on the beach this morning.”

Chapter Sixteen

Noah ended the call, got out of his patrol car and dragged himself up the brick walkway to the front door of Poppy's house. He'd moved in last summer, renting his place next door to Mac. After being up for two days without sleep, trying to help everyone as much as he could after the quake and tsunami, he was dead on his feet.

The scent of something rich and savory hit him the moment he walked inside. "I'm home."

Poppy came out of the kitchen, wiping her hands on a towel, her blond hair pulled up in a messy bun. The smile she gave him eased the fatigue, and when she wrapped her arms around him, pressing all those delicious curves against him, he sighed, leaning into her embrace. He was home.

"Did you tell her?" she asked.

"Yeah, just now."

"How'd she take it?"

"Okay." Tiana was distressed, which was understandable. As sheriff and her friend, he was distressed too.

The ankle monitor had been cut with something sharp, so it had been taken off deliberately. It bothered Noah that they'd found it near her house. If Brian was still in the area, Tiana or Ella might be in danger, and his department's resources were stretched too thin at the moment to allow him to put the kind of vigilance in place that he normally would have.

Poppy eased back to search his face. "You're exhausted."

"Yeah." He kissed her. This was his home, the place where he'd grown up, and the people who lived here were like extended family to him. He'd do everything in his power to make sure everyone was safe and warm and fed. "You've been such an amazing help through all of this."

She'd dropped everything as soon as the quake hit to assist him with coordinating search teams. She'd taken all the food from her café and distributed it to the emergency personnel and townspeople who had assisted in the response effort. She'd handed out supplies and blankets, driven stranded people to safety and stood out in the rain making pots of hot coffee, tea and hot chocolate for people at the emergency shelter in the center of town.

He loved her and her huge heart so much, he ached. "Thank you."

"Of course. Did you eat anything today?"

"Can't remember." The hours had all blurred into each other.

She made a sympathetic sound. "Come on. Get a plate of spaghetti down, and then you can crash."

He didn't resist as she towed him into the kitchen, sat him down and began serving him a helping of homemade spaghetti with meatballs. His eyes burned and his whole body was tired, but knowing he'd done some good today brought him a deep level of satisfaction and the sight of her filled him with peace. His bright, beautiful sunflower.

"Here," she said, placing the plate in front of him. She even put the fork in his hand.

He ate in silence, his brain sluggish, limbs heavy. When he was done he took his plate and started to rise but she pulled it from him, set it aside and curved an arm around his waist.

"I'm afraid you're gonna keel over on me," she said with a light laugh, and walked him upstairs. "You want a shower first?"

He shook his head. "Later." He just wanted to crash.

In the master bedroom she helped strip him, pulled down the covers and tucked them around him when he slid between them. She knelt beside the bed, gave him a gentle smile and smoothed his hair back from his forehead. "I love you. And I'm proud of you."

He smiled. "Thanks. Love you too." He could hardly keep his eyes open.

She watched him for a moment, something moving in her eyes that he couldn't decipher, but whatever it was, she had something on her mind. "You know that question you keep asking me?" she said after a loaded pause.

"What question?" His brain was barely functioning at this point. What was she talking about?

"You know. *The* question."

Oh. *That* one. The one he'd already asked three times, and each time his gun-shy sunflower had put him off, saying it was too soon. That she needed more time. "What about it?"

Her expression was solemn. Almost determined. "Ask me again," she whispered.

The fatigue vanished. He shoved up onto an elbow, watching her intently. "What?"

"Ask me again, Noah. Right now."

Hardly daring to believe this was really happening, he reached out for her hand. It shook slightly. He squeezed it, rubbed his thumb over the back of it. *Don't be scared.* "Poppy. Will you marry me?"

Her lips trembled and a sheen of tears glistened in her beautiful brown eyes. "Yes, Noah, I will."

Her fervent answer made his heart clench. On a groan

he dragged her to him, kissing her hard on the lips before he crushed her to his chest. She'd said yes, after holding him off for months. They were getting married. She was going to be his forever.

"What changed your mind?" he whispered.

She cuddled closer. "You. Watching you handle everything after the quake."

"What do you mean?"

Her shoulders moved in a little shrug. "I realized I've still been afraid that things are too perfect between us. I've been waiting for the bottom to fall out like it always has before. But now I see you would never let that happen. Or if it did because you couldn't stop it, you would be there to break my fall. Just like you were there for everyone today."

He closed his eyes, breathed in her scent. She was his forever. He was officially the luckiest son of a bitch in the world. "Yeah, sunflower. I would always break your fall."

****

The world spun briefly as Brian got out of his car and stood up. He grabbed for the seat to steady himself, knocking the vodka bottle over. Swearing, he caught it just before the last third of it could spill. He needed the liquid courage to get him through these next few hours.

They'd know by now that he was missing and would be looking for him. They might even have found his ankle monitor. If so, he was on borrowed time.

He'd moved his car three times throughout the night, in case anyone was looking for him. Leaving now wasn't an option. There were only two roads out of here. One was blocked by fallen power lines. The other still had a police presence near it.

His current hiding spot near the woods bordering Tiana's house wasn't ideal, but it would do for now. He'd been checking on her place through the night. She'd eventually shown up with some big guy, and they hadn't come out since.

Was he fucking her? The idea made Brian snort as he staggered deeper into the trees to take a leak.

Fucking Tiana was about as much fun as fucking a plastic blow-up doll. It had been fun at first but that had worn off quickly and sex with her had become like a chore. He'd had to go into his head and fantasize about other things just to get off.

Now she'd ruined his life. And he wouldn't allow that to go unpunished.

He zipped up his jeans, leaned a hand on a cedar trunk to steady himself before heading back to his car. He'd keep checking on her place and nurse the last third of the vodka, watching for an opportunity to strike.

When it came along, he was taking it.

****

Brian was missing? How the hell could he be *missing*?

Of course with the ankle monitor removed, it would be that much easier for him to slip away amidst the chaos of the earthquake. They'd found it on the beach, Noah had said. Was it too much to hope that he'd drowned, and that was all that was left of him?

Scowling, Tiana carried the last of the bags of debris to the front door and left it on the porch for Aidan to put at the curb. He and Ella had gone up to Beckett and Sierra's to borrow a shop vac so they could give her place a thorough vacuuming and make sure all the bits of glass were off the floor.

On her way back inside, her cell rang.

Evan.

The sight of his number sent her heart plummeting into her stomach. For a moment she considered ignoring it.

Pretending she'd missed the call, or that the cell service hadn't been restored yet.

Then she thought of Ella, and the crushed look on her face when Tiana told her she wouldn't get to meet her dad.

She stopped in the entryway, took a slow, fortifying breath, and answered. For Ella. "Hello."

"Tiana, thank God. Are you and Ella okay?"

He sounded genuinely worried. "We're both fine."

His relieved sigh echoed in her ear. "I'm glad. I was staying at the airport when it happened. I kept calling you, but the cell towers were down, and—"

"I know. But she's okay."

"Good. What about the tsunami? I heard it wasn't that big, but…"

"Thankfully it wasn't. Some of the businesses here in Crimson Point along the waterfront sustained a little damage, but everything else is okay."

"What about your house?"

She hoped the hell he wasn't fishing for things to add to his list of negligent things about her he was making. "Just some broken things inside. Nothing that can't be replaced. Structurally it's fine."

"That's great news." He paused. Cleared his throat. "So. Obviously we missed yesterday's meeting. If everything's under control there…any chance I could meet Ella today?"

"You'd never get to her in time. The roads are—"

"I'm almost at the coast now. Probably take me another hour or two, tops."

"Oh." She fought with herself, wanting to blast him for the shitty stunt he'd pulled with his lawyer.

"The court liaison is available. I've already talked to her. She could make an appointment anytime after two."

"What about your flight home?"

"Everything's delayed. But even if my flight was still on time, I'd rather see Ella."

Well, that was something, at least.

But she couldn't let his underhanded treatment go. "I was in Portland yesterday because I had an appointment with my family lawyer to go over the possible visitation schedule and my feelings about sharing custody."

"Oh."

Yeah, *oh*. "I hear you're compiling a list of past transgressions against me, so you can possibly get custody of Ella."

He sighed, and she could easily picture his grimace. "About that. I—"

"You swore to me when we met that you weren't going to pursue custody of any sort, and then I find out this. What the *hell*, Evan?" She was pissed. And hurt. Stupid of her to be hurt by a man who had left her a decade ago, but she was.

"Look, I was only thinking about Ella. Someone left me a file with that stuff in it, and I was concerned."

"What? A file?"

"I came out of the restaurant after meeting you and there was an envelope on my windshield with my name on it. Papers inside listed the incident with…Brian Palmer. Is it true?"

She flexed her jaw. "Yes, it's true, and he got his nose broken for it prior to being arrested. We're still waiting to see if there's going to be a trial or not. As for my family history that your lawyer may or may not use against me, you knew all of that a long time ago. And it's beyond low that you would ever try to use that as evidence to take Ella from me."

"I would only think about trying for custody if I believed Ella was in danger by being with you. I got this file, was worried, and asked my lawyer to look into everything to see if it was all true. That's all, I swear."

"Who gave you this file?"

"I have no idea."

That was unsettling. Obviously she had an enemy out there somewhere. Someone who wanted to hurt her. Other than Brian, she couldn't imagine who it was, and until this morning, he'd been watched closely by the authorities. "And you didn't think that was weird? Or think about coming to me first?"

"I honestly didn't know what to think."

"Well, Ella's not in danger with me. I would never let anything happen to her if it was in my power to prevent it, and I sure as hell wouldn't put her in jeopardy knowingly. And it's rich that you would think that when you literally abandoned her when she was a baby."

She paused, her heart thudding as her anger grew at his audacity. He'd been an absentee parent for all Ella's life, and now he thought he knew best? Fuck that.

"You were the one who started this whole process. You came to me and asked to keep this civil, for Ella's sake. I've done everything you've asked of me. I went to mediation, I agreed to proceed with this, and I met with you face-to-face. I can't believe you would ever do this to me after everything you've already done. Or *not* done, as it is."

He groaned, and she could picture him rubbing a hand over his hair the way he did when he was agitated. "All right. You're right. And I should have called you after I read the file and had time to absorb it all. I should have talked to you about all of this rather than going to my lawyer."

"Yes, you should have. Jesus, Evan. You seriously thought I would have just let any of that happen to my daughter? You know better."

"Yeah." He was quiet a moment. "I'm sorry, Tiana. I'm sorry for not asking you directly, and for causing you any more stress and concern. But please, don't take away my chance to meet Ella just to hurt me. Please."

Her heart was way too damn soft if that speech affected her. "You'd deserve it if I did."

"I know."

She pushed out a breath, feeling better now that she'd vented and had her say. Ella wanted to meet him. So, that was that. "All right, if the liaison is available, Ella can meet you this afternoon."

"*Thank* you—"

"But I swear to God, if you pull any more shit going forward, I will fight you in court with everything I have to make sure Ella won't see you until she's legal age. She and I have been through too much together. I won't allow anyone to add more to our load."

"Understood. And I agree with you."

"Good." She glanced behind her. Aidan and Ella were on their way down the lane. They were engrossed in conversation, Aidan listening intently to whatever Ella was saying. "Have the liaison text me about what time she'll be picking Ella up."

"I will. And Tiana…"

"Yes?"

"Thank you. I mean it."

"Don't screw this up. Bye."

She ended the call, shoving aside the stab of fear as she watched her daughter and Aidan walk toward her. It was done. All she could do now was hold onto what was right in front of her for as long as she could.

Chapter Seventeen

"You remember Lindsay, the lady from the court who you met at the police station a few weeks ago?" Tiana asked as she did up Ella's raincoat.

"Yes." Her daughter checked through her backpack distractedly.

"She's the one taking you to meet your dad. She'll stay while you guys talk, and then she'll bring you straight home afterward. Okay?" *And if things don't go well, you never have to see him again.* Tiana would make sure of that.

Ella was still preoccupied by whatever was in her pack. "All right."

Tiana straightened and examined her daughter for any outward signs of nerves or stress but didn't find any. No, that was all coming from *her*. Dammit.

She put on a smile even though she hated this and dreaded every moment Ella was at the meeting. Her anxiety was battering at her, whispering about all the possible things that could go wrong as a result of this. "We'll be here when you get home and you can tell us all about it."

Ella looked up, her face brightening. "Is Mac staying over again?"

She glanced behind her as Aidan came down the hallway. "Yes, if that's all right with you. His house still isn't safe yet."

"Sure, it's fine. Better than fine," Ella answered, shrugging into her backpack. "I'm taking some of my drawings to show my dad. Just in case we don't have a lot to talk about. You know how that happens sometimes when you meet someone?"

"I do," he answered, and shot Tiana a wry smile.

"I don't want it to be awkward."

This kid. She said the damndest things. "My phone," Tiana blurted, reaching for her purse, then stopped. *Crap.* "It's almost dead." She'd forgotten to charge it after her call with Evan.

"Here, she can take mine." Aidan handed his to Ella. "This is the swipe code. Do you know your mom's number? It's stored in there if you forget."

"Of course I know it," she told him in a "what a ridiculous question" tone as she tucked it into the front pocket of her jeans.

A car pulled up out front on the road and Tiana's stomach dropped. "She's here."

She went out on the front porch with Ella. The young court liaison, Lindsay, stepped out of the car and smiled at them. "Hi, Ella. You ready to go?"

"Yes. Bye, Mama, bye, Mac." Ella trotted down the steps before Tiana could get a goodbye kiss in, paused at the car to wave, then climbed into the back.

"I'll have her back by four-thirty at the latest," Lindsay promised.

"Sure." Heart sinking, Tiana waved as the woman got behind the wheel.

She stood there on the top step as the car reversed, her insides pulling into a giant knot that kept tightening with each passing second. Every instinct screamed at her to run to the car, pull Ella out and hold on tight. To never let her go. To protect her from more possible hurt.

But she didn't. She sucked it up, stood on that step and put a smile on her face as Ella turned to wave at them, her daughter's excited and hopeful expression tearing at her.

"Bye sweetheart," she called, her voice catching slightly, glad Ella wouldn't be able to tell from inside the car.

Aidan came to stand beside her as the car reached the lane and began to drive away. He wrapped a solid arm around her shoulders and tugged her into his side. "Brave lass," he murmured into her hair, giving her a squeeze.

She knew he meant her and not Ella. It made her throat tighten.

Tiana closed her eyes and turned into him, grateful for his quiet strength and the comfort he gave her. That he understood how awful this was for her. "I hate this so much." The lack of control. The inability to protect Ella just in case it didn't go well.

"I know you do, but you didn't let Ella know it, and that's what's important."

She nodded, leaning into his hold. He was right. And she would never tire of the way he felt, or how safe he made her feel. Valued, in a way she'd never felt with another man. "I just don't want her to get hurt." Any more than she already had been, and would be, when Aidan left.

He ran a hand over her back, his breath warm on the top of her head. "No. And you don't want her to leave you, either."

She sagged against him, his words piercing her, because it was her darkest fear. "I don't know what I'd do if it came to that."

"It won't. Your ex could never have anything on you that would make the courts take Ella away. And he'll never replace you, even if she decides she wants a relationship with him. Ever."

He took her by the shoulders and set her a bit away

from him to look her in the eyes. "No matter what happens, you'll always be her mother, and she'll always adore you. You've seen to it, by devoting yourself to her for her entire life. That lass knows deep in her bones how much you love her. Nothing will ever change that bond between you."

Oh, God, the backs of her eyes were already stinging, and his words just made it worse.

One side of his mouth lifted, the grin fond rather than amused, as though he could tell just how thin a thread she was hanging on by. "Come on," he said, taking her hand and leading her back inside.

"Where are we going?" she blurted. If he thought she was even remotely in the mood for sex right now, he was nuts. Wine, maybe. Several glasses of wine and maybe a relaxing bath if they had enough hot water for one now. But not sex. Even with him, the sexiest man she'd ever known.

"Out."

She scowled. "I don't wanna go out."

He raised an eyebrow at her petulant tone. "You'd rather sit here and drive yourself crazy for the next two hours?"

She sighed. *Dammit...* "You're right. Where do you want to go?"

He studied her for a long moment. Then, without a word he bent and swung her up into his arms, earning a squeak as she grabbed hold of his shoulders.

He walked to the living room and sank down on the couch with her, pulling her into his lap and wrapping her up in a fierce hug, holding her tight. "It'll be all right, lass, I promise," he whispered against her temple. "Now just let me hold onto you for a minute, and once you're settled we'll get out of here for a wee while."

****

The bumblebees were back, buzzing around in the bottom of her tummy when Ella got out of the car and followed Miss Lindsay into Whale's Tale a few minutes later.

She hadn't felt them in a while. Not since the last time she had to talk to the judge about Brian—she never thought of him as Mr. Brian anymore, not after what he'd done—which she hated doing. She wished she could just forget him and never have to talk about him again.

These bees were different than the kind she'd felt whenever Brian was around, though. Even before he'd done…those bad things in front of her, she'd felt them. Angry, hot bees that stung her insides. These ones weren't hot, they were just…buzzy.

She was glad she was meeting her dad here at Miss Poppy's shop where she knew people, so she didn't feel so alone and nervous.

"Hey, Ella," Miss Poppy called out with a bright smile, coming into the café side from the bookstore in the back carrying something in her hands.

The bees quieted a little. "Hi, Miss Poppy."

"I got a new shipment in today and I found something I thought you might like." She presented the box to her at the table Miss Lindsay sat down at. "It's a calligraphy set. It comes with an instruction manual, paper, a fountain pen and some ink refills."

Ella gasped. "It's so pretty."

"I thought you'd like it. Want to give it a try? If you like it then I know other girls will too and I'll order a few more."

"Yes, thank you." She slipped off her backpack and opened the calligraphy set while Miss Poppy and Miss Lindsay talked for a minute.

"Ella, you want your usual?" Miss Poppy asked her.

She looked up from the instruction manual she'd been

engrossed in. "Yes, please."

Miss Poppy tapped her on the end of her nose gently. "Coming right up, cutie."

"Let's take a look at all this, since we're a bit early," Miss Lindsay said, taking out the pen to put a cartridge in it. Ella liked her. She smiled a lot and she actually listened when Ella talked. A lot of adults only paid partial attention or talked down to her, which annoyed her.

They were busy working on the letter A in the workbook when Miss Lindsay looked up. "Oh, I think your dad's here."

Ella's heart jumped in her chest. She put the pen down and swung around on her chair to face the door just as a man walked in. Her mom had showed her a picture of him. He looked like a nice man, with brown hair, and when he stopped to smile at her, his blue eyes were the exact same color as hers.

"Hi, Ella," he said and started toward them.

Ella's cheeks began to burn as blood rushed to them and her heart was beating too fast. The man shook hands with Miss Lindsay and sat down, his leather jacket making a creaking sound. He smelled nice, but not as nice as Mac. And she'd never felt nervous around Mac. "What are you working on?"

She couldn't find her voice. She was too busy staring at him. Trying to see bits of herself in his face. He was handsome and seemed like he would be kind. Why would he have left her and her mom and not cared about them?

He didn't seem to mind that she didn't answer. His smile got bigger and the look in his eyes grew softer as he watched her. As if he was trying to see his face in hers too. "You're even more beautiful than the pictures your mom showed me," he said.

The burning in her face got worse. He was really her dad? She looked at Miss Lindsay, who gave an encouraging smile. So she turned her attention back to…her dad.

“Are you a musician?” That’s what her mom had told her. Ella tried not to ask about him very often, though, because whenever she did her mom’s face went all tight and her tone got annoyed. She didn’t want to upset her mom.

“I am.”

“Do you play instruments, or just sing?”

“I sing and play guitar. Electric and acoustic. I can show you some video later if you want. What about you? Do you play any instruments?”

“I play the recorder for school, but I don’t like it. I like to dance.”

“Ah. I’ll bet you’re a wonderful dancer.”

She hid a smile and ducked her head, feeling warm like the sun had just come out from behind the clouds to shine on her.

Miss Poppy came over with their drinks and food and took Ella’s dad’s order before he turned back to her, his eyes kind. “I appreciate you meeting with me, Ella. I’ve thought about you so often.”

She lowered her gaze, her eyes settling on the gold wedding band on his left hand. “Are you married?” How come he’d married some other lady and not her mom? Her mom was a nice lady.

“Yes, and I have young twin boys. Your brothers. Would you like to see them?”

She gasped. She had brothers? Her mom hadn’t told her that. “Yes.”

She stared in fascination at his phone’s screen as he showed her some pictures. Her brothers were babies, but they were cute. “They have the same eyes as us,” she said, unable to help the smile forming on her face.

“Yeah, they do,” her dad said, his voice a little funny, and when she looked up, his eyes were shiny.

After that her face wasn’t hot anymore and the bees went to sleep.

Her dad told her stories about her brothers and their

home in California. They lived close to Disneyland.

"I haven't been there yet," Ella told him, taking a sip of her chocolate milk. Miss Poppy always put extra chocolate in it for her. "Mom said she'll take me there someday."

"It's a pretty neat place. The boys are too young to go yet, but in a few more years maybe you can show them the ropes."

They ate lunch together. Ella answered questions about school, her dance, and she even took out her drawings to show him, too. Miss Lindsay didn't say anything at all, just ate her sandwich and listened. She was a great listener. Maybe that's why the court had given her this job.

"What about you, Ella," her dad said as they finished up. "Do you have anything you want to ask me?"

She hesitated. There was something, but she wasn't sure she should say it.

"Anything you want to know. Ask away."

She glanced at Miss Lindsay for permission and received an encouraging nod. So she blew out a breath and toyed with the edge of her drawing before speaking. "Why did you leave?"

Everything froze. Or at least, that's what it seemed like.

Her dad was like a statue as he stared at her in surprise, and her face got hot again. She shouldn't have asked him. Now she'd ruined everything and he might not want to see her again. Her stomach started to hurt and the bees woke up.

"That's a fair question," he said softly after a horribly long moment. He leaned back in his chair, his eyes fixed on her.

She risked a peek at his face. He didn't seem mad. He seemed almost...sad. So sad that even the bees felt sorry for him and settled down again.

"Your mother and I had you when we were really young. I wasn't very mature then. I was selfish and not ready to be a dad to anyone, not just you. That probably sounds awful to you, and it is. I was. I left you and your mom because I wanted to be a musician so badly, and I didn't think I could do it if I stayed with you. But I thought about you all the time. And since I had your brothers, I couldn't stop thinking about you."

He paused, watching her, and her pulse thudded in her ears. "I'm a different person now. I'm not asking you to forgive me for leaving you and your mom, but I want you to know I'm sorry. And I want you to know that it wasn't your fault. It was mine. I promise you didn't do anything wrong."

Ella swallowed, her eyes going blurry. She'd wondered sometimes, wondered what she'd done wrong when she was a baby to make him leave. That maybe she'd been a bad baby and wouldn't stop crying or something.

She blinked fast, trying to force the tears back. "It's okay," she whispered, even though it wasn't. But she didn't want to upset him. She liked him and wanted him to like her too.

"It's not," he said, "but thank you. And I'm glad you got to meet me now, instead of back then. Back then you wouldn't have liked me much, but now you might."

Even though she'd just met him she could hear the slight teasing note in his voice. She looked up at him, shared a little smile.

After that, the rest of the visit was easy. She asked more questions about baby Eddie and Alex, asked about their dog Sammy and told him all about Walter and Bruce, and how she had wanted a dog for as long as she could remember but now she wanted Bruce more than anything. Cats were easier to take care of anyway.

"It's four o'clock," Miss Lindsay said with a soft smile. "Time to go, Ella."

"Oh." She didn't want to, but she knew her mom would worry if they didn't get home soon. Ella couldn't wait to tell her and Mac all about the visit. Well, maybe she'd just tell Mac. She didn't want to upset her mom.

She stood, then stopped and held out a hand to her father, because it was good manners to shake hands when you met someone. "It was nice to meet you."

He grinned and shook her hand. "Very nice to meet you, Ella. What do you think, would you like to meet up for lunch or something again next time I'm in town? Maybe we could talk on the phone if you want, too. Whatever you're comfortable with. You can talk it over with your mom first."

"That sounds good." Better than good. She had a *dad*. Not the same kind of dad as most kids had, and she didn't love him the same way she loved Mac or even Mr. Beckett, but he was her dad and no one could change that.

She couldn't wait to tell the kids at school about this on Monday.

She said goodbye to him and Miss Poppy and held Miss Lindsay's hand on the way out of Whale's Tale, feeling like she had swallowed a bite of sunshine. She was all warm inside, and happy. As soon as she told Mac everything, she would go see Bruce and Walter and tell them all about her dad too.

"Let's get you home, Ella," Miss Lindsay said.

"Okay. I want to tell Mac everything."

"Is Mac that man who was on the porch with your mom?"

"Yes. His house was damaged in the earthquake, so he's staying with us." She was about to say he was her mom's boyfriend, but she wasn't sure so she didn't say anything, just in case.

But she really, really hoped Mac would be her mom's boyfriend, because she wanted Mac to be her *real* dad. The one she lived with and saw every day. The one she talked to and asked about tricky math questions.

Mac listened to her. He paid attention. Didn't just brush her off like her mom's other boyfriends had, only being nice to her in front of her mom.

If Mac was her dad, he would *never* leave her and her mom.

In the back of the car she buckled her seatbelt and took out her calligraphy book to read on the drive home. Mac probably wasn't very good at calligraphy but she'd bet her mom was. Her mom could do lots of cool things.

"Okay, I'll drive you straight home then," Miss Lindsay said as she pulled out onto the street.

Ella didn't pay much attention to where they were, she was too busy reading the instructions on how to make the letters for her name.

"Ella?"

"Hmm?" She looked up, realized Miss Lindsay was waiting for an answer to something. They weren't on Front Street anymore. There were no more shops and she couldn't see the ocean, just trees and the occasional house. They were close to her house. "I didn't hear you. Pardon?"

"I said I'll talk to your mom for a few minutes and then—"

Ella gasped when something slammed into the back of their car. The seatbelt jerked hard against her shoulder. The calligraphy book shot from her fingers.

"Oh my God," Miss Lindsay cried, and turned the wheel.

They skidded. Ella tensed, grabbing for the door handle as the car spun. Her head jerked sideways, a cry ripping from her as something hit them a second time.

Tires squealed. Ella froze and held on as they spun faster, afraid to move, her gaze shooting to the window beside her at the car that had hit them.

A swarm of hot, angry bees poured into her stomach

when she saw the driver's face through the back window. A scary face that she sometimes still saw when she had bad dreams at night.

Brian.

Chapter Eighteen

Gotcha.

The elation pumping through his system almost made Brian dizzy, penetrating the fog of all the booze he'd consumed.

This was it. After almost two fucking days living in his car, unable to leave, trapped like a rat in a maze because of blocked roads and the possibility that the cops were looking for him.

He'd started to worry about whether he'd ever get out of here to start his new life. That he'd be apprehended again and have to spend the rest of his life in prison. That he'd die there.

But now she would pay.

Everything had changed when the woman had come to pick Ella up a little while ago. As soon as the car had started backing out of the driveway, he'd known what he had to do. He'd raced back through the woods to his car and made it to the intersection on the opposite side just as she turned off Salt Spray Lane.

Now all his patience had paid off.

He would catch Ella, and wait for Tiana to come for her. Then he could kill her. Or both of them.

Wait, maybe he'd kill Ella in *front* of Tiana first, make

her watch, so he could drink in her pain and use it to live on if he was locked up for the rest of his life.

His breathing was erratic as he jumped out of his car and raced for the other vehicle, riding the biggest high of his life. He'd never felt a rush like this, and it wasn't merely the alcohol in his bloodstream. Not even when he'd been forced to satisfy his urges when they became too strong.

No. This was powerful. Vindication and vengeance all in one.

The front end of the car Ella had been riding in was crumpled where it had plowed into the telephone pole. He could see the deployed airbag in the front. The driver was pushing at it. And in the back…

A pair of huge blue eyes stared out at him through the rear window.

He latched onto that terrified gaze, adrenaline punching through his veins, giving him an added burst of speed. There were a few people around, watching from down the sidewalk behind him, but he didn't care.

A fresh wave of rage swamped him when he thought of how his life had fallen apart while everyone else's just went on as normal. He couldn't stand that Tiana would get away with doing this to him. He wanted to hurt her. Hurt her as much as he could, and that meant taking Ella.

It was the little bitch's fault, after all. If she'd kept her stupid mouth shut, none of this would have happened. Well, now he would show her what the real meaning of suffering was.

An engine raced behind him, then tires screeched. He didn't slow, didn't look around, all his focus on Ella. The soles of his shoes pounded over the pavement, his elevated breathing loud in his ears.

In the backseat Ella spun around, leaned over and quickly pushed down the locks. As if that would save her.

He laughed and grabbed the front passenger door handle before she could lock it and wrenched it open. Ella screamed and scrambled into the back to cower against the door.

"Don't!" the female driver cried, appearing dazed as she tried to climb over the console to block him.

Brian punched her in the face, the satisfying crack of knuckles against bone singing up his arm. Her head snapped back and she lay still, moaning.

Drawing back his arm, he locked gazes with Ella, feeling as if he was floating. "You're mine," he snarled, and lunged between the front seats to grab her.

She yanked the lock up and pushed the door open at the same moment he reached for her. His fingers closed around the back of her hood. She cried out and wriggled out of the hoodie before he could grab her, slid out and darted onto the road.

Brian bellowed in rage and followed, propelling his body through the open door as she reached the opposite sidewalk. "You little *bitch*." He tore after her, caught her around the waist and clapped a hand over her mouth to stifle her shrieks.

She fought him like a wet cat, biting and clawing but he crushed her to him and turned for his car.

"Let her *go*, you bastard!"

The enraged male voice had barely registered when a heavy weight slammed into him from behind. He lost his grip on Ella as he fell, the breath momentarily whooshing from his lungs as he hit the ground. Fire streaked over the side of his face, knees and palms as he skidded over the pavement.

Strong hands grabbed his shoulders and flipped him over. He blinked up into Evan's incensed face just as a fist came hurtling toward his nose.

He turned his head just in time and slammed his hands out, knocking Evan off him. The other man fell on his side but grabbed Brian again, dragging him down once more.

Brian let loose with a flurry of punches, absorbing the blows he got in return, barely feeling the pain. Evan wasn't going to stop him. Ella was *his*, and both she and Tiana would pay for what they'd done to him. For what was going to happen to him.

He drove his fist into Evan's gut, making the other man double over with a pained grunt. Brian scrambled to his hands and knees, narrowly avoiding Evan's hand as it swept out, trying to trip him.

"You bastard, leave her the fuck alone," Evan rasped.

Brian didn't answer. He shoved to his feet, already searching for Ella, his heart jackhammering against his ribs. People would have called the cops by now. He was running out of time.

Out of the corner of his eye he caught the flash of her pink shirt and blond ponytail just as she disappeared around the corner up ahead.

Swearing, he raced for his car, hopped in and gunned it. "No way, little girl," he panted, steely determination driving back the fear and uncertainty eating its way through the alcoholic haze. He'd already come this far. He had to see this all the way through.

He had this one last chance to even the score, and he was taking it. "You're mine," he repeated, speeding after his target.

****

"We didn't get very far, did we?" Aidan said with a smirk as Tiana settled beside him on Beckett and Sierra's couch.

"No, but you're right, I needed to get out of the house and this way I've got company to distract me."

He gave her an affronted look. "And what am I? I'm not capable of distracting you?"

Her heart softened, fluttered. She smiled. "You're lethal at it. But in a different way."

"Sure I can't get you guys anything else to eat?" Sierra asked as she came in from the kitchen to hand Tiana a glass of white wine and placed a platter of cheese and crackers on the coffee table.

"No, this is perfect, thanks," Tiana said. It was only when Sierra's sharp eyes moved between her and Aidan and settled on her with an unspoken question that Tiana realized she was pressed up against his side.

Busted.

She gave Sierra a tiny smile and received one in turn, but her friend was way too classy to say anything in front of Aidan. Tiana expected to be fully grilled later, first by just Sierra, then again later in front of her, Poppy and Molly. She didn't mind. Aside from Lizzie, these women had become her closest friends. "Where's Walter?"

"Beckett took him out for a walk. Old guy usually hates walks, but it's better than being surrogate mom to the kittens, I guess, because he seems happy enough to get out of here now."

"You talking about Beckett or the dog?" Aidan asked.

"Funny," Sierra deadpanned.

They stayed and visited for a while. They helped feed the growing kittens some wet food and Tiana kept checking her watch. How was it that time could move so slowly sometimes?

"Are you leaning toward letting Ella have Bruce, or what?" Sierra asked her.

"Leaning. Haven't quite made up my mind, though."

"I hope you'll let her have him. She's been an amazing help and she loves him to death." Sierra covered a yawn for the third time in ten minutes.

Tiana nudged Aidan. "Well, we should get going," she said to Sierra. "Aidan promised me a walk on the beach before Ella got back, to clear my head."

"Aye, I did," he agreed, and pulled her up off the couch.

"Are you really wanting a walk on the beach? Or did you change your mind about a different kind of distraction?" he asked as they walked up the lane together a minute later, bouncing his eyebrows.

She laughed. "I'm tempted. But I think we should take a walk."

"All right." He laced his long fingers through hers, tugged her closer to him. "Letting the anticipation build will only make you want me more later."

She raised an eyebrow. "Pretty sure of yourself."

"Aye." He shot her a charming, sexy grin. "I know exactly where all your sweet spots are now."

Yes, he certainly did. And the thought of him putting that expertise to good use later sent a flood of heat spearing between her thighs.

Determined not to let her worry about Ella spoil the afternoon, she tipped her head back and closed her eyes. "That sunshine feels so good," she murmured. Opening her eyes a moment later, she was startled to find him staring at her with such longing that her pulse tripped. "What?"

"You're so damn beautiful," he said with a slight shake of his head.

Blood rushed to her cheeks. "I—thank you," she said, barely stopping herself from brushing off the compliment. Was this real? Could she actually trust her feelings and instincts this time? Or did she only feel this way because it was new, and because he was leaving in another two weeks?

She stopped walking and faced him, the question nagging at her. They'd both been hurt before. Had both gone through their share of heartache. "Can I ask you something?"

"Of course you can."

Her heart picked up speed. "This…thing between us," she began, unable to put a definition on it. "I've never felt anything like it. Have you?" She held her breath, awaiting his answer.

Heat and possessiveness filled his eyes, building the want inside her. "Never." He raised their joined hands to his lips, pressed a lingering kiss to the back of hers, his gaze on hers.

A smile spread over her face, his admission lowering the walls around her battle-scarred heart. "Ever?"

He shook his head, his lips still on her hand. "Not ever." He lowered her hand and cupped the back of her head with his other, bringing his mouth down on hers.

Her eyes closed as need shot through her, as intense as this crazy, stunning chemistry and deep connection between them.

Her cell phone started ringing.

She broke away, scrambling to pull it from her front pocket, expecting to find Aidan's number on the display. But it wasn't Ella calling.

"What's wrong?" Aidan asked.

She stared at the screen, torn. "It's Evan." Should she answer? Did this mean the meeting had gone well, or badly?

Does it matter? He's probably going to be part of Ella's life now, whether you like it or not. It'll be much easier on everyone if you can be a grown up and put your own feelings aside for Ella's sake.

Taking a steadying breath, she answered. "Evan. How did it go?"

"*Tiana.*"

The sharp edge of fear in his voice ripped through her like a lightning bolt, making her heart lurch. "What? What's the matter?"

"Brian's after her. He must have been watching us."

All the blood drained from her face. "What?" she

whispered.

Frowning in concern, Aidan took hold of her shoulder.

"Jesus, he chased after the liaison's car," Evan continued. "I followed him but he crashed into them—"

"*What*?"

"—and tried to drag Ella from the car. She got away and I tackled him, but he broke free and chased after her."

The world tilted on its axis. Aidan grabbed her, his expression and voice urgent. "What is it?" he demanded.

"Did you call 911?" Tiana demanded, too focused on what Evan had said to answer Aidan.

"Yes, the cops are on their way. Shit, I—I lost sight of her."

Her mind raced. "Where are you?" she demanded, icy panic raking over her skin.

"Cedar Ridge Drive, about two blocks off Front Street. Last I saw, she was running west toward the water."

"I gotta go," she rasped out, her heart in her mouth. "Call me if you find her."

"Wait—"

She hung up, wanting to scream, her heart threatening to explode. "Brian attacked Ella," she blurted out. "He's chasing her. She's on foot, maybe coming this way."

Aidan's jaw set. "She's got my phone. We can track her using my phone." He snagged her phone, grabbed her hand and started running up the lane.

"Who are you calling?" she said, on the verge of tears.

He didn't answer, her phone pressed to his ear, his expression grim and determined. "I need you to trace my phone," he said to whoever answered. "Ella's in trouble. We need to get to her before Brian does."

Chapter Nineteen

He was getting closer.

The breath sawed in and out of Ella's lungs as she ran, her leg muscles burning and her heart slamming so hard against her ribs it hurt. She could still hear Brian behind her, chasing after her through the woods like a hungry bear.

No matter what, she couldn't let him catch her. She'd seen that terrible look on his face when he'd tried to grab her in the car. If he caught her, he would hurt her. She knew it.

It was dark and shadowy in the woods and she wasn't sure where she was. She stifled a sob and kept running, almost blinded by the tears of fright. She had to get through this band of forest. Then she could find a path that would take her home. Aidan and Beckett would scare Brian away.

"Get back here, you little bitch!"

He was almost close enough to catch her now, crashing through the underbrush.

A wave of terror broke over her. She put on a burst of speed, darting between the trees as fast as she could go. Her foot snagged on a branch and she tripped, falling.

No! Brian was almost to her now.

She scrambled up and took off in another direction.

Please, no. Please don't let him catch me.

Maybe if she could put more distance between them she could find somewhere to hide and lose him.

"I'm gonna get you!"

She choked back another sob and kept going. It was getting brighter in here now, the trees thinning out. And just ahead, there, she could see the edge of the forest. There was a road.

She broke from the trees and tore across it, searching around for a place to hide. There were no houses here but she recognized the area. The lighthouse was off to the right. It had lots of rocks around it. If she could get there, maybe she could hide.

But she was getting tired, her heart and lungs ready to burst. She was slowing, and Brian was still behind her. She wasn't sure how much longer she could keep going.

It startled her when Aidan's phone buzzed and rang in her pocket but she couldn't risk slowing to pull it out to see who it was or ask for help. Aidan? Her mom? Her dad?

Keep running.

Thoughts raced through her mind. Her dad had seen what Brian had done, and tried to stop him. Maybe he'd called her mom, or even the police. Someone would come to help her if she could just get away from Brian.

Panting, she raced for the path that led down the cliff to the base of the lighthouse. She knew all the paths down there. There would be plenty of places to hide, and once Brian gave up she could make it around the point and home using a path farther up the beach.

She slipped and almost fell twice on the way down the sandy incline. The wind whipped at her, cutting through her clothes. Her teeth chattered, her muscles shuddering as she risked a glance behind her. Brian was at the top of the cliff now.

He spotted her, charged down the path toward her.

Ella raced for the rocks at the base of the cliff. The wind was even stronger here, icy and sharp.

Gasping for breath, shivering all over, she climbed between a large group of rocks and crouched down, trying to make herself as small as possible. All around her the wind moaned through the rocks, cold water splashing up through the gaps every time a wave hit them. It sluiced over her tennis shoes and soaked the legs of her jeans, making her even colder.

She stifled a whimper as Brian reached the rocks. He stopped, his head whipping back and forth as he searched for her, and the expression on his face was every bit as scary as it had been in the car.

She huddled there, unmoving, hardly daring to breathe. She wanted to go home. She wanted her mom and Mac.

Don't let him see me. Don't let him—

Even though she hadn't moved, something must have given her away because Brian's gaze locked on her. A horrible, evil smile split his face and he started toward her.

No!

Ella shot to her feet and spun to flee, but it was too late. Her foot had barely touched the next rock when something caught her ponytail and yanked her head back. She fell. Brian grabbed her. Dragged her backward, his evil laugh sending chills down her spine.

Her screams were ripped away on the cold wind, taken out to sea where no one could hear them.

****

It took every bit of restraint Tiana had not to rip the phone from Aidan's hand as he and Beckett stared at it. "Have you got her?" She was dying inside. Was frantic to find Ella and get to her before Brian did.

"There." Beckett pointed to a dot on screen.

"She's heading down the path that goes below the lighthouse," Aidan said, and took off running. Tiana charged after him.

"I'm getting a boat," Beckett yelled back.

Aidan raised a hand in acknowledgment but didn't slow. He was way faster than her, his long, powerful legs outdistancing her in no time. But he was taking the wrong route.

"Wait! Go this way!" she shouted.

He looked back at her and she pointed to the right. "There's another path here that goes down to the beach." She started down it without waiting, and he soon caught up. Only locals knew about this one.

The path was narrow and tangled with vegetation. Her shoes slipped a few times but Aidan caught her. Together they rushed down the steep incline, causing small landslides of sand and rock as they went.

The lighthouse stood atop the towering cliff top to their left. Below them, the ocean roiled in the cold spring wind, waves crashing against the rocks at the end of the point.

Tiana scanned the base of the cliff below the lighthouse, searching for a glimpse of her daughter. "Can you see her?" She had to shout to be heard over the wind. It whipped her hair around her like a fiery halo, obscuring her vision. She shoved it aside, jammed it inside the collar of her jacket, making her way down the path as fast as she could.

"Not yet, but she has to be there."

Recent rains and the quake had damaged the path. It stopped halfway down, blocked by a steep ravine and a jumble of rocks that must have tumbled down the cliff.

Aidan ran past her and leapt across it, landing in a crouch on the other side. He turned back toward her, held out a hand. "Jump. I'll catch you."

Ella was in danger and needed her. That was all it took to make her jump.

She backed up a few yards, took a running start and launched herself over the ravine, her gaze locked on Aidan's hand. He caught her outstretched hand and yanked her forward just as she landed on the opposite edge, would have fallen backward into the ravine if not for his strength.

"There, I see her!"

She stopped breathing and wrenched her head around to follow his outstretched arm. There on the rocks at the base of the cliff, she spotted a flash of pink. "Ella," she cried and started running, her legs like rubber.

And then her blood iced over as Brian came into view. He lunged for Ella.

"I'm going after her," Aidan said, and took off.

"Yes, go, *go*," she urged him, her heart in her throat. She skidded her way down the loose sand, not even bothering with the path now.

Aidan had already reached the bottom and tore up the beach. She stumbled when she hit the beach, but shoved up and sprinted after him, fear and helplessness choking her. Goddamn it, they were too far away. Too far away to get to Ella before Brian took her.

The sound of a boat's motor cut through the rush of the wind. Beckett was streaking across the water toward them, angling toward shore. He waved an arm at them, calling them to the boat.

Tiana hesitated. Ahead of her, Aidan changed direction and headed for the water as Beckett came closer to shore, bringing the boat alongside an outcropping of rock.

Tiana followed, clambering across the black basalt formations. Aidan reached back to grab her hand, hauling her over the largest one. Beckett had one hand braced on the rock nearest the boat, the other on the wheel.

Aidan lifted her, all but tossing her over the side. She scrambled in just as he jumped in beside her and Beckett hit the throttle, cranking the wheel around to speed away from the rocks toward the base of Lighthouse Point.

Tiana clung to the side of the boat and kept her gaze trained on Ella. "Oh God, baby," she choked out. Brian had grabbed her.

Rage and determination punched through her, making the hairs on her arms stand up. "*Fight*, baby. Keep fighting." She would kill him for this. Kill him with her bare hands and gladly spend the rest of her life in jail as long as her daughter was safe and he was gone.

Aidan was poised beside her, both hands gripping the side of the boat. "She got away," he yelled.

A surge of pride swelled inside her as she watched Ella scramble away from Brian. "*Yes*, baby. Hold on. Hold on, we're coming." They were getting closer now. Maybe thirty seconds from reaching the rocks and Beckett wasn't slowing.

She saw the exact moment Ella spotted them.

Her daughter froze, costing her precious seconds of lead time, and began waving her arms frantically. Her mouth opened and closed as she screamed something, and even from this distance Tiana could see the terror in her expression, her eyes so wide the whites showed all the way around.

Agony splintered through her. The crushing pain of helplessness when the person she loved most in the world was in danger and there was nothing she could do.

Brian lunged for Ella again. Caught her. "No!" Tiana cried, wanting to vault over the side of the boat and bash his head against the rocks. White hot rage blasted through her.

I'll kill him. I'll fucking kill him with my bare hands.

Beckett slowed the boat slightly, angled the bow as they approached the deadly outcropping of rocks. "I'll get us as close as I can," he shouted back to them.

Tiana didn't look at him, totally focused on Ella.

Her daughter slipped. Fell.

Tiana sucked in her breath. *Get up. Get up, baby.*

Ella managed to get to her feet. Brian was a step away, lunging for her.

No…

Time ground to a near halt, the scene playing out frame by frame as though Tiana was watching a movie at half speed.

Ella's head turned as she looked over her shoulder at Brian, then swung back around to stare at them in the boat. Her expression changed, filling with determination. And in that single heartbeat Tiana knew what her daughter was about to do.

She clutched Aidan's shoulder, fear rolling over her like a dark wave. "Oh my God, no, she's going to—"

Ella launched off the tallest rock and dove into the water.

Tiana made a terrible, high-pitched keening sound, like something a wounded animal would make. *Ella!*

She set one foot on the side of the boat and dove in after her without thinking. Aidan's shout echoed in her ears a split second before she hit the water.

The cold hit her like a thousand knives driving into her body, sucking the air from her lungs, momentarily paralyzing her.

Her brain finally kicked back into gear and she aimed for the surface, sucking in a tortured breath of air when her head breached the water. She was a strong swimmer but the ocean was powerful and cold.

A wave slapped her in the face. She choked, flailed in the water, the weight of her sweater and shoes dragging her downward.

She clawed her way back to the surface, scanning desperately for Ella.

"Tiana!"

She glanced over her shoulder to see Beckett steering

the boat toward her, his face grim. Aidan wasn't with him.

Ignoring the boat, she turned onto her belly and began swimming for the rocks as fast as she could. Ella. She had to get to her—

A flash of pink caught her attention off to the right. A half-second later Ella's blond head popped up above the surface.

"Ella!" she cried, and started swimming for her. The current pulled at her, the cold turning her limbs numb and sapping her strength far too quickly.

Aidan's head broke the surface next to Ella's.

Tiana sobbed and kept swimming toward them.

Beckett had angled the boat around. He was closing in on Aidan and Ella.

Still swimming, Tiana watched as Beckett reached over the side of the boat, and Aidan lifted Ella toward him. Beckett pulled her daughter to safety and the towering wave of emotion crashed over Tiana, unleashing a torrent of tears.

Out of the corner of her eye she glimpsed a rock jutting out of the water. She swam for it. Grabbed hold and clung to it, panting and shivering.

Ella was okay. Everything would be fine now.

A gasp wrenched out of her when something grabbed her hair and yanked back with vicious force. A split second later she was underwater.

Blindly she reached back to grab at whatever had caught her.

Her flailing hand met a fist clenched around her hair. She twisted her head around to see.

A jolt of terror streaked through her when she saw Brian's enraged eyes staring back at her under the water.

Chapter Twenty

Aidan's heart rate slowed a fraction as Beckett hoisted Ella over the edge of the boat to safety. *She was safe.*

He slid back into the frigid water and immediately turned around to search for Tiana. She'd jumped in before he'd even guessed what she was about to do. But she was nowhere to be seen.

His heart pumped desperately in his chest. "Where's Tiana? Do you see her?" he called to Beckett.

"Over there," Beckett said, pointing to Aidan's right.

He bobbed in the water, searching. The wave in front of him bottomed out, and he glimpsed her red hair immediately. She was clinging to a rock sticking out of the water about fifty yards from shore.

Thank you, Jesus. Pure relief sluiced through him. Finally able to breathe again, he began swimming toward her.

He'd only taken half a dozen strokes when her head suddenly snapped back and she went under.

Alarm shot through him. "Tiana!" What the hell?

She didn't come up.

Fuck.

He dove under, swam faster, and what he saw beneath

the waves made his heart constrict in sheer terror.

Brian. The bastard had her. Was trying to drown her.

Adrenaline roared through him, giving him added strength.

He kicked and pulled against the water with all his might, desperate to get to her. The water was freezing. His limbs were already numb, all his muscles shuddering in an effort to conserve warmth. He stayed below the surface to avoid the waves but the current was pulling him out to sea. And he and the boat were too far away from Tiana to get to her in time.

Too. Fucking. Far.

A roar of rage and denial built in his throat as he plowed his way through the water, fighting to get to her. She was kicking and twisting, desperately trying to throw Brian off her. She managed to break free for a moment, and his heart soared as she shot to the surface.

He followed, took a breath of air with her. "Tiana!"

Her blank gaze locked on him for an instant, then Brian surfaced and shoved her back under.

Aidan dove back under and swam for all he was worth, the muscles in his legs, arms and back burning. *Hold on, sweetheart. Almost there...*

He gave a hard kick and reached out with both hands, gripping her shoulders tight. With a guttural snarl he ripped her out of Brian's grasp and drove his foot forward, ramming it into the bastard's gut, knocking him off her. Then he shoved Tiana upward, kicking again, building momentum as he propelled her toward the surface to get her head above the waterline.

His head broke through the water a split second after hers. He grabbed her other shoulder to steady her, his legs scissoring to keep them afloat.

She clung to his arm, choking, thrashing. "Tiana," he rasped out, holding her up so she could clear her lungs and get air. Beckett was nearby in the boat but they were too close to the rocks now for him to get to them. Aidan had to get her to land.

"Mac! Over here!"

At the shout to his right he glanced over to find Jase in the water, swimming toward them with strong, sure strokes.

"Give her to me!"

Aidan pushed Tiana in his direction, keeping one hand on her as he swam. He was numb, the cold quickly draining the strength from his muscles.

Jase was there in a matter of seconds. "I've got her. Let go."

Only because Aidan was numb and exhausted and trusted Jase with his life, he did, releasing his death grip on Tiana's arm. Jase took over, immediately turning around to tow her to shore. Aidan followed, the cold sapping what was left of his strength reserves.

But seconds into the swim he spotted Brian surface mere yards from the rocks on the north side of the point.

An unholy rage swept through him, followed by icy resolve.

You're mine, *ya slimy wee bastard.*

The growl was low and guttural in his head. Undeniable, shutting out all other thoughts. Brian wasn't getting away. Not after everything he'd done.

Without conscious thought he changed direction, dove under and swam for Brian, the cold and numbness fading beneath the tide of righteous fury pumping through him. He surfaced less than ten yards from the bastard.

Brian's head whipped around, his eyes bulging when he saw how close Aidan was. He spun back around and tried to flail his way to shore, but that wasn't fucking happening.

Aidan shot out a hand and grabbed a fistful of the bastard's hair. Yanked as hard as he could, pulling him under the water. *How's it feel, you pathetic piece of shite?*

Brian reached back to claw at his hand but Aidan didn't give an inch. He kept a solid hold on him, keeping Brian under until he thrashed with panic, on the verge of drowning. Aidan released him with a shove.

They surfaced a second apart. Brian was flailing, choking. Panting, Aidan turned away and swam for the rocks, letting the arsehole fend for himself.

A fist swung out toward his face. Aidan jerked aside at the last moment, narrowly avoiding the blow. Brian came at him again.

Aidan spun around to face the bastard and blocked the next punch, then answered with one of his own, his knuckles slamming into Brian's jaw. The waves battered them, crashing around them, sending them hurtling toward the rocks ahead.

Brian took the brunt of the impact, his head ramming into the rocks. He jerked and stilled for a split second.

Carried by the overwhelming power of the waves, Aidan crashed into him a heartbeat later, the force of it momentarily jamming the air from his lungs. As soon as he could breathe again he wrenched Brian up and forward, dragging his head above water.

Blood spilled down the guy's face from where he'd cut his head on the rock.

"Ya fuckin' *bastard*," Aidan snarled, gasping for breath, his body exhausted, his strength spent. He drew his numb fist back anyway, and drove it straight into the fucker's slack face.

Brian's head snapped back. Aidan didn't even feel the impact. He drew back for another shot, then realized the wee shite wasn't moving. Brian was hanging like a sack of flour in his grip, pinned against the rock by the force of the waves crashing against them. A deadweight.

"Mac!"

Jase was running over the rocks toward him. Aidan kept hold of Brian until Jase got there and dragged his limp body up onto the rocks. Aidan grabbed hold of the one closest to him and hauled himself up, his chest heaving, and lay there for a few moments, spent.

Slowly he got to his hands and knees. Jase had Brian stretched out on his back on a flat rock. He was performing chest compressions.

Aidan wasn't sorry the bastard had inhaled a lungful of seawater and bashed his head against the rocks.

Still gasping, he summoned the strength to turn his head, his gaze searching for and finding Tiana. Noah was with her. She was okay. And Beckett was speeding Ella to shore in the boat.

Aidan closed his eyes and dropped his head, his heart expanding until he feared it might burst.

As long as his girls were safe, that was all that mattered. As for Brian…

Aidan hoped the bastard died and spared Ella the trouble of enduring a trial.

****

Tiana couldn't stop shaking as Noah wrapped her up in a blanket. It cut the wind but didn't warm her. She was numb all over, shaking so hard her teeth chattered and her breaths came in ragged gasps.

Noah was talking to her, his voice urgent, but she wasn't listening. Her attention was divided between the boat carrying Ella, heading away from her to shore, and on Aidan just in sight on the other side of the point. He was on his hands and knees, his head bowed in exhaustion.

Close by, Jase was doing compressions on Brian's chest.

Just let him die, she thought savagely. She wanted him to die. He deserved it. She only wished it could have been slower and more painful. And by her hand. That monster had tried to take her baby.

"Tiana, *look* at me."

She forced her gaze to Noah's. "I'm o-k-kay," she grated out. "W-want Ella." She needed to hold her daughter. Craved it with every cell of her being.

His worried expression softened. "She's okay. Beckett's still with her and paramedics are on the way. I'll get you to her as soon as I can, but I can't if you're hypothermic." He rubbed his hands briskly over her back, her arms, trying to warm her.

"A-Aidan. N-need Aidan."

"We need to get you away from the water and out of the wind so we can warm you up."

It was then she noticed the people coming down the cliff path toward them. Men wearing sheriff's deputy jackets, and firemen carrying medical supplies.

She shook her head, the motion jerky. "A-Aidan," she insisted. She wasn't leaving without him.

Noah grunted in annoyance, held her gaze for a second, then bent to hook an arm under her knees. "You're as stubborn as my sister. I'll take you to him for a minute, but when the firemen get here, they're taking a look at you."

She didn't argue, wrapping her arms around his neck, her gaze riveted on Aidan. He was watching her too, and pushed back to sit on his heels. He was shaking hard, his chest heaving. She wanted to go to him. Hold him. Thank him for what he'd done. Warm him with her body heat and never let him go.

"She wasn't going to cooperate until she saw you," Noah said to Aidan as he made his way across the rocks with her.

Aidan slowly pushed to his feet, shivering so much it made her want to cry again. When they got close she pushed at Noah's shoulders. "P-put me d-down," she begged.

Noah lowered her to her feet, keeping an arm around her waist as she wobbled, meeting Aidan halfway. His arms closed around her as she swung her blanket around them both.

She grabbed the back of his neck with one hand, her icy fingers clamping tight while she pressed her face into his chest and hugged him around the back.

"Y-you ok-kay?" he demanded, shaking even harder than her.

She nodded, managed to choke out a yes and kept clinging. He'd been in the water longer than her. Without him, she would have drowned and Ella might have too. "You s-saved us," she whispered, so overcome with gratitude and emotion for this man that she wanted to weep.

"H-how's Ella?" He looked over his shoulder.

"Safe. N-need to s-see her."

"Right after the firemen check you both out," Noah promised, waving the other first responders over.

Tiana tamped down her impatience as two firemen approached her. Two immediately moved past her to Aidan, and two others to Brian, taking over CPR from Jase. The firemen peeled off her sodden clothes, put her in sweatpants, a sweatshirt and thick socks, then wrapped her up in more blankets.

Their friend made his way over the rocks to them wrapped in his own blanket, panting from the prolonged exertion. "Is h-he dead?" Aidan demanded.

"Not yet." His aqua gaze cut between them. "You guys both okay?"

"Yes, but I need to see Ella," Tiana said, holding Aidan's hand. It was every bit as cold as hers but even though she couldn't feel it she needed to touch him. She needed to see her daughter *now*.

Finally, they were allowed to start for the beach. A firefighter carried her, steering clear of whatever was going on with Brian while Jase and Aidan walked beside her.

"I just need to see my little g-girl," Tiana said to him, her heart racing.

"I understand. She's all right. Just wet and cold and shaken up."

God, the trauma that child has sustained already. Tiana bit her lip. Partway up the beach a group of first responders were gathered around someone, presumably Ella. She needed to get to her daughter.

The awful pressure in her chest expanded and pushed up into her throat, shoving against the backs of her eyes. She blinked to clear the haze of tears, shivering as the wind whipped around her. Once again, she'd failed to protect her daughter from a mistake she'd made.

Ella. My poor, sweet Ella...

The effort of carrying her across the sand began to wear on the fireman. He was slowing, his breathing strained and he kept shifting his grip on her.

"It's okay, put me down," she insisted, pushing at him.

"You sure?"

"Yes." She was cold and tired but if she didn't run to Ella right this instant, she would explode.

He set her down on the damp sand. Without waiting for either Aidan or Jase, Tiana broke into a lope, going as fast as her wobbly legs would allow. The firemen and paramedics gathered around Ella saw her coming and made way.

As soon as her gaze landed on her little girl, huddled in a blanket in the midst of all the first responders, a sob tore from Tiana's chest.

"M-mom," Ella cried, and stood up.

Tiana dropped her blanket, her numb feet racing over the sand for those last few torturous yards, and then Ella was in her arms.

A low, wounded sound ripped from her lips. She clutched her daughter to her, one hand on the back of Ella's little blond head to hold her daughter's face to her chest, her free arm locked around Ella's waist.

She couldn't get a single word out, the feel of her daughter safe in her arms breaking something inside her. Locking Ella to her, she fell to her knees.

Uncaring of the spectacle they made, she rolled to her side there on the sand, buried her face in Ella's hair and cried, hard, agonized sobs ripping through her. Ella clung tight, the muscles in her little arms shaking with the effort.

Someone lifted them upright. Pressure and warmth slowly registered.

When the sobs finally eased enough to allow her to open her eyes, she looked up into Aidan's face. His cheeks were streaked with tears as he cradled them both to his chest, his big body sheltering them and blocking the worst of the wind.

Tiana leaned her head on his shoulder and closed her eyes, pressing fervent kisses to her daughter's wet hair, every part of Ella's face she could reach.

The wind receded even more. She looked up to find Poppy, Sierra and Molly there. The women wrapped them in quilts and Molly gave them all hot tea to drink from a thermos. They'd brought warm clothes and shoes as well.

Everything after that passed in a complete blur.

Tiana refused to let Ella out of arm's reach when an ambulance crew met them at the top of the cliff. They were taken to the hospital to be checked out.

Tiana stayed with Ella as her daughter relayed the entire harrowing tale to Noah, who wrote it up in a report. He'd told her that Brian had died on the beach, that based on the liquor bottles they'd found in his car, his blood alcohol level was likely way above the legal limit, making him succumb to hypothermia faster.

She was glad he was dead. And she hoped hell was real, because she wanted him to suffer the worst torture it could throw at him for the rest of eternity.

"Miss Fitzgerald?" a nurse said to her, pulling her out

of her ruthless thoughts. "There's a man here asking to see you and Ella. He said he's her father."

The word *no* immediately shot into her mouth, but she stopped it before it could come out. Evan had his faults but Ella had clearly enjoyed his visit and he'd tried his best to protect her, tackling and fighting Brian.

She swallowed her own feelings and put the question to Ella. "Do you want to see him?"

Ella nodded and sat up straighter, her expression anxious. "He was hurt."

"All right," Tiana told her nurse. "Send him in."

Evan came in a minute later, his face bruised from his struggle with Brian. His gaze shot from Tiana to Ella and his face filled with a mixture of grief and relief that softened Tiana's hardened heart. "Oh, God, sweetheart," he breathed, dropping to his knees in front of Ella to cup her face in his hands. "Are you all right?"

"I'm okay. Mac and Beckett saved me."

"Well then, I owe them big time." He reached his arms out, then hesitated, watching Ella. "Can I hug you?"

A tiny smile curled her lips upward. "Yes." She leaned forward and wrapped her arms around Evan's neck, and Tiana had to look away for a second, her throat tightening.

She couldn't hold on to her bitterness. It would only do more harm than good and Evan clearly cared about Ella. This had to mark the start of a new beginning for all of them—if Evan proved he'd really changed.

"I'm so glad you're okay," he whispered, then his eyes came back to Tiana. "Both of you," he added.

Ella let go and sat back, seemed to sag in her chair as she met Tiana's gaze. "Where's Mac?"

"They're checking him over in another room." She intended to cover that man with kisses the moment she was alone with him again.

"I want to go home now. I'm tired."

"I know, baby. We'll go as soon as the doctor says it's

okay." As soon as Ella's core temp came up to normal.

Ella drifted off into a doze. Tiana sat beside her, stroking her hair. "She's been through so much," she whispered, then bit her lip.

"But she's safe now."

She looked up at Evan. Nodded.

He sat forward, clasping his hands and resting his elbows on his knees. "You're one hell of a fierce mom, Tiana. Diving into the water to save her." His smile was genuine, full of admiration. "Our daughter's lucky to have you."

For some reason his words pushed her near tears. "Thank you."

"It's the truth. And please don't worry about the custody issue. I swear I won't try to take her from you. She belongs here with you. I'll be satisfied with seeing her once a month or whenever your schedules permits it."

"Do you mean that?"

"Yes."

She believed him.

Evan stayed for a little while longer. Tiana found it easier to be around him as the minutes passed, and the goodbye was only mildly awkward. She was never going to be friends with him, but she could deal with him being involved in Ella's life as long as he proved to be a good father now.

Finally the doctor cleared them to leave. Aidan was waiting for them in the hall. He gathered them both into a fierce hug that was returned twofold.

Ella wound her arms around his neck and her legs around his waist, refusing to be put down, so he carried her down to the entrance where Beckett waited for them in his truck. He drove them home, asked if they needed anything, then left.

"Hot showers all around?" Aidan said to her and Ella.

"I want a bath," Ella said.

"I'll get her settled," Tiana told him. "You go shower."

She stayed next to the tub in the spare bathroom while Ella had her bath, refusing to leave her for even a moment. She studied every single detail of her daughter's face, drinking them in. Every time she thought about what could have happened, that she'd almost lost Ella, panic shot through her veins.

"Am I going to have to see Missy again?" Ella asked her.

Tiana's college friend in Seattle, the child psychologist. "Maybe. Would that be a bad thing?"

"No, I liked her." She sighed, rested the back of her head on the edge of the tub. "I just want to have a normal life."

Oh God, her little girl sounded so grown up. "Me too, sweetie." She took Ella's hand, squeezed it as she smiled. "Only normal from now on, I promise."

Ella eyed her, a calculating gleam there. "Maybe if I had a cat, it would help. You know, give me something to focus on after all this."

Manipulative little brat. Tiana fought a smile. Lost. "All right. You can have Bruce."

Ella shot upright, her eyes wide with excitement. "I *can*?"

"Yes, you can." Tiana would have given her any damn thing she'd asked for at the moment, so a pet her daughter clearly adored was a simple request to grant.

"Oh, thank you," she breathed, launching forward to envelop Tiana in a wet, enthusiastic hug. "You're the best mom *ever*. I can't wait to tell Miss Sierra."

"Tomorrow. Right now you're getting dried off, bundled up in warm clothes, and put to bed."

"Okay. Can I sleep with you and Mac again?" she asked.

"Sure." Tiana had planned on it anyway. She needed both of them close to her tonight.

Aidan was freshly showered and dressed in sweats when Tiana carried Ella into the master bedroom a few minutes later, her daughter half asleep on her shoulder. "She's exhausted," Tiana whispered, "but she wanted to sleep with us."

"Bring her on over." He climbed into the bed and pulled the covers down, reaching for Ella.

This time there was no jolt of alarm at the thought of Ella being next to him in the bed. Nothing but tenderness and a feeling of rightness as Aidan took Ella from her.

Tiana's heart turned over at the way he gently positioned Ella against his chest and tucked the blankets around her slender shoulders. Ella yawned and cuddled closer, already sliding into sleep.

Because her daughter knew even on the deepest subconscious level that she was safe with him. Tiana knew exactly how that felt.

Aidan looked up at her, his warm gaze raking over her. "You must still be chilled. Go have a shower."

This time there wasn't even an ounce of hesitation about leaving Ella alone in the bed with him. And that felt amazing.

She took a long, hot shower, continually battling to force the awful images from today out of her head. After blow-drying her hair she put on her thickest, warmest pair of socks, a sweater and yoga pants, then brushed her teeth and went back into the bedroom. Ella's soft, even breaths greeted her.

"She's out cold," Aidan whispered, folding the covers down on Ella's other side for Tiana to slide in. "Dropped right off to sleep in the middle of telling me about Bruce. You caved, did you?"

"Like a badly constructed snow fort."

"If it matters, I fully support that decision. Feel warmer?"

"Much." She climbed in beside her daughter and settled on her side to snuggle in close, her top arm draped over Ella's ribs to curl around Aidan's waist. He rolled toward her more and wrapped a strong arm around her back, his big hand splayed across the middle of her spine.

It was still light outside, the sunset filtering through the window above the bed. She searched Aidan's eyes, falling into them. Into him.

"I've fallen for you, lass," he murmured. "I didn't plan on it or even want to. But I think I fell months ago, and today I knew for sure."

Her heart hitched, then swelled, a sweet, warm ribbon of elation threading through her. "Me too." She lifted her hand to stroke her fingers over his bristly cheek. "Now what the hell are we going to do?"

"We find a way."

He made it sound so obvious and simple, but it wasn't simple. She'd gone into this knowing he would be leaving at the end of the month. Had gone into this relationship with the strict understanding that their time together had a definite expiration date, hoping her heart would be safe.

Instead, she'd lost it to him completely.

She shook her head, a torrent of grief welling up to twist her insides. "How am I supposed to live without you when you go?" she whispered miserably. Ella was going to be devastated too.

There were so many logistical problems and hurdles for them to combat if their relationship even had a prayer of continuing. He would be gone overseas for at least six months, maybe up to nine if things dragged out on his assignment, fulfilling the terms of his contract with his friend's security company.

He could come back here to the States to visit, but without a work visa he couldn't earn money and would have to return to Scotland eventually. And now that Evan was seeking a legal parenting time agreement, even though he wasn't a bad guy, Tiana couldn't see him allowing her to pack Ella up and move them to Scotland.

Aidan smoothed a hand up her spine to slide into her hair, his fingers rubbing over her scalp. "It's less than a year. We'll figure it out. I'm not letting you go. I'm not letting *either* of you go," he added, looking down at Ella with an expression of such fierce devotion that Tiana almost started crying again.

He'd risked his life to save them today. Without hesitation. Without any expectation of thanks or reward. And Tiana knew he would do it all again if necessary.

This. *This* was what true love felt like. Safe and fulfilled in ways she could never have imagined, even as it threatened to fracture her heart into a thousand pieces.

Even though it was going to rip her to shreds to see him go, she wouldn't have changed any of it for a single second.

Chapter Twenty-One

Two weeks later

"Did you like the French toast, Mac?" Ella asked him as she hopped off the stool at the kitchen counter to take her plate to the sink.

"I did, aye. It was brilliant." She and Tiana had made it for him, with chocolate chips and whipped cream on the side.

She beamed at him, came back to throw her arms around him and press a kiss to his cheek. "Good. I'm going to go read now."

The lass melted him without even trying. He was going to miss her almost as much as he would her mother when he left, and he was still trying like hell to find a permanent solution that would allow him to come back to them for good. "All right."

Tiana stood at the sink doing the breakfast dishes, her back to them. She'd been quiet all morning, a little distant even, as though she was trying to pull back from him already. It would be kinder to let her, but he couldn't. She was his and he wanted to imprint himself on every cell in her body before he left. Because he would find a way back to her.

She stiffened when he came up to settle his hands on his waist, her spine going rigid. Seconds passed, only the sound of rushing water from the tap filling the void.

He reached past her to shut it off and took the plate from her wet hands, then wrapped his arms around her and nuzzled the side of her neck, ignoring the tension in her body. "The dishes will keep," he murmured.

He'd spent the past two weeks falling asleep beside her, waking her with caresses and kisses until she was wet and needy and he could slide into her from behind and rock them both to heaven. While she was at work during the day and Ella at school, he'd helped his mates out with repairs around their places, trying to formulate a plan that ensured he came back to his lasses as soon as humanly possible.

Tiana swallowed audibly. "I just… I need to keep busy." Her voice was as taut as her muscles. "I'll finish these up while you pack."

He was dreading the moment he said goodbye. There was no way to make it hurt less, for any of them. "All right." He kissed the side of her neck, then her cheek.

Ella's door was shut when he walked down the hallway. She seemed to be handling everything that had happened well, with two video chat appointments per week with Tiana's child psychologist friend in Seattle. With Brian dead any threat against her or Tiana was gone.

Noah and his team had uncovered certain things about Brian's activities over the days leading up to his death. He'd been at the same law office as Evan and had somehow put it all together and decided to hurt Tiana by leaving the file. It had his fingerprints on it. Aidan hoped the bastard was roasting in hell.

In the master bedroom Aidan started gathering all the clothes and other items he'd brought over during the past two weeks. Tiana had helped him pack up everything else at Noah's old place yesterday.

He looked up when the door closed. Tiana stood with her back against it. They stared at each other in silence for a long moment, latent hunger arcing between them, then she reached behind her and turned the lock quietly.

He dropped the shirt in his hand and faced her, his heart thudding hard against his sternum as he stalked toward her. Wrapping one hand in her hair, he tipped her head back to search her eyes. They were wet with unshed tears, the green and hazel even more vivid than usual. He made a low sound and covered her mouth with his.

She clamped her arms around his neck, holding on so tight as she opened for him, meeting the thrust of his tongue as he wrapped his free arm around her hips and hoisted her up. Her legs locked around his waist, bringing her core against the hardness of his cock.

He crossed the small distance to the bed and fell on top of it with her, plunging both hands into her hair while he devoured her mouth. She grabbed at the bottom of his shirt and yanked. A seam ripped.

They went at each other with greedy hands, both of them urgent, desperate. When they were both naked he caught her hands and pinned them on either side of her head, waiting for her to relax a little. Surrender.

Her quiet sob ripped him apart.

"Don't," he rasped out, squeezing his eyes shut as a wall of grief rose inside him. He couldn't bear to see her cry and know he was the cause of it. He'd never meant to hurt her. Hadn't meant to fall this hard. But they both had. Now they had to pay the price.

"I can't lose you," she choked out, tightening her legs around him. As if she couldn't get close enough.

Ah, shite.

He slanted his lips across hers, possessing her mouth as he longed to possess her body. By the time he got the condom on he was riding the edge of control, ready to explode.

He barely had the presence of mind to cover her mouth with his as she lost it, bucking in his arms, clenching around him with a choked, keening cry. He kept moving, kept stroking between her legs until she grabbed his hand to stop him and then gripped him tight around the back.

"Come in me," she whispered, a desperate edge to her voice.

Aidan caught her wrists, bringing them over her head and held them there, staring down into her eyes as he plunged in and out of her. Demanding. Forceful. Way rougher than he had ever been before, but he needed it, and the way she softened and melted for him as if she knew it sent him rocketing over the edge.

He threw his head back and clenched his teeth together, a throttled groan escaping as he locked deep inside her and let go.

When the pleasure faded enough for him to breathe, he released her wrists and settled his weight on his forearms. Her eyes were wet again as she stared up at him, but that sharp edge of grief was gone, replaced by a soul deep sadness that he would give anything to be able to erase.

"I love you, lass," he whispered raggedly. "Desperately."

She pressed her lips together for a moment, regaining control, then nodded. "I love you the same way."

That's why this hurt so bloody bad. He'd thought he'd been gutted when Ginny walked out on him. This was a thousand times worse. It was like he was literally bleeding inside and nothing could staunch it.

"People do year-long separations all the time in the military," he said, trying to put a positive spin on things. "My contract's less than that, even worst-case scenario. It'll be over before we know it, and hopefully by then I'll have an answer about my work visa here." No matter what happened, he would find a way to come back to them.

"But you'll be in danger that whole time," she whispered, her expression stricken.

He didn't want her to worry about him constantly, and tried to ease her mind. "I'll be fine, lass. This time I'm on a private security detail, not out doing combat ops like I did as a Royal."

She cupped the back of his head and tugged him into a kiss, then tucked his face into the curve of her neck. "I just want it to be over."

He didn't know if she meant the upcoming agony of the goodbye, or the contract he had to fulfill. "Maybe I should go to the airport alone."

"No," she said fiercely. "I'm not giving up one second of the time I have left with you."

He wished he could have reversed their positions and held her like that for hours, stroking her hair and skin, but he had to leave in twenty minutes or he'd risk missing his flight.

He drove Tiana's car to the airport, her beside him and Ella in the back seat.

Tiana held his hand the entire way. They made several attempts at conversation but they all fell flat, and even Ella was uncharacteristically quiet. It seemed like it got harder to breathe with each mile they drew closer to the airport.

"Maybe you and your mom can come to visit me in Edinburgh when I get back from my assignment," he said to Ella. "I could show you the old town and the castle. You would love it."

"I'll be ten by then," she said, making it sound like it was a decade from now instead of six to nine months.

"Aye, you will. And taller too, I'll wager." It made him sad to think of all he'd be missing out on with them.

Tiana's hand tightened around his when the sign for the airport came into view. He squeezed back, pulled it to his lips to kiss it. "Want to just drop me at the curb?"

"No," both of them answered simultaneously.

It felt like there was a lead weight in the center of his chest as they walked into the terminal together. Tiana and Ella insisted on staying with him while he checked himself and his bags in. But they could go no farther and he'd waited as long as he could. His flight was boarding shortly and he still had to clear security.

Two long faces awaited him when he turned around from the counter, and the sight of them so sad was like a knife to the gut. "Hey, it's not forever," he told them, trying for a light tone. "It'll go by so fast, you'll see. And you'll be so busy with Bruce once he comes to live with you next week. Lizzie's coming to stay with you after her trip as well." She was thrilled that he and Tiana were together, as were their friends and his parents, who desperately wanted to meet her and Ella.

Neither of their expressions changed. He grinned. "You two could give Walter a run for his money right now with those expressions."

Rather than laugh or even crack a grin, Tiana bit her lip and Ella made a little hitching sound.

Ah, God. How had he gotten so damn lucky to find them? And now that he had, there was no damn way he was giving up on making a life together somehow. "Come here," he murmured, and gathered them both close.

Ella reached her arms up to try and wind around his neck and started crying.

"Hey," he said in an anguished whisper, hoisting her up in the crook of his arm. She jammed her face into his neck and clung to him like a monkey, her little shoulders shaking with the force of her sobs.

"I want you to s-stay and be my forever dad," she cried.

Aidan closed his eyes and hugged her as tight as he dared without hurting her, tears burning his eyes like acid. "Ah, lass, I want that too," he said in a rough whisper.

Tiana laid her head on his shoulder, her arms wrapped around them both. "Just be safe and always remember that we love you," she said.

"I will, I swear it. And you both remember how much I love you, too."

This was awful. A million times worse than he'd imagined. It felt like there was a raw, gaping hole in his chest where his heart was supposed to be. Not far from the truth, since he was leaving it behind with his girls.

A voice over the PA system announced that his flight was boarding. He had to move his arse if he was going to make the plane.

"Ah, Christ, I have to go," he whispered, giving them both one last fierce squeeze. Then he let them go.

He kissed the top of Ella's blond head that smelled of her special detangling shampoo, then cupped Tiana's cheek in his hand. He swallowed, his vision blurred by the sheen of tears he couldn't hide. "My bonnie red-haired lass. I love you. And I'm coming back to you when this is done. This isn't the end. We'll talk as often as we can—there's phone, text, email..." He would find a way to make it work. There had to be a way. He was going to spend the rest of his life with her.

She slid her hands into his hair, her lips clinging to his for one last, lingering kiss. Then she stepped back and he could literally see the steely cloak she protected herself with drawing around her. "Be safe."

"Aye, always." He picked up his carryon, paused to look at her one last time. "Bye."

The smile she put on broke his bleeding heart in half. "Bye."

He didn't allow himself to look back, glad neither of them could see the tears he'd been fighting back begin to fall.

Epilogue

Eight months and three days later

Edinburgh

"Aidan, did you dust the top shelves for me in the bookcase?"

He didn't look up from the book he was reading in a lounge chair in the living room. He'd only arrived at his parents' house last night, fresh off a flight from Afghanistan on what had felt like the longest deployment of his entire life. Every Hogmanay his mum turned into a cleaning cyclone and they'd all learned to go with it. "I did."

"And the top of the kitchen cabinets? You know I can't reach those, even with the stepladder."

He turned the page, only paying partial attention to her. "Aye."

His mum bustled in a moment later wearing her red dress with the MacIntyre plaid shawl draped around her shoulders, holding the traditional smoking juniper branch in one hand. She waved it around and muttered some Gaelic, "purifying" the room.

He shook his head. "We just spent the better part of

three hours scrubbing this place from top to bottom, and now you fill it with smoke."

"It's tradition," she argued, and hurried toward the kitchen to purify it too.

The book he was reading was okay, but it couldn't hold his attention. Tiana and Ella were flying in from Oregon in two days, and after not being able to touch or hold his lasses for so many months—no amount of video chats or calls or emails could match that—finally seeing them in person again was pretty much all he could think about.

Ella had proven incredibly resilient in how she'd recovered from all that had happened with Brian, and Evan had stayed consistently in contact, even coming up to see her once a month. Aidan was literally counting the hours until they arrived.

"Did you put the whisky and the shortbread by the door?" his mum called out a moment later from the kitchen. "It's quarter to midnight. Maggie and the girls should be here any minute, and I want everything to be ready for first footing."

"It's all ready." His dad was far smarter than him, hiding upstairs until she'd finished the redding of the house.

The front door opened and his little sister Maggie tramped inside with her husband and teenage girls. "Made it! It's so pretty out there with the snow falling, but I hate driving in it."

Aidan hugged her and the girls. "Good to see you lassies."

"Same to you." His sister beamed up at him. "Glad you decided to wear your [illegible] this year."

"Mum insisted." He didn't mind so much as he didn't get the chance to dress up all that often anymore.

"Look at you, all dressed up with nowhere to go," Heather said and gave him a big kiss on the cheek.

"My turn," Sophie said, and gave him one on his other cheek.

"And you both look far too grown up for a fifteen and seventeen-year-old." He looked at his brother-in-law. "It's not too late to lock them both away yet. We'll let them out when they're twenty-five."

"Not that again," Sophie groaned. She was the baby but looked at least nineteen and Aidan had already put the fear of God into the boy she'd brought over to meet them last night.

"I know how boys think, lass."

"Well, what David now thinks is that he's never coming over here again while you're around. He's terrified."

Aidan grinned. "Aye. That's a good thing."

"Good, everyone's here," his mum said, marching back in with the smoking juniper branch. She waved it at everyone, making them all flap their hands in front of their faces and cough.

"Granny, ugh, that's so old school," Heather complained. "Who does that anymore?"

"Och, shush." She waved it a few more times for good measure, twice more over Sophie's head, maybe to purify thoughts of David out of her hormone-addled brain, then tossed the branch into the fire crackling away in the hearth. She kissed Maggie and the girls, then Graham. "All right, come and eat something before the bells."

They gathered around the table to help themselves to bites his mum had made for them, talking and laughing while they waited for the stroke of midnight. They'd celebrated Hogmanay this way every year for as long as he could remember, but tonight there was something missing.

Two people, to be precise. And each of them owned a half of his heart.

"A toast," his dad said, raising his glass. They all raised theirs. "I wish you all love, peace and prosperity in the New Year. Lang may your lum reek. Happy New Year."

"Happy New Year," everyone chorused.

He'd missed this more than he'd realized. Being surrounded by family in his childhood home and taking part in their traditions, especially Hogmanay, which was a much bigger deal than Christmas in Scotland, but especially Edinburgh. But this year his enjoyment was diminished by the absence of the two people who had come to mean everything to him.

He'd surprised Tiana and Ella with the plane tickets on Christmas Day, and even though he loved his family, his lasses were his world now. He couldn't wait to introduce them to everyone and show them around his city.

The past eight months had been the longest of his life. Even with frequent video chats and phone calls, it wasn't the same as being able to wrap his arms around them.

His green card application was moving forward, and he had enough money saved up that he could move back to Crimson Point for the better part of a year before needing to make more. Hopefully by then, something more permanent would be decided.

He and the others gathered around the fire with a drink while they waited for the clock to tick down. At the one-minute mark his mum got ready to start the countdown, watching the second hand with her eagle eye. "Ten! Nine!"

They counted down the remaining seconds together. At the stroke of midnight they all cried Happy New Year and did another round of hugs and kisses.

The doorbell rang. Everyone glanced at Aidan, then each other, grinning.

"Ah, wonder who the first foot is this year," his mum said. "Maggie, you answer it." She gave his sister a shove toward the door.

Maggie went over to answer it. "Ach, it's a redhead! That's bad luck."

"That's a doaty old superstition and you know it," Sophie scoffed.

Maggie looked back at them. "Should I let her in anyway?"

"That's up to your brother," his mum said, grinning from ear to ear as she shoved him toward the door.

What the hell was going on? Confused, Aidan crossed toward the front door, freezing in shock when he saw Tiana and Ella standing on the doorstep, huge smiles on their faces and snowflakes dotting their hair and shoulders.

"Oh my God," he blurted, his face splitting into a smile even as emotion punched him in the chest.

Off to the side his sister had her phone out, recording the whole thing, and moved aside as Aidan rushed past her to grab his girls.

Tiana and Ella both laughed and threw their arms around him, engulfing him with their familiar scents and love. "Surprise," Tiana whispered, hugging him tight.

Aidan couldn't believe it, his chest tight, full to bursting. "How?" he managed, still holding them close as he walked them inside and kicked the door shut behind them.

"Your mom and sister helped us once we found out when you were flying in," she told him, easing back to smile up at him. She looked like an angel standing there, her cheeks and nose pink from the cold.

"You wore a kilt!" Ella cried, delighted.

"Aye." And now he knew why his mum had insisted. She was a good one.

"I love it," Tiana added with a suggestive smile that made his mind go blank and sent blood rushing south of the border. "You look so hot."

"Oh, and I brought you this." Ella shoved a piece of coal up into his face, her expression unsure, her little forehead wrinkled in a frown. "In America you only get coal in your stocking at Christmas if you're really bad, but I'm supposed to give this to you anyway."

He laughed. "It's to go in the fire, love. It's tradition to bring someone a piece of coal or shortbread when you visit after the bells first thing on New Year's Day."

"Oh." She beamed up at him. "Then here you go." She put it in his hand.

He kissed the top of her head, then shoved the coal into his sporran and grasped Tiana's chin. After staring into her gorgeous, different-colored eyes for a long moment, he planted an ecstatic, lingering kiss on her cold lips. He relearned the shape of her lips, the feel of them as they warmed and gave way beneath his.

Whistles broke out behind him, followed by laughter.

"Is that considered 'appropriate' behavior in front of your teenage nieces, Uncle Aidan?" Sophie called out.

To hell with appropriate, he hadn't seen his woman in eight fucking months, and he didn't care who was watching. He plunged his hands into her hair and kissed her until she started to laugh and pushed gently at his chest.

Finally he lifted his head, unable to wipe the stupid grin off his face. "God, I've missed you both."

Her mismatched eyes glowed with pure joy as she gazed up at him. "We've missed you too. Now maybe you could officially introduce us to your family?"

"Sure." He hooked an arm around her, grasped Ella's shoulders with his free hand and turned them to face his family. More hugs and kisses ensued.

As soon as his family was finished with her he pulled her in front of the fire and proceeded to warm her up in his own way, cupping her face between his hands as he covered it with kisses. Her delighted laugh filled him with warmth and lust, and he was grateful for the sporran at the front of his kilt that hid his body's reaction.

"For goodness' sake, Aidan, let the poor girl breathe," his mum said with a laugh, whacking him on the shoulder.

He raised his head, pleased to see the heat and need in

her eyes, her cheeks even pinker. “Love you, lass.”

Her smile was so beautiful it hurt. “Love you back.”

God, he couldn’t wait to get her alone. “Please tell me you’ve booked a hotel room,” he whispered. He wanted to do things to her that required privacy and not being under his parents’ roof. With Ella there he’d have to be creative to make it work, but he would find a way.

“Yes. I can’t wait to see if you’ve got anything under that ridiculously sexy [illegible]. And your mom’s already offered to keep Ella here for the night. They’ve talked on the phone a couple times, so Ella’s comfortable with it.”

“I adore that woman.”

She laughed softly. “So, are you going to show us what Hogmanay is all about?”

“Aye.” Smiling, he reached out a hand to Ella, his heart so full it ached.

While everyone bundled into their coats, he ran upstairs to grab something and met them at the door. Holding his lasses’ hands, the whole group began the trek through Dean Village toward Princes Street while light snow fell around them.

“It’s like being in a story book,” Ella said in wonder as they walked the snowy, cobbled street past the Victorian-era and older buildings.

“It is,” he agreed. “Wait until you see Old Town and the castle.”

The streets were full of people, the Hogmanay *ceilidh* in full swing as they walked up The Mound toward the heart of the old city center.

“Wow,” Tiana said with a laugh as they reached the Royal Mile. Ella looked around her with wide eyes, taking in the spectacle. Bonfires dotted the street along with musical performances and people dressed up as Vikings and Highland warriors danced and paraded past the ancient shops.

Aidan bent to Ella. "Down that way is Holyrood Palace. And up there, that's Edinburgh Castle." He pointed to the right.

She gasped, her eyes full of wonder as she stared at it. "Can we go see it?"

"I'm sorry lass, they'll be packing up after the fireworks. We won't get in tonight, but I'll take you soon." He turned to his mum. "There's something special I want to show Tiana down by St Giles Cathedral. Maybe we could catch you up in a few minutes by Greyfriar's Bobby?" He raised his eyebrows.

His mum went into action immediately, coming over to crouch in front of Ella with a smile. "Would you like to come with me and the girls for some shortbread and a hot chocolate, Ella? We can get some and then I can take you to a café nearby where the author of the Harry Potter books used to write in."

Ella gasped. "I *love* Harry Potter."

"Was hoping you did." She gave Aidan a wink, then smiled at Tiana and reached out a hand to Ella. "Come on, then. Aidan and your mum can meet us in a bit."

Ella didn't even hesitate. She wrapped her mittened hand in his mum's and walked off without a backward glance.

"Wow, she really likes your mom," Tiana said.

Yes, and thank God for that. Aidan snagged her hand and tugged her in the opposite direction, his heart pounding. "Come with me."

He led past the Heart of Midlothian to the far side of Parliament Square where there were a few quieter corners, away from the twinkling lights and burning torches.

"What do you want to show me? You're being all mysterious," she said with a wry smile.

Guiding her into an alcove, he stripped off his winter coat, pulled the first box from the front pocket and went down on one knee in front of her.

Her face sobered instantly, her lips parting in shock as he opened the box to reveal the diamond ring inside.

His heart hammered against his ribs. Not from nerves. From pure excitement and pride. She was everything he'd ever wanted and more. He'd known before leaving Crimson Point last spring that he wanted to spend the rest of his life with her. "Will you make me the proudest of men and be my wife?"

She put a hand to her heart, gave a watery laugh and thrust her hand out at him. "Yes. In a heartbeat."

He was on his feet in an instant, pulling her tight into his body while his mouth came down on hers. He kissed her with all the love and pent up longing in his heart, plunging his tongue between her lips to stroke hers. Clinging. Counting down the minutes until they were alone in her hotel room bed and he could sink between her thighs the same way.

Soft laughter broke through thc haze of lust fogging his brain. He looked over to find Maggie there with her phone. She gave him an enthusiastic thumbs up, a huge grin splitting her face. "Got it all! Congratulations."

Tiana smiled and pressed her face into his chest. "I can't believe it."

"It's all real. I'm moving back to Crimson Point with you. And once we're married, it'll help my case for permanent residency. So you're stuck with me for the long haul."

"I love you. Now put that gorgeous thing on my finger so we can go tell Ella. She'll explode. And then I have to call Lizzie."

He slid it onto her finger, raised it to his lips and kissed her knuckles, gazing into her eyes.

She sniffed and blinked fast. "Oh my God, I'm so happy," she whispered.

"Me too." He kissed the tip of her nose. "My bonnie red-haired lass."

Her smile was full of an adoration that filled him to bursting. "I love it when you call me that."

"Good. Now let's go find Ella. I've something for her as well."

It felt like he was floating as he walked his future wife back to the Royal Mile and left along George IV Bridge. His mum's face lit up when they arrived out front of The Elephant House a few minutes later, her eyes immediately dropping to Tiana's hand. She bit her lip, gave Ella a little push toward them.

"Hi," Ella said, a hot chocolate in one hand and a piece of shortbread in the other. "What did you see?"

"Something beautiful beyond words," Tiana answered. "And I've got a secret."

"What kind of secret?" Her eyes glittered with interest.

Tiana grinned and held up her left hand, wiggling her fingers to show off the ring. "Aidan asked me to marry him and I said *yes*."

Ella's eyes went wide, shooting to Aidan. "You did?"

"Aye. And I've something important to ask you as well."

He took out the second box from his pocket and went down on his knee before her, hiding a grin at the stunned look on her face and the soft gasps that sounded around him. He opened the lid to reveal the little ring on its velvet bed.

White gold, with her birthstone set between his and Tiana's. "Will you be mine as well, Ella?"

She looked up from the ring into his eyes, and swallowed. "So you'd be my forever dad?" Her voice was rough, the hope in her face enough to crush his ribcage.

A bittersweet pain pierced his heart. "Aye, lass. Forever and ever," he vowed, overcome with love and protectiveness for this precious wee one who had given him her trust in spite of everything she'd been through.

Her lips trembled, her little face twisting. Instead of

replying she nodded, choking back tears.

"Ah, lass," he began and reached for her, distressed to see her reduced to tears by him declaring his love for her.

She dropped the hot chocolate and biscuit and launched herself into his embrace.

Aidan caught her, closing his eyes to absorb the feel of her hugging him so fiercely with her little arms.

"Aww," his mum, sister and Tiana all chorused together. His sister was probably filming this too, but he didn't check, too busy holding his daughter.

Ella squeezed him tighter. "I love you, Mac." Her voice was hoarse with tears.

"I love you too, my wee darlin'. Can I put the ring on your finger now?"

"Yes." She let go and leaned back to tug her left mitten off, her lips curving upward despite her tears.

Aidan slid the ring onto her finger. "There. A perfect fit."

She hugged him again, her face buried in his neck. "Yes, we are."

His eyes were wet when he met Tiana's gaze over Ella's shoulder, but he was smiling.

His lasses. His whole world.

And he was the lucky bastard who got to spend the rest of his life loving them.

—The End—

Dear reader,

Thank you for reading ***Rocky Ground***. I hope you enjoyed it. If you'd like to stay in touch with me and be the first to learn about new releases you can:

Join my newsletter at:
http://kayleacross.com/v2/newsletter/

Find me on Facebook: https://www.facebook.com/KayleaCrossAuthor/

Follow me on Twitter: https://twitter.com/kayleacross

Follow me on Instagram: https://www.instagram.com/kaylea_cross_author/

Also, please consider leaving a review at your favorite online book retailer. It helps other readers discover new books.

Happy reading,
Kaylea

Excerpt from

Stealing Vengeance

Valkyrie Vengeance Series

By Kaylea Cross

Prologue

Trinity Durant tucked the package safely into the bodice of her cocktail dress and slipped out of the guest suite into the top floor hallway of the posh hotel like she owned the place. Black and simple, the dress was sexy and short enough in front to allow her full motion of her legs should a quick getaway become necessary.

Not that she expected to have to make a run for it tonight. But she was always prepared, nonetheless.

She smiled at a couple she passed and headed for the stairs. Her target—Richard Goerner, a man with important CIA contacts and a past to hide—was currently down the hall screwing his mistress in another suite, allowing Trinity plenty of time to slip in and retrieve what she'd needed from the safe in the closet. As a bonus, it had also allowed her to send a video link of them entering the room to his new young socialite wife.

Trinity hoped it got splashed all over every social media outlet out there. The slimy bastard and all his corrupt government buddies deserved public ridicule and humiliation once their dirty deeds were unearthed.

Down on the second floor in the large, adjoining ballrooms, the party was in full swing. A ritzy gala supporting a children's charity, featuring a guest list made up of celebrities, politicians and government officials. Anyone and everyone who had power and money in Washington. With any luck, the package tucked into her bodice would have several of them panicking by morning—but especially the man upstairs.

She bypassed the party and headed for the hotel entrance, struck by how easy this was compared to the jobs she used to take on. So many times she had been forced to take the place of the mistress in the upstairs suite right now, using the powers of seduction she'd been trained with to get what she needed. And sometimes, the job ended only when she'd added another kill to her count.

That was then. Now she had a new life. One where she called the shots, and only took on assignments she was comfortable with. And a wonderful man to share it with.

Her left thumb went unerringly to her bare third finger, naked without the weight of the diamond engagement ring. Warm night air surrounded her as she walked out of the air-conditioned building. A few steps from the curb, the burner phone rang from her evening bag. She pulled it out and answered without looking at the display. Only one person had the number.

"Did you get it?" the familiar male voice asked when she answered.

"Of course I got it," she said, feigning insult. On a difficulty and risk scale of one-to-ten, tonight's op had been a zero-point-five on both counts. But hopefully one of the most important of her career.

"Good. I'll pick you up at the rendezvous point."

Which they should have set up a few blocks closer, she thought wryly as she tucked the phone away. Easy for him to set the RV point earlier—he wasn't the one walking three blocks in freaking four-inch heels. Heels that concealed stiletto blades in them. Because a girl could never have too many weapons on her.

By the time she reached the appointed intersection her feet were killing her, but her steps never faltered and her gait didn't change. A Valkyrie never showed pain or weakness on a job—not even a former one.

She folded her arms and shot a mock glare through the BMW's tinted windows as it pulled to the curb in front of her. The lock popped up and the passenger door swung open.

Her boss, Alex Rycroft, leaned across the front seat, silver eyes gleaming as he grinned at her. He was "retired" and happily married with a toddler at home, but took on certain things as a consultant from time to time. "You look gorgeous."

"Flatterer," she muttered, fighting a smile as she slid into the passenger seat and shut the door.

He smoothly pulled out into the evening D.C. traffic and headed toward the river. "How was the party?"

"Scintillating."

He grinned. "I'll bet. Here." He handed her the transmitting device.

She pulled the tube of lipstick from the bodice of her dress, unscrewed the base and pulled out the flash drive she'd made of the hard drive. It slid easily into the device. After entering the code she hit send, and the piece of electronic wizardry did its thing. "Who are we sending this to, anyway?"

"Two people I trust. Whoever cracks the encryption first, wins."

"Let's hope I got what we need this time."

He'd been frustratingly vague about what it was they were after, but for him to have taken this on in the first place meant it was important, and he'd approached her specifically, saying she had a vested interest that would be revealed in time. This was her third op of the mission, all involving stolen, encrypted files he wanted recovered. The first one had been in San Fran. The second in New York City. Now this.

"Third time's the charm, right?" he said.

"That's what they say." Trinity reached up and removed her long brown wig, then breathed a sigh of relief as she slid off the sadistic heels. The shoes were sexy as hell, but horrible to wear. Obviously invented by a man. "Oh, *God,* that feels good." She leaned back in the seat, watching the lights and traffic out the window, relaxed but alert, and simmering with impatience to find out what was going on. "Wherever you're taking me, there had better be wine and cheesecake."

"I'll order you some from room service," Rycroft promised, a smile in his voice.

He was a good man. A hard man with a legendary reputation both in Special Forces and with the NSA. But he was fair. If you were motivated and dependable and delivered results, there was never a problem. After the people Trinity had worked for in the past, that was a revelation.

They rode in comfortable silence until they reached a hotel and he turned into the underground parking garage. She didn't bother asking him where they were going because he wouldn't answer, and because she trusted him. So she followed him into the elevator and down the hall to a room, which he unlocked with a key card.

"After you," he said, his silver eyes gleaming with secrets and a hint of a smile.

Not sure what to expect, Trinity stepped inside. She drew up short, barely concealing her shock when she saw they weren't alone.

The two women waiting for them both jumped up to greet her, big grins on their faces. "Surprise," they chorused.

She laughed and reached for the slender brunette first. "Wow, a reunion." They were the closest thing she had ever had to sisters. And they had been through so much together.

Briar DeLuca returned the hug a little stiffly, so much less awkward about it than the former sniper would have been a few years ago. "Yep. Not sure what he's got up his sleeve, but I know it's gotta be good."

Georgia was there to hug her next, blond hair cut to her shoulders, pale blue eyes bright with glee. "Nice to see you."

"You too. Where's your mysterious husband at, anyway?"

"He's around," her friend answered evasively, and they both grinned.

"So, wine and cheesecake all round?" Rycroft said from behind them.

Trinity faced him and arched an eyebrow. "What's going on?" If he'd brought them all together for a secret meeting, then something big was up and she wanted details.

He gestured to the chairs in front of the flat screen TV. "Sit and I'll fill you all in."

When everyone was settled he leaned back against the desk and folded his arms across his chest, still broad and hard with muscle even though he was now in his mid-fifties. "I have confirmation that the Valkyrie Program was still operating up until several weeks ago."

Stunned silence met his words, and the mood turned dark. Trinity exchanged shocked glances with her fellow Valkyries before focusing back on Rycroft. "That's impossible."

He shook his head. "You three and the others who trained with you were part of phase one. But there was a phase two as well, initiated a few years later, and it kept going even after Balducci and the others were brought down."

Will Balducci—a former trainer and would-be senator who had betrayed them all for money and influence several years ago. He had put hits out on Briar and Georgia's handlers. Tried to kill them both to cover his tracks.

Trinity was glad he was currently rotting behind bars. But apparently the decay within the CIA went even deeper than she or anyone else had realized.

"They changed the name and buried everything deeper," Rycroft continued. "I'd just been informed about it and authorized an off-the-books investigation, then the trail went cold. Everything stopped, almost overnight. Then I found out why."

He pulled out his phone, typed in something and held it out so they could see the picture on the screen. It showed a young woman probably in her twenties, her face bluish, eyes closed on top of an autopsy table. "Her name was Martina. And she had a very interesting tattoo on her left hip." He swiped to the next photo, showing a symbol they were all intimately familiar with.

It was about the size of a silver dollar, positioned on her left hip. A black crow with a sword clutched in its talons, with the word *Valkyrja* written inside a stylized scroll beneath it. Each Valkyrie received it upon "graduation" from the program.

"Her death was reported to U.S. intelligence a few weeks ago. She was killed by a quick-acting isotope used exclusively by Chinese operatives. Divers found her in a back alley Dumpster in Shanghai."

Trinity shifted her gaze from the phone to him. His expression was somber. As somber as she'd ever seen it, and a warning tingle started up in the pit of her stomach. Alex Rycroft had seen and done it all. If this had brought him out of retirement, it was huge.

"Her name and picture were sent to a Chinese mobster one day before her death," he continued.

"By who?" Trinity asked.

"That's what we need to find out. Because Marina is just one of four dead Valkyries who have turned up over the past month—ever since the media got wind of the program. Each murdered in a foreign city after completing a job. So far, all the evidence points to them being killed by the organizations they targeted."

Silence greeted his words, all of them absorbing the gravity of the statement. Valkyries were notoriously difficult targets. Nearly impossible to find, and hard to kill. Because they were ghosts, and only a few people knew their true identities and locations.

Until now.

A cold wave of anger spread through her. Someone had deliberately leaked the operative's names and locations once the public had gotten wind of the program. A program that to her and everyone else's knowledge had been shut down years ago.

Rycroft regarded all three of them in turn before continuing. "Here's what I know. Whoever leaked these files is involved with the program, and they're no longer with the CIA. They're likely a talented hacker, because it would take an electronic wizard to get hold of those files. Whoever they are, our target is operating alone from the outside, and I'm currently analyzing anyone who might be involved. But whoever this is potentially has files on all former and current operatives, and is selling them off piece by piece to our enemies."

"To kill us off one by one," Briar finished.

He nodded. "That's how it seems right now. And that's why I'm asking for your help to stop the bleeding before it gets any worse. Nobody knows better than you three what needs to happen. The clock is ticking. We're in a race to find the hacker, mitigate the damage, and then bring in the at-risk Valkyries before they're taken out."

"I'm in," Trinity said without hesitating.

Rycroft nodded at her, then looked at Briar. "You're a new mom, so I would never ask you to do field work. But I want you to work logistics with a small, hand-picked team I'm putting together."

"Yeah, of course I'll do it," Briar answered, her espresso-brown eyes burning with resolve.

"What about you?" Rycroft asked Georgia.

"I'm in too. Whatever you need."

"Good." One side of his mouth lifted, then his expression straightened. "Zahra got one name by complete accident, and we're trying to locate her right now." He swiped on his phone again, then held it up so they could see the new photo. "This is Megan Smith," he said, showing a young Caucasian woman with chestnut-brown hair. "She was last operational in Europe, but with the media fallout surrounding Balducci's trial, she went to ground. We have no idea where she is, but we need to find her, and fast, because her name was leaked to a terrorist organization two days ago."

Trinity studied the picture, trying to place her. She was fairly certain she'd never met the woman. But it took a Valkyrie to catch a Valkyrie, and Trinity was going to be the one to find her. "I'll go."

The meeting lasted another half hour while they went over logistics and a plan of attack. As soon as they got a hit on Megan Smith's location, Trinity would be on the next flight out of D.C.

Rycroft stopped her at the door on her way out of the hotel room, searching her eyes. "Is Brody home?"

"He's due home tomorrow night." And he wasn't going to be too happy when he found out what she had just agreed to.

His smile was sympathetic. "Good luck."

On her way down the hall she rubbed her thumb over the bare spot on her left ring finger, thinking of her fiancé and then Megan.

Brody might not understand, but she had to do this. She had no choice.

Holding Megan's image in her mind, she strode for the elevator.

Wherever you are, I'm going to find you. And then I'm going to set you free.

—End Excerpt—

About the Author

NY Times and USA Today Bestselling author Kaylea Cross writes edge-of-your-seat military romantic suspense. Her work has won many awards, including the Daphne du Maurier Award of Excellence, and has been nominated multiple times for the National Readers' Choice Awards. A Registered Massage Therapist by trade, Kaylea is also an avid gardener, artist, Civil War buff, Special Ops aficionado, belly dance enthusiast and former nationally-carded softball pitcher. She lives in Vancouver, BC with her husband and family.

You can visit Kaylea at www.kayleacross.com. If you would like to be notified of future releases, please join her newsletter: http://kayleacross.com/v2/newsletter/

Complete Booklist

ROMANTIC SUSPENSE

Valkyrie Vengeance Series
Stealing Vengeance

Crimson Point Series
Fractured Honor
Buried Lies
Shattered Vows
Rocky Ground

DEA FAST Series
Falling Fast
Fast Kill
Stand Fast
Strike Fast
Fast Fury
Fast Justice
Fast Vengeance

Colebrook Siblings Trilogy
Brody's Vow
Wyatt's Stand
Easton's Claim

Hostage Rescue Team Series
Marked
Targeted
Hunted
Disavowed
Avenged
Exposed
Seized
Wanted

Betrayed
Reclaimed
Shattered
Guarded

Titanium Security Series
Ignited
Singed
Burned
Extinguished
Rekindled
Blindsided: A Titanium Christmas novella

Bagram Special Ops Series
Deadly Descent
Tactical Strike
Lethal Pursuit
Danger Close
Collateral Damage
Never Surrender (a MacKenzie Family novella)

Suspense Series
Out of Her League
Cover of Darkness
No Turning Back
Relentless
Absolution

PARANORMAL ROMANCE

Empowered Series
Darkest Caress

HISTORICAL ROMANCE

The Vacant Chair

EROTIC ROMANCE (writing as ***Callie Croix***)

Deacon's Touch

Dillon's Claim

No Holds Barred

Touch Me

Let Me In

Covert Seduction